PROLOGUE

When you have the money nearly in hand, it's not wise to insult your victim--especially when the woman you just called a stupid blonde bitch looked like she wanted to strangle you already. The junkie waving the gun at Rachel Ingles had done just that. Now she was livid and he was her sole target.

Until then, Rachel had been obediently filling the thief's grungy duffel bag with money from the register as he had demanded. The elderly owner of the health food store had been watching helplessly, hovering somewhere close to a state of shock. Now, Rachel was slowly dumping the money out of the bag and onto the floor. The would be criminal's jerky movements had increased in agitation. He started to stutter. "Wh.. What ar.. Wha.." He couldn't seem to form a coherent word.

She stared intensely, her vision narrowing and her eyes darkening to a shade that was closer to black than the bluish green they usually were. Her breathing became heavy. Aside from the man's profuse sweating and tell-tale withdrawal shakes he was too stunned to move. Reason had drained from her consciousness. She had no room for thought. She was pure focused energy and she had decided that her kickboxing classes were about to pay off.

*****

When describing the events to the police, no one was exactly sure what made the thief fall to his knees sobbing; the shock of the gun going off in his hands or the thud of her heel as it impacted against his chest. It wasn't until hours later, when emotions and adrenaline had drained away and reason had finally returned that Rachel realized the stupidity of what she had done. *Oh hell, not again.*

CHAPTER 1

Rachel struggled to close the heavy door of her rusted out muscle car. When it finally gave way, she could only watch helplessly as the corner of her coat wedged inside; locked. "Shit!" She cursed, quickly yanking it free. She checked it for damage and let out a sigh of relief when she found it hadn't ripped. She couldn't afford to lose her last remaining good coat, especially with this unusually bitter cold spring hanging on for dear life. "Enough with the Lion!" She called out looking skyward, then as she straightened up she added. "Where's the ruddy Lamb?"

With a heavy sigh she looked towards the granite building looming in front of her. She used to love how its historic majesty, oddly mixed with the chic modern façade accents. Lately she was getting sick of the sight of it. She had been here too many times of late and today it seemed to be taunting her. She already felt as if all its occupants had their judging eyes trained on her as she approached. Her mind raced as she tried to think of a way to explain how this one wasn't her fault either.

"They guy had it coming!" She sighed in exasperation, staring towards the top floor windows as if waiting for an argument. When she didn't get one she clutched her coat tighter, as she shivered against the biting cold wind. She stayed huddled like that a moment longer, before finally straightening her shoulders and shrugging off the self-doubt. "What's to explain, I didn't lose the contract, the store owner retired. It's not my fault he wasn't used to seeing a woman defend her own honor." She declared aloud as if responding to the building's judgement.

With renewed determination she marched into the building, through the smoky glass entrance doors and up the heavily scuffed tile staircases to the office at the top of the third-floor landing; Suite 301 of the Brockton Employment Agency. The building had elevators, but she always took the stairs. The elevators that the building management referred to as antique, were really just decrepit and painfully slow. Rachel had no patience for waiting. When she reached the Agency's entrance, she took deep breath for courage and pushed forward, through the solid oak doors. A satisfied smile teased the corners of her mouth as she looked around; time to get to work.

The agency offices took up two floors. The main floor was crammed with cubicles and was flooded with sunlight from the window lined walls surrounding them. Overlooking the main floor was a lofted balcony level that housed the executive offices and conference rooms. It was here where agents met with businesses to analyze their needs and help them evaluate the right fit for their needs. It was also where they evaluated a potential temp for each role.

The Brockton agency prided themselves on being selective with their temps. They didn't present just anyone for the role. Whether it was selecting from their stable of permanent temps or one of the ones that came to them hoping for a contract to hire position. They would only be given a lead if the agent felt they were the right fit. Rachel was one of the permanent temps. She was intelligent, worked hard, had a lot of marketable skills and lived for the freedom that being a permanent temp offered. This made Rachel a favorite at the agency.

Considering that lately her contracts seemed to be ending earlier than expected, and she was here a little more often for a new gig, it was a good thing they still found her easy to place. This was the case today. She wasn't expected back on the market for another two months, so she knew they wouldn't have her on the open to hire list yet. That might make getting a quick placement near impossible. Her bank account might not survive that, so she kept her fingers mentally crossed. Not that Irish luck seemed to follow her, more like run in the other direction, but she was going to hope for it just the same.

She scanned the room. After a moment her smile morphed into coy grin as she homed in on her target. She had to move fast if she didn't want to end up waiting through lunch for the next opening. Without wasting another second, she rushed over and plopped down in the gleaming metal chair.

"Hello Amy." She started, casually stretching back in her seat to get comfy. "How's tricks?" A playful glint glowed in her eyes.

Amy looked up at the sound of her voice and groaned. "Oh no, what did you do this time?"

Rachel immediately sat up straight, taking a defensive posture. "Why do you immediately assume it was something I did?"

"Because it's always your fault Rachel!" Amy blurted, the fondness clear in her light teasing voice.

"That's not fair. Everyone lost their job this time, not just me. The owner decided to retire, so he no longer needed me to do his payroll. How could that possibly be my fault?"

"He only retired because you scared him into it. Attacking that thug in front of him? He was 78 years old. Women aren't supposed to do that in his world. I'm not sure if he was more scared by the junkie who thought the place was his personal pharmacy or you and your Kung Fu."

"Kickboxing."

"Whatever! It was only after that he decided to close shop and retreat to a world he understood better." Amy confirmed triumphantly.

"Okay maybe I had a little to do with speeding up the owner's decision, but honestly, that creep insulted me. A girl has a right to stand up for herself." She fiddled with her chair trying to adjust its height to better fit her long legs. "Besides, it's not like the guy looked that bad, a few bruises at most. The police said he likely passed out from the effects of his withdrawal, nothing to do with my kicking him at all." She crossed her arms defiantly.

The two women stared each other down before finally bursting into uncontrollable laughter. Amy shook her head, her soft spiraling burgundy-red curls bouncing off her cheeks, emphasizing her defeat. "Ok not your fault every time, but you have to admit, if you weren't so damned smart I would have a really hard time placing you so often." Amy tried to sound reproachful, but her smile gave her away.

"Who says every job needs to make it to the resume?" She responded with a wink and a smile. She was glad she was able to speak with Amy today. If anyone had a chance of placing her without much notice, it would be Amy. Amy's leads were always top notch. It didn't hurt that they had become best friends over their last two years together. Which in turn meant that she didn't have to explain how much her bank account needed immediate placement.

She noted that Amy's current hairstyle was a dramatic deviation from her usual shock-effect look. This time it seems Amy had gone for what could only be described as a throwback to the old Hollywood glamour. The burgundy had toned down any left-over bright red from the last time she had seen her. Amy was the only agent who could get away with her non-corporate attire and usual outrageously colored hair. She produced the strongest billable numbers for the agency so she was given more leeway in the agency's dress code interpretation. Plus she always looked great no matter how she tried to cover it up. Amy had soft delicate features, and could look good in a clown suit, which is what her last hair color came close to looking like.

Rachel on the other hand was no ugly duckling, but she always envied women that seem to look soft and feminine no matter what they did. Her features were bolder and more dramatic. Her lips were full with a permanent pout. Her eyes couldn't seem to decide if they were blue or green or somewhere mixed in between and they had a hard edge to them. Even her cheekbones were well defined. It all came together to create a sculptured look that could at times overwhelm you with a strength that she often felt obligated to live up to. The only thing that saved her was her long sun-kissed straight blonde hair. This gave her a softer naïve look that she never failed to use to her advantage when she could.

"Well, I suppose you can fill me in on the rest of the details of your early termination over lunch. I assume I'm buying." Amy said matter-of-factly; more as a statement of fact than a question.

"Well if you insist!" She smiled as her stomach growled as if on cue.

"Alright then, let's work on getting you into your next gig quickly 'cause I'm starving." Amy let out a light airy giggle. "To be honest, I'm glad you came in today." She said leaning in and lowering her voice. "I was not looking forward to another sandwich in the lunchroom listening to endless stories from the usual choir of disgruntled wives that gather in the back."

Amy pinched her face and mimicked her best whiny voice. "My husband doesn't listen to a word I say. Blah, blah, blah." She rolled her eyes and turned back to her computer.

Rachel didn't bother to stifle her laughter as Amy clicked away at her keyboard, searching for the perfect lead. She let her thoughts wander as she often did when she was bored. After what felt like only a few seconds, but was probably more like 15 minutes, she was jerked back to reality by Amy's delighted shrieks.

"I found it." Amy squirmed in her seat. "I knew I had one in here for you. It's absolutely perfect." Amy's seat squeaked as she spun her seat around to face her friend. "All you have to do is answer phones. How could you possibly get into trouble with that?"

Rachel's smile brightened. "This day is looking up already, who knows I might even be able to pay my rent on time." She giggled, picking up on Amy's contagious enthusiasm. "Set it up." She said bolting upright in her chair.

"Don't you want to hear about the company?" Amy looked bewildered.

"After all this time, I trust you. Besides I'm starving, so whatever it is I'll take it so we can get out of here!"

Amy let out a snort. "Great, give me a few minutes to set the appointment up, then we can go eat. Any time that won't work for you?" Amy asked then answered as soon as she saw Rachel's expression. "Right, the sooner the better. Why don't you wait in the coffee room? I'll grab you as soon as I wrap things up."

"Coffee!" Rachel smiled, jumped up and headed off in search of black gold as Amy often called it. The break room was not typically open to the temps, but she had been with the agency for so long she was like one of their staff. She loved the familiar smell of the break room. The distinct smell of coffee, mixed with the warm mix of muffins and other treats that were often shared here. She poured herself a coffee. It was one of her few vices so she felt the need to indulge herself with all the added she spoils could pile in it; double cream, triple sugar. Calling it a drink was probably stretching it, the way she doctored it up it might as well be a dessert.

She cradled her mug and sank into the larger of the two worn leather couches in the room. She had long legs so this was the only one where she could actually stretch out and relax in. She snuggled in and took a long glorious sip. The steaming hot liquid comforted her and her attention drifted towards the windows across the room as the sound of a car horn blasted in the distance. Before long her mind was wandering through a series of "What if's" until one eventually caught her interest and she followed it into a new story line. Before she got too far along in the plot, she was jolted back to reality when Amy popped her head around the corner to grab her attention.

"Pssst." Amy looked around quickly before continuing. "Let's get out of here before Brad comes down and sees us." Amy's voice was low as she discretely signaled for her to come quickly.

Rachel giggled conspiratorially as she hopped up, gulped the last of her coffee down so she could slip her mug in the dishwasher and rush out the door with Amy. They snuck along the walkway quickly, ducking as they neared anyone who looked their way. Neither one uttered a sound. One of the hazards of spending more time at work then home is that work soon replaces your home life. Consequently begins the life of endless drama. Where coworkers feel out their relationships as they deepen to friendships and sometimes more intimate relationships, then back to professional colleagues as balances shift with office politics and the dynamics of an ever changing work place.

Inevitably there are those that seem to dance around each other in mischievous courtships that continue on until one of them either acts on their feelings or simply gives up and moves on. In this way, Brad was Amy's dance partner, only they were both too stubborn to admit it. Of course it didn't help that he was her boss, well technically that is, no one really told Amy what to do. She was the best and could pretty much set her own rules which she usually did, much to Brad's dismay.

Rachel was aware of this dynamic so she didn't need to ask why they were pulling this particular kind of exit. They continued to duck and weave their way out, successfully avoiding any confrontations. Once outside they headed directly towards Amy's silver Audi. Rachel didn't bother to offer to drive; she knew Amy would never get in her beat up car.

"I got you an appointment for 4:30 this afternoon." Amy explained as they rushed through the parking lot so as not to be stopped should anyone, namely Brad, decide to chase after then. "That should give us plenty of time to catch up over lunch before you have to go get ready. Here's the address." Amy handed the appointment sheet to Rachel.

Rachel scanned the address, looked at her watch and rolled her eyes; she knew Amy was serious. It was 1:45; plenty of time to eat, race home, shower and still make a 4:30 across town. Not. Obviously the reasoning Amy was using was based on her seemingly magical ability to always be ready. Rachel was about to protest, but one stomach rumble and she quickly forgot the late hour and was focused back on food.

"Plenty of time." She confirmed, tucking the paper in her pocket. "Easy in. After all, it's not like I have to work up a sweat answering phones right?"

"Exactly, easy in, easy contract. No trouble at all!" Amy suddenly found herself very worried upon uttering those words. This was

Rachel Ingles after all, and this wasn't the first time she had uttered words to that effect.

CHAPTER 2

Rachel rushed into a parking spot close to the building and checked her watch, 4:29. "Well, definitely cutting it close, but certainly not the first time." She affirmed to herself with a smile. Although she was still in a great mood from her lunch with Amy, she had to take a deep breath to calm her nerves. After all her rushing around to make it on time, it didn't help that her car was being more temperamental than ever.

Most of the time she didn't bother fighting with the rust encrusted door and instead chose the more direct route of hopping in and out the open car window. Which was pretty easy for her to do. Although she wasn't a gym queen, she did play a variety of sports on a regular basis and had her kickboxing class 3 times a week, which kept her mind occupied and her body relatively shapely, despite the extra sugar habit. This time however, with the job interview ahead and laundry day still a few days away she thought better of risking it.

She shoved the door with as much force as she could muster and still avoid any visible bruises. The door groaned and squeaked in complaint but finally gave way, leaving her having to catch herself from tumbling onto the pavement. She righted herself as she stepped out of the car, sighed and slammed the door. "One day." She threatened as she scowled at the heap in front of her. "One day I'm replacing you with a car that actually works." With that threat, she laughed and rushed into the building. She blinked adjusting to the light and checked her watch. She'd hit the front reception desk at 4:30. She smiled to herself in amazement, but as she looked around her surroundings she started to frown.

The air felt stagnant and there was a hint of cleaning products, Windex maybe. There was no one around to be seen and the phone seemed to be ringing off the hook. She leaned forward over the desk, craning her neck as far as she could past the desk, but the entrance was L-shaped making it impossible to see past the reception area without walking around the corner. She bit her lip and sighed as she looked around again for signs of anyone nearby. There was no one. She called out.

"Hello?"

After another minute when still no one appeared and she could no longer stand the incessant ringing, she tested the situation further, much louder this time.

"Helllllllllllooooooooooo."

She paused a moment, then louder still. "Yo! Hellooooooo Baaaby!" She called out with an intensifying staccato tone and smiled, amused by her own ridiculousness. "Well, clearly I'm in the right place. A receptionist is definitely needed here." She confirmed aloud, then set her messenger bag on the counter, hopped behind the empty desk and picked up the phone.

She hesitated a moment before speaking in order to read the backwards reflection on the glass entrance door. "Stafford Financial." She finally answered. "How can I help you?" She spoke with as much of a bubbly sounding voice as she could muster without making herself ill.

"Finally!" shouted the angry male caller through the receiver. "I keep getting an error on this damn machine of yours. I want someone out here to fix it today." He rushed on without letting

Rachel respond. "Nobody can get any money out of it. What good is a cash machine when nobody can get any God damn money out of it?" Rachel had to hold the phone away from her ear so as not to bust an ear drum as the man's shouts got louder. "I've been calling for hours. I've pressed zero to get out of voice mail so many damn times I think I broke my finger." The man was obviously way past what could even be described as anger.

Rachel winced at his voice and tried her best to maintain a soothing tone. "I really apologize for the problems you're experiencing and I assure you I'll get you someone to help you right away. Let me just put you on hold for a moment so I can get someone on the line who can help you, is that alright?"

The caller grunted angrily. "Just don't leave me too long, I'm sick of waiting." The caller grumbled once more but didn't protest any further.

Rachel looked around at the phone system for a moment. It wasn't anything she recognized. She knew this caller did not need to be accidentally hung up on, so instead she gently set the receiver down on the desk, shrugged her shoulders, hopped out of the chair and headed around the corner. She stepped into the main room and into what she could only describe as a pit.

There was a circular row of shoulder high cubicles surrounding the center of the room with various other odd sized cubicles strung throughout the rest of the room in no particular order. Along the far edge of the wall were a row of partially glassed in offices, some were lit and some were not. Throughout the pit area were streaks of people that seemed to be running on fast forward, like in a strange movie.

She started forward but stopped in her tracks. There were people shouting across the room at each other rather than picking up the intercom, there were fax machines going like crazy, yes literal fax machines. Of course they could have been some very old printers, she couldn't be truly sure she had never seen an actual fax machine before. Overall, a general feeling of chaos radiated throughout the room. Not sure who might be who and with no one paying any particular attention to her she figured her best bet was to avoid the pit and opt for one of the quieter far offices.

She headed swiftly around the pit area, not wanting to leave the obviously distressed caller waiting for too much longer. Figuring one was as good as the rest she popped her head into the first lit office with an open door she could find. The male occupant had his head lowered, obviously reviewing a report of some sort. He had vivid blonde hair and looked to be in his late thirties.

"Excuse me, I hate to disturb you," she started politely, "but I have a rather upset caller on the phone that says his cash machine isn't working. I wonder if someone can come out front and speak with him."

"ATM." He grunted disgustedly, without looking up from his report.

"Pardon?" She responded in confusion.

"It's not a cash machine," he spoke with disdain, "we don't operate coin or token dispensers. We sell Automated Teller Machines. A. T. M's." His agitation edged his voice louder as he had spelled out the acronym as if speaking to a child. "Why the hell don't you just transfer him to the service department for God's sake?" He was shouting now when he finally lifted his head up from his papers and was able to take in the full view of Rachel's standing dumbfounded in his doorway. He looked at her for a moment, obviously puzzled by her presence, but shook it off and continued. "Well?"

Rachel kept her composure, despite the fact that her normal reaction right about now would have been to knock this guy's block off. She was after all supposed to be having a job interview right now, so instead or arguing she offered her explanation in her calmest and sweetest voice. Kill 'em with kindness was her motto of the moment. "Well I might have done that, sir, but I have no idea where your service department might be. Nor for that matter any knowledge that you might even have a service department, because I don't actually work here. Besides that fact, I'm not really sure how to transfer a call on your phone system or what extensions I would even transfer him too. So there's that." To complete her passive rant she tossed him her sweetest smile.

The man stared at her, stunned for a moment, before some sort of recognition of the facts started to sink in. "You don't work here." He said, more as a fact than a question.

Rachel shook her head in response. "Not yet." She delivered in the same matter of fact voice.

"But..." He started to mutter out, but Rachel cut him off.

"Look, I don't mean to be rude. I can explain it all in more detail later, but I think someone really should speak with the man on the phone right now now before he gets any angrier." She emphasized her point by stepping back out of the way leaving a path open for the man to come through.

With a look of instant awareness he jumped to his feet. "Oh yes of course. Come with me." He directed as he rushed from his office, past the pit area and out to the front desk. Rachel stayed close behind, as her own energetic gate easily kept pace with his.

When they reached the reception desk, she unceremoniously

retrieved her stuff off the counter and took a seat in one of the reception area waiting chairs. The man temporarily ignored Rachel and immediately the picked up the phone to speak with the expectedly even angrier man on the other end of the line.

She studied him from her new vantage point. He sat against the edge of the reception desk instead of in the chair as he spoke to the caller. His face grimacing painfully, leaving her to assume that the man on the other end must have decided to give him the full extent of his vocal rage. She felt some momentary sympathy for him as she had faced it earlier and it wasn't pleasant. He looked to be just over six feet, lean, but filled out his shirt nicely, indicating he kept himself in good shape.

"Yes, sir," he began in a low calming voice, "I agree that is not acceptable." He paused as he listened to the caller's response. "I truly apologize, but I assure you that I will make sure this is taken care of for you today." He nodded in sympathetic agreement with what the customer must have been relaying to him, he let the man continue on until he was done.

He shifted his stance and adjusted the phone in his hand to get more comfortable. "Yes, as I said, it will be taken care of today. I will see to that personally. Now what is your merchant ID and your call back number?" He asked, leaning back and grabbing a pen and a pink post-it. "Yes I have it." He continued, as he quickly wrote it down. "I will have the service department call you as soon as they have dispatched a technician. Again I apologize for your wait, but I will make sure your problem is resolved."

After he hung up the phone he sighed heavily, rubbed his brow and stood up leaving the front of his hair slightly askew. He looked over at Rachel and smiled as he rolled his eyes in relief. "That was fun." He offered sarcastically. Rachel smiled supportively in response. He raised his finger indicating he would be right with her, before peeling off the top post-it and slipping out-of-sight the direction they had just come from.

Rachel took a deep breath. "Well I can see this place will be quite the adventure." She whispered to herself with a hushed chuckle. She leaned back in the chair to relax and finally took in her surroundings. The entrance walls were painted in a pale shade of mauve, so pale you only glimpsed the purple in the reflections of light that streamed through the front glass entry doors. There were lush blooming plants placed at welcoming intervals throughout the room. The walls, doors and windows were accented with a dark silvery grey that richly enhanced the wall color.

The logo stenciled on the wall behind the reception desk was done in the same accent color. "Subtle." She said aloud as she nodded in approval. Then she noticed an ATM sitting in the far corner by the front entrance. She smiled and went over to take a quick look. It had a small footprint, like the ones found convenience stores, though this one was much cleaner, lacking the graffiti and whatever else they were usually covered with. She shuddered and decided not to imagine what some of the stains they often had might consist of. Just as she was poking her head around the back of the machine for a closer look the man she had grabbed for the phone call had returned. He startled her, making her jump when he spoke.

"I see there is no end to your involvement in our company." His voice held an obvious hint of amusement and his handsome face was cocked at an angle indicating his curiosity.

She straightened and turned towards him. "Well, I aim to please!" She said as she flipped him a salute before firmly planting her hands on her hips.

He smiled and leaned casually against the front of the reception desk, facing off with her. "So do I get to hear how you've come to add this drama to my day or what?"

She chuckled. "Most certainly, my name is Rachel Ingles and I'm here for a job interview."

He raised a questioning eyebrow as he casually crossed his arms. "Oh, for what?"

She smiled coyly and tossed a nod towards the empty receptionist chair behind him. "Well, for receptionist I assume."

With this he glanced over his shoulder to acknowledge her observation. "Well, you've definitely come to the right place then."

Finally acknowledging the strangeness of the events that had just occurred she let her arms slip to their sides and softened her demeanor to a more professional tone. "Well I really am here for the receptionist position. I was sent here by the Brockton temp agency. I had an appointment scheduled for 4:30 with a Mr. Tanner." He offhandedly glanced at his watch as she spoke. "I was here on time," she immediately added in defensively, "but the phone call took a while. You see there was no one at the desk and I couldn't stand to listen to the ringing phone, so I had to answer it."

He held up a hand in protest and smiled. "No, I'm sorry it wasn't that. I just hadn't realized that it was so late in the day already. I feel like I still have a million things to do and its pretty much the end of the day, that's all." Now he felt like it was his turn to explain. "As you can see we truly do need a receptionist. Our last one quit 'unexpectedly' last week and we've had no one that we could spare to even fill in until we got a replacement." He shifted nervously. "I did have every intention of having someone sit out here this afternoon so you wouldn't be left standing around," he sighed and shrugged before continuing, "but the day just got away from me."

"So I take it I was to meet you?" Rachel asked hesitantly, not wanting to assume any more than she had already today.

This seemed to jolt him out of his casual attitude. He moved towards her, hand extended. "Oh yes, I'm sorry, it looks like I must apologize once again to you, Rachel, was it?" She nodded in response.

She took his hand; his grip was firm yet gentle, and she thought she caught the hint of a wink in his crystal blue eyes. A player, she thought briefly before mentally slapping herself for her quick judgmental thoughts.

"I am Mr. Tanner, Josh Tanner. Sales manager and head of operations. I guess you could say I'm in charge of this crazy place and before you ask, yes I was expecting you, but I think maybe this worked out even better."

She tipped her head to offer a sideways glance. "How so?"

"Well, you certainly showed you can handle stress with grace and poise and new situations with skill. What else do I need to know?" He affirmed by raising his hands. Rachel stared at him as she contemplated what he was saying. She slowly nodded her head. She didn't want to make any assumptions. He took her uncertainty at face value and continued. "You're hired, that is if you still want the job, but from what I've seen, you're a natural."

Rachel mulled this over for a moment. "Oh hey I still want it," she started hesitantly, "but don't you want to see my resume, check references, that kind of thing?"

Josh chuckled. "Oh that," he said rolling his eyes, "what would a reference tell me that I haven't already seen. You're not afraid to dive right in that's for sure and more than anything else, you can stand up to me." He smiled, then dropping his voice into a more somber tone he continued. "Seriously though, from what Amy Renalds told me, I already know your qualifications. We have dealt with Ms. Renalds enough times to know that she would never consider sending anyone to us that didn't already pass our required back ground checks and that she hadn't checked out personally." He leaned back against the counter and casually rested a hand on it. "Look from what I've seen here today and with the agency vouching for you, I have all I need to make my decision. So I say again, the job's yours if you want it."

Rachel smiled all traces of doubt gone. "Well you are definitely right about Amy, Miss Renalds," she corrected herself, "her reputation in this business is everything to her." Josh simply nodded along, patiently waiting for her response. She straightened back her shoulders and walked closer to Josh. "When do I start?"

Josh once again looked at his watch and ran his fingers through his expertly styled spiked hair. "Hmm, let's see, you busy at 9:00 am tomorrow?"

CHAPTER 3

Rachel plopped down on her couch, tossed her head back and stretched out to reflect on the day's events. After a moment she giggled and shook her head in quiet disbelief. Then she looked across the room towards her darkened computer and cringed. "I should be over there, writing, instead of lying here." She scolded.

She wanted desperately to be a fulltime professional writer, a paid one. It was the main reason she stuck with temping, that and the fact that she got bored easily. Temping gave her the freedom to work when she needed to and yet not take her work home with her. Lately though, she spent more time temping and less time writing, but that wasn't for lack of time, more lack of confidence. That and a case of writers block.

Now, staring through the fading light of the day at her dark computer monitor, she felt it taunting her. She wanted so desperately to write for the sake of writing. If anything just to know the craft hadn't abandoned her, but the fear of writing something less than brilliant currently paralyzed her. She turned back and stared at her messenger bag that she had so carelessly tossed by the doorway upon returning from her 'interview'. She sunk further in the couch, letting her head drop back against the cushions as she laughed aloud.

"I should write about today. Or better yet my last job fiasco." Then she shook her head in defeat, thinking back to her first rejection letter. "We do not believe that this would ever happen to a real person, it's too contrived." They had said. *Yeah, like anyone would believe what had happened at her last job wasn't made up, who would believe her* she thought to herself.

She continued to stare it down in defiance. "Screw it!" She finally exclaimed, leaping off the couch and over to her computer. Who cares if they think it's implausible at least I'd be writing something!" With that she turned on her computer, letting out a satisfied sigh as the familiar tune announced its readiness. With only a moment's hesitation and an anxious knot in her stomach she opened a new document.

She started and restarted the first sentence what felt like a hundred times, but after the fifth attempt she smiled. Before long, her imagination driving her on as the fantasy of her story mixed with the reality she knew. Suddenly she felt that familiar rush of emotions. It felt good to be writing again, and all those internal critical voices seemed to just fade away as she lost herself in the beat of her rhythmic typing.

Finally, when she had to stop for the sixth time to work out various kinks in her neck and hands and could no longer concentrate, she was forced stop for the night. She found it hard to shut the computer off, in fear that if she did she wouldn't be able to pick it up again, but when she saw the flicker of the clock changing time she jumped to action. She looked at her wristwatch for confirmation of the time, 3:01 am. "Yikes, work!" She reminded herself as she begrudgingly shut it down and rushed to get ready for bed.

"I really have to find a way to get creative at earlier hours." She teased herself as she looked in the mirror and tied back her hair. "Either that or find a job that will let me work when my muse wants to." She shrugged, then plopped a gallon of toothpaste on her toothbrush and jammed it in her mouth. "You mean like writing." She mumbled to her reflection, her mouth full of minty foam, and giggled. She was her jovial self again as she rushed top speed for bed, the last week's events on paper and out of her mind. Too bad her new job didn't have anything exciting to offer her story she mused. Oh well, at least the boss is cute. She stopped and gave herself a quick lecture in the mirror. "Oh no you don't, that is even worse trouble getting mixed up with the boss! He is NOT cute!"

CHAPTER 4

Rachel groaned as her alarm clock blared, the announcers annoying voice ruining her beautiful dream. She couldn't remember what it was about, but she knew it had to be better than the annoying commercial that was now shouting in her ear. Of course she was sure she wouldn't have been this irritated if she had not stayed up past 3 am. Despite her grogginess a proud grin crossed her face as she thought back, "Oh well, you only live once." She proclaimed aloud as she rolled out of bed and stumbled down the hall to shower her eyes open.

She cringed as the bright bathroom light stung her eyes. Too tired to complain, she bent down and turned on the shower. Any normal person would have realized being this tired called for a cold shower, but who ever claimed she was normal. Besides she stood firm in her belief that the hotter the shower the more she could force the aches and cramps out of her shoulders, and therefore the more she might be able to function normally.

She quickly undressed, gargled and then when the room was sufficiently dense with steam, she stepped into the welcoming shower and fought the urge to sleep; trying to focus this early was the worst part of being a night owl. Realizing being late on her first day might not be the best move. She finally forced herself to shut off the shower.

As she stepped out she remembered the down side of really hot showers; the room temperature outside felt a hundred times colder. "Eek!" She squealed loud enough to wake the dead, or at least any neighbors that might still be sleeping as she hopped out. Her shivering body could barely pull the towel off the rack, but somehow she managed to wrap it around herself and open the door. Where she immediately proceeded to let out another scream; the hallway was even colder than the steamy bathroom.

“Okay, awake now. Awake now!” She cried as she streaked quickly down the hallway to her bedroom. “Oh man, this job better be worth this torture.”

*****

Rachel raced into the parking lot and slid out the open window of her car; she didn’t have the energy to fight with the door today. She checked her watch. “Two minutes to spare, getting better.” She nodded with pride to herself. Then she leaned back through the window to fetch her bag; legs dangling out over the door as she stretched to reach it. After snatching it up triumphantly, she jumped back out and instantly found herself up against an immoveable object. In shock, she just about lost her footing and was immediately caught by a set of strong male arms.

“Quite some entrance; trying to top yesterday already?” Her heart skipped at the sound the man who had caught and rescued her from falling. She steadied herself and turned around to see the solid object she had backed into had been the solid chest of Josh Tanner. She smiled in recognition and brushed herself off in an effort to hide her embarrassment.

“Ah well you know how it is, a girls gotta have some excitement in her life.” She laughed nervously.

Josh took a step back and gave her the once over. “Why is it I get the feeling you don’t have to look too hard for that?” He cajoled, half joking, half serious.

"Must be an overactive imagination." She concluded for him an innocent look glow about her face, still flushed from her efforts with her bag.

He raised his eyebrow, mockingly. "Must be." He added with an enticing smile.

She automatically returned his smile, finding herself drawn in by his inviting eyes and silky voice. They stood staring for a moment, then without warning, she shivered and found herself averting her eyes. She was mentally slapping herself, Not Cute, she reminded herself. Josh looked puzzled, but before he could say anything she gave him a casual smile. "Guess I better hurry if I don't want to be late for my first day." With that she turned and headed to the entrance.

Josh shook his head and chuckled under his breath. "Yes, but you're not supposed to be ahead of me!" He taunted, with a wink and a smile as he passed her at a jog. She ignored her competitive urge to race by him that screamed through her as he beat her to the entrance. This was after all, her boss and she should behave, at least for today.

A devilish grin crossed her lips when she found herself staring at his ass. Her smile turned into a smirk when he turned and stood holding the door open for her, all the while ensuring he had left only enough room that she would have to brush against him to get through.

"Well, I guess I should get someone to show you how this place works so you can get started learning the ropes." He said casually as she neared. "Although at the rate you're diving into the company I'm sure you'll be moving up faster than I did."

She smiled as she brushed by. "What makes you so sure I want to stick around here long enough to move up?"

Josh stiffened as he followed her in, letting the door close automatically behind them with a click. He studied her in silence for a moment as she turned to face him. After a few seconds he tossed her a sly grin and a knowing wink as he neared. He stopped in front of her and leaned in until he was a few inches from her face and spoke in a low voice. "Because you find it intriguing." He declared, in such a way that indicated instead of "it" he really meant "me".

He lingered a moment longer, letting his warm breath brush against her, then he turned and walked past her. As she turned to follow, he glanced over his shoulder and as if knowing just which button to push, he added, "Besides, I dare you to."

She laughed at his childhood taunt, but she had to work hard not to respond. A dare was a tough one for her to resist, but she resisted. After all, the now empty reception area didn't do much to convince her that this job would ever be exciting enough to keep her interest. She gave it a month, tops.

Josh smiled at her doubtful look. "How about we start with getting you trained enough so that you can stop calling our ATMs, 'cash thingies'."

Instead of protesting that she had just been repeating the caller's words, she simply smiled and nodded. "So where do we start?"

"I think it's best if you know the types of people that will be calling and who they'll need to speak to. I wish I had the time to give you some proper training sessions, but I'm swamped right now." Josh turned on his heels and started through the reception area towards the back. "Come on, I'll give you a quick tour first, then leave you with someone who can run you through the basics."

He rounded the corner with Rachel in toe. They passed by the washrooms that he pointed out for her, and pointed to the lunch room, then stopped at the main open pit area that she had avoided yesterday. She took a deep breath and took it all in. The room was already bustling at a pace nearing chaos, it made the previous day's activity seem like nothing. Her mouth slightly agape, she received a quiet chuckle from Josh as he nodded her on. They pushed forward into the overcrowded area. She wasn't sure where to look first, Josh narrated for her.

"This is the technician's area. First thing in the morning and end of day is the most hectic here as far as bodies go. Most of these guys are out in the field all day installing new ATM locations, answering service calls from merchants who report problems, like that caller yesterday or doing preventative maintenance to keep the machines working properly." His tone and manor was strong and confident, he was clearly in his element explaining the business and he was all professional. "Right now they are all here to pick up their assignments and map out their routes. Once they head out, this area will settle to the quiet buzz you saw yesterday. It will contain just the techs that can do support over the phone."

Rachel nodded, but she quickly realized like the activity before her, most of her next few days were going to be a blur as she tried to absorb all the information she would need to not sound like an idiot when she spoke to anyone. She chastised herself for not taking notes. "If I hadn't seen this, I wouldn't have described yesterday as quiet, but I see what you mean."

Josh rested an encouraging hand on her shoulder and smiled. "Don't worry, a few days in this and it will start to make sense. For now, just listen and take it in. Here let me introduce you before they head out to the warehouse to load up their trucks." Josh tried to signal the big guy closest to them over, but he was busy struggling to wrap up a large odd looking device with a clear plastic packaging that looked suspiciously like Saran wrap. It was the size of a shoe box, the base of it was formed with solid metal plates and it was about the size of a file drawer stood on its end. From there it was covered in a series of metal rods and plastic cogs that held in place two rubber tracks.

"Punt!" Josh yelled above the din and the rather awkwardly large man stopped what he was doing and looked up. "An ATM with a broken cash dispenser isn't much good to us. Where's the bloody packaging it came in?" The technician stared dumbfounded and simply shrugged. Josh rolled his eyes and looked towards the smaller, more defined man sitting atop the last desk. He had been sorting through a stack of papers but had stopped to watch the exchange between Josh and the guy called Punt.

The man sighed and looked over at Punt and spoke in a heavily Spanish accented voice. "Punt, check the warehouse, it's likely with the other parts boxes." Punt shrugged again and trudged off towards the back entrance. He looked to Rachel like he figured the Saran wrap was good enough and anything else was a waste of time, but he would do it anyway just to avoid being yelled at again. The smaller man then turned his attention back to Josh. "Who you got there boss man?" He said smiling towards Rachel. Josh stepped forward and motioned Rachel closer.

"Guys," he started proudly, "this is our new receptionist, Rachel. Rachel," he said as he looked from her back to the group of technicians, "this is the heart of our business, tech support. Without these guys the money doesn't come in, literally." He added with a chuckle that the guys knowingly returned. He started his introductions by pointing first to the man who had asked the question. "That rather overly confident man is Miguel, he's the head of our service department and right now he should be getting these guys their assignments so they can get on the road." Josh added with a friendly chastising tone which Miguel promptly ignored.

"Don't listen to this blow hard, he's all talk. Welcome Rachel. You need anything, you come to me. I'm the only one who knows anything anyway." He puffed up his chest and Rachel gave him a friendly smile.

"You wish." Chortled the youngest of the group, who happened to be sitting close enough to throw a friendly jab Miguel's way. "Don't listen to him Rachel. Without me they wouldn't have any smarts in this group. I'm Jackson and you can come to me if you need anything, anything at all." He said broadening his chest as if the next thing he would do was to thump his fists against it and let out a Tarzan yell.

This one she assumed was the pretty boy of the bunch. He couldn't have been more than 19 or 20, but seems he had ego enough to fill the entire building. Rachel smiled at him as well. He was full confidence, but clearly harmless. He had an air of sweetness about him that probably allowed him to say almost anything and get away with it. As the rest moved in with similar introductions she quickly felt right at home. She was used to working with blue collar guys like this and while they all loved to show off, they were usually the most welcoming and easy to get along with. Better than the bunch of stuffed shirt lawyers that she had worked for last year. They were all ego and thought they were above everyone unless it suited their interests, for the most part, though there were one or two that she had gotten along with ok.

She wasn't sure she would remember all the guys names but did make sure to repeat them back at least once in an effort to try none the less. Beside Jackson, there was a much older man, perhaps in his late 30's. It was hard to tell though as he had a face that was clearly weathered by more than just time. His name was Martin. Across from Martin was another heavily Spanish accented unassuming man. Hard to size up, but probably aged between Jackson and Miguel and sized somewhere in between the two. He was introduced as Hector.

After Hector, Miguel introduced the last two who had remained seated due to their headsets. They were Bob and Phil. Miguel explained that they were working the help desk today and if she got any calls for a technician she would transfer them to one of them. Phil, he explained, always worked the phones, but that Jackson and Bob usually switched off; One in the field and one working the phones with Phil. After he finished the introductions he sat back onto the desk he had been sitting on when they first arrived.

"Welcome to the Bull Pen Rachel." Miguel said as motioning his hands in a sweeping gesture around their area.

"I can see why you call it that." Rachel said giving them all the once over and receiving a chuckle from the group in return.

"Well shall we?" Josh asked as he motioned her onward. Rachel nodded and waved goodbye as they moved on. As they walked out of ear shot she whispered to him. "Who was that other guy, the one you called Punt?"

"Oh that's John. Everyone calls him punt." Josh noticed the puzzled look she had on her face, but simply offered her a shrug and an odd game reference. "You only punt in a game when you have to." Rachel nodded slowly as they walked on, but her bewildered look remained.

The rest of the tour was pretty much a blur. He pointed out the location of the various supplies she might need, the copier, long rows of metal filing cabinets and locked metal storage cabinets that he had explained contained the paper journals from all the ATMs. He pointed out two large cross-cut shredders, which were located on opposite sides of the main cubicle areas surrounding the bull pen. Those he said were required to meet audit rules regarding the destruction of the encryption keys; he explained further what encryption keys were, clearly they were not actual keys but codes on a paper for something, but she forgot most of it.

Then they came to the rows of offices, past the entrance to the warehouse area, opposite to the bull pen. They stopped briefly in front of a rather large and currently empty corner office. This, Josh explained, is for the CEO and owner of the company when he chose to come by the offices. For the most part the office was always dark. The only indication he might actually exist, Josh explained, was his assistant who sat in the cubicle kitty corner to his office.

As they continued on, she came to realize that most of the offices we shared offices that the various commissioned sales staff would use when they came onsite. While most of them worked out of their homes, there was usually one or two that were always in the offices at any one time. He passed by his office which needed no narrative for her to recognize before rounding the corner towards an area closed off to the rest by two large swinging doors.

This was the accounting department. It was much more organized and quieter than the main areas. She felt like she had to be extra quiet when she was standing in this part, almost like she was in a library. She was introduced to the staff briefly and then quickly ushered out. They seemed to like their quiet. Next they headed to their last stop on her tour. The squared row of cubicles that seemed to act as a buffer between the quiet of the accounting department and the craziness of the Bull Pen.

"This is the settlement department." Josh explained as they approached. "At the back there is Judy, she handles all the cardholder disputes that come in from the banks and processors. One over from her is Leanne; she does merchant reconciliation and disputes. Over here is who I need you to meet." He finished as they approached the cubicle closes to them.

Josh leaned on the corner of the cubicle. The woman with long black hair looked up from her computer and upon seeing Josh she almost purred as she smiled up at him. Her smile turned instantly cold when she noticed Rachel standing beside him. Josh didn't seem to notice her quick change in demeanor or if he did, he didn't care. He went on to introduce them.

"Rachel I want you to meet Coralene." He gave them both what Rachel had already realized must be his trademark school boy grin and continued. "Coralene runs the settlement department here. I will be leaving you in her more than capable hands so you can get the training you need to get you started." Josh adjusted his stance in order to face her. He spoke in a clear precise tone. "Rachel is our new receptionist. I need you to show her the ropes and make sure she gets what she needs to take over that role."

"Of course Josh." Coralene replied sweetly as she leaned forward, causing her breasts to squeeze at the top of her scoop neck yellow sweater as they pressed against her bent arms. Josh again seemed to take no notice of her extra attentions and turned back towards Rachel. Coralene gave Rachel a menacing stare and looked her up and down.

Rachel met Coralene's gaze head on with her own sweet indifferent one. She figured Coralene to be around the same age as she had guessed Jackson to be, perhaps a year or two older. Not much more than 21 or 22 anyway and not worth her getting riled up about the young ones clear possessive attitudes towards her boss. If Josh didn't care, she certainly wasn't about to.

"Rachel, I'll have to leave you with Coralene for now. I have a few conference calls I need to be on, but I'll be sure to stop by later to check on you." He moved closer to her as he spoke.

Rachel smiled and nodded. "No problem." She said turning back to face Coralene who had had already sat back in her chair with a pout. "I'm sure Coralene and I will be just fine." She threw Coralline a sweet smile which was not reciprocated.

"Great. I can't tell you enough how glad I am you could join us." He said giving her a gentle pat on her shoulder. He then turned back to Coralene who immediately spun her chair around to face him, leaving the tops of her thighs exposed as her black skirt slid up with the movement. "I've already taken her around to meet the rest of the staff, so if you could get her started at the front desk that would be best." His voice was light and professional but he didn't wait for her to respond. He simply gave them both his easy smile and strolled off towards his office, leaving Rachel and Coralene alone.

Rachel took a deep breath and straightened her shoulders. She had temped in enough offices to know how to handle the young Coralene's of the world. "I really hope I'm not too much bother. I'm sure as head of the settlement department you must be swamped so I can't tell you how grateful I am that you can take the time to help me like that." Coralene's pout slipped off her face. She uncrossed her long naturally tanned legs and stood beside Rachel. A cautious, but proud grin crossed her bright red lipstick laden lips. Rachel grinned knowingly, go for the ego boost off that worked the best.

"Let me introduce you to my team, they'll cover you during your lunch breaks so you'll get to know them quite well. After that I'll show you to the most important place in the office." Rachel tilted her head. Coralene just laughed herself. "The coffee machine. Rachel beamed and nodded her heart felt agreement. At least they had something in common. With coffee to look forward to Rachel was easily able to smile through the rest of Coralene's charming ways.

Coralene pranced down the corridor of cubicles, her red stilettos weaving on the carpet. She stopped at the last one in the row. The mousy brunette, who Rachel recognized as Judy, was busy on the phone. Coralene impatiently tapped her long red tipped fingernails on the top of the cubicle. Judy waved her off and absently nodded to the caller on the other end of the line. She listened in silence, adding only the occasional 'uh huh' to indicate to the caller that she was still there. After a loud sigh from Coralene, Judy covered the receiver with her nail bitten fingers and whispered. "What's up?"

"I need you to train the new receptionist." Coralene replied in an annoyed tone. Judy rolled her eyes and pointed to the phone. Coralene crossed her arms and stomped her foot before finally prancing back down the way they had just come. Coralene lifted her nose as they passed Pam's cubicle. Rachel smiled as the middle aged woman looked up and shook her head disapprovingly before nodding towards Rachel.

Coralene continued past the small group of interns who were working the phones to generate sales leads, smiling only at the lone male in the bunch. Rachel followed quietly, biting her lip and looking around innocently, trying her best to stifle a laugh. She didn't need to be friends with Coralene, but she certainly didn't need any trouble either. Laughing at Coralene would have been trouble.

They finally stopped at Leanne's cubicle. Leanne quickly minimized her game of solitaire to expose a half filled spreadsheet, likely cursing the carpeted floors for stifling Coralene heels. She was about to grab for the phone when Coralene abruptly stopped her. "I need you to train the new receptionist." She commanded, not bothering to use either of their names. Leanne sighed, but before she could speak Coralene continued. “and don’t bother pretending you’re too busy.”

Leanne spun her head around to face them, sending waves of bleached blond curls past her face. She pulled an errant strand from her mouth before speaking. “Why do I have to?” She whined between chews off her bubble gum. Though not as young as Coralene or Judy, Leanne was clearly at the same maturity level as the other two and maybe somewhere around 26. Rachel sighed, invoking an angry glance from Leanne, so she quickly returned a sweet smile and Leanne quickly went back to ignoring her again.

Coralene tapped her foot impatiently. “Because I said so.” Rachel rolled her eyes, unnoticed, as the two stared each other down. She suddenly felt very old, even though she couldn’t have been much older than Leanne. Leanne easily gave in. Coralene was the leader after all. Leanne gave Rachel a quick annoyed glance, then nodded to Coralene who immediately grinned proudly before prancing off down the corridor. Leaving Rachel without her coffee and Leanne without her game of solitaire. They were not a happy pair.
Leanne stood up and they both trudged off; neither leading the way as an air of boredom and apprehension overtook them.

*****

Training hadn’t improved the situation, if you could call it training. Between her bubble gum popping instructions on phone system and her complaints of having too much work to do to be expected to train someone, Leanne did manage to give Rachel the basics. All ATM support calls go to the technicians and she learnt their extensions. Any investors who claim they didn’t get paid their money from the ATM go to the accounting department. Investors she explained owned their own ATMs but use Stafford Financial’s sponsorship into the bank networks so their money flowed through the company, minus a sponsorship fee. Any cardholders or merchants, which she learnt were store owners, who claim they didn't get money from the ATMs go to Judy unless she's busy, then, and only then, do they go to Leanne. They only go to Coralene as a last resort.

Leanne had also managed to muster up the energy to get her a badge that was the only thing that identified her as staff and therefore allowed to go into the back offices unaccompanied. She also learnt that her main function was to verify staff and ensure visitors were signed in, given a guest badge and ensure that someone accompanied them into the back and that under no circumstances was anyone to go in back without a badge or accompanied by someone with a badge. After that Leanne's attention was impossible to keep, so aside from learning how to turn the phone system on and off automatic answering Rachel couldn't get any more information from her.

After a few minutes of awkward silence, she switched the phone onto automatic and turned to Leanne who was busy stretching her now stale smelling gum around her finger. "Probably time for a coffee break right about now don't you think?" Leanne's eyes suddenly brightened, but she seemed hesitant, so Rachel continued. "I mean, I know how much work you have waiting, surely we can stop here and take a break. You've done a great job training me, I'm sure I can handle it from here on."

That was all the coaxing Leanne seemed to need and she hoped up, tossed her gum in the trash, barely and spoke. "Follow me." Rachel smiled, leapt out of her chair and followed close behind Leanne. She hadn't gone this long without a coffee in years and didn't think she could feign interest any longer without it. Now she didn't have to.

*****

With Leanne back at her desk and a very sweet and very thick coffee in hand, Rachel was finally able to function. It hadn't taken her long to pick up the phone system and learn the main extensions, so with time on her hands she decided to poke around the computer system so she could actually try learning something about Stafford. She preferred this method of training anyway, self training. Most people didn't bother to spend much time on training a temp so she was often left to her own devices. Learning as much as she could by combing through the materials that companies often left on their networks but rarely remembered was even there. It took a while to find anything interesting, but once she did immersed herself in reading and spent the times she was not on the phone or drinking coffee, reading.

She hadn't given much thought to ATMs when she had used them, but now she found their simple complexities fascinating. The fact that so many people touched each part of the transaction from start to finish. How revenues were divided amongst all the parties involved by literally splitting them down to the half pennies. She had even stumbled onto some old reports that detailed the costs to run an ATM. The Visa network registration fees alone were over 10 thousand dollars a year that Stafford and its clients paid.

She became so fascinated in trying to figure out how, with so many parties involved and so many hidden fees, an ATM could charge only two dollars a transaction and still be profitable, that she lost all track of time. Which is why she was startled when Josh came up behind her and spoke.

"I see snooping is a habit with you." Josh gave her an amused smile when she jumped at the sound of his voice. "I'm going to have to keep a closer eye on you." He added with a wink.

Rachel turned and flashed him an innocent smile. "Just making sure I learn enough to be a valuable employee." Josh exhaled in disbelief. "Okay, so maybe a little snooping. It's sort of fascinating, I never knew ATMs involved so much." She admitted. Josh crossed his arms. "What? Can't a girl be a little curious about her new company?"

"I doubt you've ever been only a little curious." He teased. Rachel bit her lip, not able to come up with an argument to that. Josh laughed smugly. "I guess you've never heeded the warning about curiosity and the cat?"

Rachel shrugged. "Without curiosity, I'd never learn anything."

"And so just how much have you learned?" He said as he leaned against her desk.

"Enough to know there is a lot more I could be doing around here to help you."

Josh cocked his eyebrows and eyed her suspiciously. "One day and already bucking for a promotion?"

"Maybe I'll give it two days before that." Rachel laughed and Josh quickly joined in, but still didn't totally lose the look of suspicion he questioned her with earlier. She shrugged. "Ok, ok I'll wait a week."

CHAPTER 5

"So? How's it going?" Amy Asked hesitantly as she twirled her fork around in her salad. It wasn't clear why they continued to call their get-togethers lunch. They spent more time talking than any actual eating and some weekends, more drinking than talking.

"Fine." Rachel replied quickly, "and you can relax now I am not here for another job!" She continued with a hint of laughter in her voice.

Amy sighed in animated relief and they both broke into laughter. "But seriously, how's it going, I haven't heard much from you lately?"

Rachel looked around as if worried someone would overhear. "Well I don't want to jinx it, but it's pretty damn good." Amy raised her eyebrow in disbelief. "No really. I think this could be a job that could make me give up temping. I really have a knack for this ATM biz." She sat up straight, with a proud look on her face. "In fact they just moved me up from receptionist to sales & operations support. I'm helping with settlement reporting, sales contract processing, heck they even have me doing tech support every once in a while!" She laughed excitedly.

Amy sat back in her chair watching her friend chatter on and nodded. "Well I'm happy for you. I'm not sure I believe you won't get bored," Rachel was about to protest but Amy continued over top of her. "But I'm happy if you are happy there." Rachel smiled in gratitude. "Guess I'm going to have to find another couple of temps though, with you out of the pool, I'll lose all my work tracking down jobs for someone at a moment's notice!" Rachel slugged her in the arm and they both broke into more laughter. "So who are you working for?"

"Amy." She groaned. "It was only a few months ago you got me the job, how could you forget where I work?"

"No, you goof. I mean you said you're in a support role now, that usually means you are supporting someone, so who is it?"

Rachel laughed at herself. "Oh that. I'm helping Josh, the operations manager, slash head of sales, slash my boss." She answered animating the 'slashes' with her fingers.

"Josh? Quite friendly aren't we? Huh?" Amy's expression demanded only the juicy stuff.

"Yes, Josh Tanner, I call him Josh, but so does EVERY body else." Amy seemed to slump in disappointment. Rachel picked up a small bit of her food and casually added, "But he does have a great ass." before stuffing it into her mouth. She acted nonchalant but delighting in the light that bounced back into her friend's eyes as her mouth practically fell open in disbelief. Amy squirmed in her seat waiting for more. Rachel simply shrugged and continued eating, this time Amy slugged her.

Rachel rubbed her arm and pouted, trying to stave off her laughter. Amy sighed exaggeratedly until she finally continued. "Honestly, there really is nothing to tell. Yes, he has a nice ass like I said and there is the odd flirty wink or comment now and then, but he's my boss. And I'm really trying NOT to get into trouble this time; especially with my new title." They both let out a light chuckle at that. "Besides I am learning so much so quickly and working such long hours that there doesn't seem to be time for anything to go on, but at least he's nice to look at."

Amy waved her hand quickly over her head before grabbing a quick bite of food as if to say "Whatever" and let it go at that, for now. Suddenly she jumped in her seat and looked at her watch. "Shit." She exclaimed. "I gotta go sweetie." Amy answered Rachel's mid-bite puzzled gaze by rolling her eyes. "Brad's called some 'urgent' meeting that I just 'have' to be at and I'm late for it. He's gonna kill me." Amy finished with her face buried in her purse.

"Why should this time be any different?" Rachel teased. Amy simply shrugged in response as she pulled out her wallet. Rachel watched her as a devilish sparkle touched her eyes. "Speaking of nothing going on, what's with the Brad thing? You made any moves yet?"

Amy looked up at her and groaned. "As if." She protested unconvincingly. Rachel cocked her head. Amy giggled as her face flushed, but she shook it off quickly. "I really do have to be there." She offered apologetically. "I promised I'd be there early and as it is I am just going to make it on time, if I go now." She added quickly as she gobbled up another quick bite, downed the rest of her drink and threw some money on the counter for her part of the bill. Then she leaned over and gave her friend a quick hug and raced off, waving briefly as she rushed out.

"Next time you don't get out of the question so easily." Rachel called out after her, invoking a barely visible devilish grin from Amy before she ducked around the corner out of sight. Rachel continued to watch after her for a moment before she too registered the time and waved hurriedly for the check. She threw down enough to cover the rest of the bill and a tip and rushed out the door to avoid being late herself. Her wallet liked this being regularly employed thing, she might have to keep it up.

****

She rolled into the parking lot, glanced at her watch and let out a sigh of relief as she turned the loud rumbling engine off and smiled. "You may not look too pretty, but you've sure got power, hey boy." She said aloud as she stroked the steering wheel.

"So it's not just boys who talk to their cars?"

Rachel jumped at the sound of Josh's voice suddenly sounding through her open window. She turned to face him, her hand reflexively over her racing heart. "Jeez Josh you scared the crap out of me. What are you trying to do give me a heart attack?" She scolded gently.

"Sorry. Guess I've never seen a woman talk to her car before and I just had to see for myself." He paused a moment stepping back from the car. "So are you coming out of there or should I leave you two alone?"

She smiled. "I don't know," she started, patting the dash gently, "he's always been there for me it's hard to walk away from such a good thing."

Josh cocked his head and gave her a provocative grin. "Not even for me?"

She shivered, uncertain why, so she quickly shook the feeling off and fell back on her more familiar sarcasm. "Leave this big powerful guy for you? Hmm." She rubbed her chin as if thinking very hard.

Josh crossed his arms defensively. "Ouch, you really know how to hurt a guy's ego don't you?"

"Practice." She confirmed without hesitation and then as if making her painful decision she sighed. "Alright, I guess I could tear myself away." She let out a laugh as she slid out the window. Josh raised his brows quizzically at her exit move. She shrugged and stood beside him as she looked back at her beat up old car. "He maybe powerful, but he's still old and stubborn and I find it best most days just to leave him be, because if I don't," she paused, then leaned in and lowered her voice, "he gets kind of testy." Without further explanation she smiled and headed into the office, leaving Josh to shake his head.

She stopped halfway there and glanced back, catching him staring at her ass. She smiled and without letting him know that she had caught his less than subtle stare, she called out. "Coming?" Her face held an innocent expression, but her voice held a slight hint of a taunt. It was a subtle double-entendre that only a few would have picked up on in that situation. Josh was not one of the few, but Rachel wasn't surprised, like her sarcastic quips, she was used to most of them going unnoticed.

Josh nodded and jogged towards her. "Why yes of course, I would never keep a lady waiting, especially after she gave up so much to be with me." They shared another laugh and headed inside. Josh pulled ahead and once again held the door open for her in such a way as to force Rachel to brush against him to pass.

This time though she purposely slowed down as she passed and moved closer than she had to, brushing her shoulder across his chest. Once again an unexpected shiver ran through her. She could almost feel Josh smile and that made her jump back, not enough to raise suspicion, but enough that she was no longer touching him. She was frustrated by her reaction. She usually never backed down from situations like this.

If there was one main reason she and Amy got along so

well it was because of their love of the game. Not the games people play during relationships where they end up spending more time hurting and hiding from each other than actually enjoying themselves, but the harmless flirtation games that go on between single men and women in everyday life. Harmless fun, more often used to challenge your Whit than for actual romantic gain. More like practice for the real thing and the only harm to come is usually just a bruised ego.

It was all pretend and Rachel had it down to an art. Besides it fit with her strong exterior. She was not supposed to be the shy blushing type, so her reaction didn't sit well with her. Again, she shook off the strange feeling and tried to reason with herself. *I'm sure it's just because he's my boss. Besides it's been so long since I had a boss worth flirting with that I must just be out of practice. Lord knows the old guy at her last job was not flirt worthy.* Her confidence returning, she smiled and continued inside, with Josh following behind.

As they passed through the front they nodded at the scowling Coralene who had witnessed the exchange at the door. Since she was moved to her new role with Josh, they hadn't replaced her with a new receptionist yet, leaving Coralene's department to fill in at the desk full-time. Judy had called in sick today, meaning that Leanne had actual work to do, that left Coralene as the only one to cover the desk. Clearly she took the responsibility as a demotion which didn't help her disposition towards Rachel.

Not that she had been any friendlier than when they first met, but she had at least been willing to give her the extra work at reception that had led to her promotion in the first place.

It also hadn't helped Rachel's case with her when she opted to spend more time with the technicians than the other girls in the office. Which Coralene had taken as a challenge to her position as most favored by the men in the office. What Coralene didn't know was that she simply found the technicians more interesting than the silly games that Coralene and the woman seemed to like to play. The guys in the bull pen were just all about raunchy jokes, bad dad jokes and sports, much more entertaining to chill with.

As Josh approached, Coralene turned in her chair towards him, her signature move it seemed, ensuring a full view of her upper thighs in short cut skirt. Her angle also ensured he would have a direct view down her low-cut tight shirt, so when Josh gave Coralene little more than a wave as he passed by she focused her displeasure on Rachel. Rachel chose to focus her attention on Josh's backside, resisting her childish instinct to stick her tongue out as they turned the corner out.

"So what kind of trouble are you getting into today?" Josh continued, oblivious to the silent exchange that had just occurred and that that suited her just fine.

She smiled, but quickly brushed off the urge to continue their earlier banter. "Actually its funny you bring that up. I have been meaning to talk to you about something odd that I came across when I was analyzing the transaction reports, but I wasn't sure if it warrants concern or if it's just due to my inexperience. I wasn't going to bother you with it, but since you brought it up."

Josh took her switch in attitude with a little bruise to his ego, but quickly settled into a business tone. "And you only just started your new position." He absently ran his fingers through his hair, a slight pout had settled over him. "It's not a bother, if something brings up a question then it's worth looking at." He shrugged his shoulders, leaving a light waft of cologne in the air. "If it turns out to be nothing, at least you'll learn something. I'd rather you ask than discover it was something later on when it might be too late to fix it."

Rachel nodded. "Yeah, I guess you're right."

"Of course I'm right. I'm always right." He smiled, his posture straightening. She let out a small laugh. He ignored her laugh and continued on. "Why don't you show me what' bothering you and we'll sort it out together?"

"Alright, give me a little time to gather the reports and I'll meet you in your office. Perhaps after your meeting?"

Josh quickly looked at his watch. "Shit. I just about forgot about that. What would I do without you?"

"It is why you hired me." She declared, with her shoulders back and stance tall. Then she headed toward her office to organize her thoughts. Josh smiled and rushed off into his to join in his conference call.

On the way to her desk she stopped in to chat with the guys in the bull pen. During her many years as a temp Rachel usually didn't make too many friends at her work places. It wasn't that she rude, in fact she was usually well liked, but she found it considerably easier to stay a temp if she didn't get too closely entwined in the lives of the people she worked with. This place had been different, at least with the technicians, she had a good rapport with them and she had learned a lot collaborating with them and she had gotten know a bit about their personal lives.

"Hey Phil." She mouthed silently as she passed by. Phil was on the phone, so she took a seat on Miguel's desk and waited for him to finish up. She poked through some of the tickets on the clipboard while she waited. They were busy today a lot of service tickets open. Just then Phil hung up the phone, sat back and pulled off his headset. Rachel set the clipboard down and smiled. "You're alone on the phones?" Phil nodded. "Where's Jackson?"

“In the field. He had to go out about an hour ago.”

“That busy?”

“That’s an understatement.” He adjusted his headset and leaned back.

“I thought you guys just hired a new tech.”

“We did, Patrick something or other. I think he’s Cajun or Caribbean.”

“Cajun is a type of cuisine and Caribbean is a region.” She teased.

“Well whatever he is I can’t understand a damn word he says. All I know is new guy or not with Miguel gone AWOL, we’re down a man, leaving me to man the phones alone.” He added spinning around in his chair.

“Miguel’s skipped out again?”

“Yup, third time this month.” She was about to complain, but the phone interrupted her. “Don’t get me started.” He complained as he put his headset back on.

“Well if you get overloaded, transfer a few calls my way, I’ll help out where I can.”

“You’re a doll.” He smiled and waved before pushing answer button. “Tech support.” He said into his headset.

She returned his smile, picked up the clipboard and motioned that she’d take it with her. Phil smiled and mouthed a thank you before answering the caller’s question.

With Miguel gone and Phil being the only one on the phones, she knew no one would have followed up on call sheets yet today. She took the clipboard back to her office to log the notes from the tickets into the incident system and ready herself in case Phil may need to pass calls over to her. She took the long route to her office, not wanting to deal with Leanne's attitude, which wasn't any better than Coralene's now that she actually had work to do. It didn't help that Josh had given her an office instead of a cubicle.

*****

When she finished logging the last incident into the computer she sat back in her standard issue ergonomic office chair and rubbed her eyes. She had managed to enter all but two tickets from the clipboard, and those she had purposely left aside to discuss with Miguel; when he decided to show up that is. They didn't make sense, so before she logged them in they would have to be corrected.

She stretched in her chair and started to pull out some of her reports. She sighed and looked at the time on her phone. Josh should be done his conference calls any time now. She realized it was going to be a daunting task tracing him through her logic. This translated to needing a strong cup of coffee. Grabbing her mug she rushed to the kitchen to rinse it out all the while praying that someone else had a similar thought and had already brewed a fresh pot saving her the wait time.

She just about squealed with joy when she found the pot full. She inhaled the unmistakable aroma of just freshly brewed coffee. She loved that smell. She filled her cup, took a sip and smiled. Double cream, double sugar and Strong, just the way she liked it. It was fresh too, probably brewed no more than 5 minutes ago, she thought to herself. If there was one skill she had down to an art, it was her ability to tell almost down to the minute when a pot of coffee had been brewed. Amy had teased her affectionately about it but even Amy couldn't deny the number of times she so close it was scary.

With her new prize in hand Rachel headed back to her office where she found Josh casually leafing the papers on her desk. He was resting on the corner of her desk and looked up and smiled as soon as she appeared in the doorway. He had the kind of smile that seemed to drop about 20 years off his face and leave you with a sense that you were looking at a playful teenager that had been running around his dads office pretending he was the boss. Rachel wondered how anyone took him seriously. Then she laughed to herself as she realized he probably used just that perception to get ahead under the radar, just like she had used her blond stereotype image to fool people into underestimating her when she had to.

"And what brings on this amused laughter?" He asked casually with the unmistakable smug glint of someone who already knows the answer. Rachel lifted her coffee mug slightly, proudly displaying her prize in response. Josh seemed to flinch with disappointment; it was obvious this was not the answer he had assumed. "Ah we have an addict do we?" He teased but didn't wait for an answer. "Don't worry, it's not considered an addiction in this line of work, it's a necessity." With that he stood up. "I see you have a lot here I guess we better get started.

"I was getting it sorted to bring to you." She said apologetically.

He waved her off. "I was in the area."

She laughed and took at seat back at her desk. She leafed through the papers until she found the one she wanted. "It started with the monthly reports. I was trying to balance off our field numbers with the numbers from the processors, to reconcile the figures, make sure everything balanced before I input it."

"See there's your mistake, they never balance." He said half teasing, half serious.

She paused as Josh pulled over a chair. He leaned forward as she pointed to her notations on the page. "Yeah, see that's what I thought at first, that it was the difference in the float, the timing difference between when a merchant runs his end of day and when the processors run theirs, but that's not it." Josh looked skeptical. She scooted her chair closer to him. "Maybe it's because I'm new at this but the fact that it is so hard to reconcile these numbers had been making me crazy. I like numbers to match, so I've been racking my brain trying to come up with a system that would make it easier. I thought I had finally managed to come up with one that worked, but now I think there's a problem with it. I was hoping to maybe bounce some ideas off you to see what you thought." Josh nodded and she smiled and started passing him her papers and notes one by one.

Josh looked through each one that she handed him. She explained how she arrived at the different reports and figures. Showed him where she had managed to compensate for the timing differences. Then she showed him the specific days and ATMs that didn't fit the pattern. The amounts and days varied by no particular pattern, the differences were small but too large to be attributed to just a single ATM or dispenser error.

By the time she was done explaining Josh looked worn. He sat up, ran his fingers through his hair and shook his head in amazement. "Well, you've certainly been busy since you first came here. I have to admit I'm impressed." He sat back in his chair and just watched her, momentarily stunned. "Now don't get me wrong, you've been very impressive up to this point or I wouldn't have promoted you so quickly, but I guess I didn't realize." He stopped, struggling to come up with the words he wanted.

She sat up straight in her seat to match him and cut him off before he could continue. "Didn't realize what, that I had the brains to back it up?" She said half mockingly half insulted.

Josh stood up and again sat on the corner of her desk, this time facing her. His boyish grin was back. "No, not at all, that's not what I meant. It's just that well, you've done a lot here and I guess I just got so used to the way things were done that I stopped looking for ways to improve them. You just reminded me that there could be other ways to do things around here." She beamed at the compliment, everybody loves a good pat on the back, why not indulge herself.

He smiled once more, took a breath and continued. "Well like I said, this is great work, but I guess I don't see the problem." She looked confused so Josh continued. "You said you wanted to show me this to ask me about a problem with it, so where's the problem? It looks like you just haven't worked out the kinks from your calculations, you are trying to cover a lot of data in a short time." Josh finished while moving his arm casually over the papers that lay scattered across her desk as if to emphasis his point.

Her eyes lit up, and she sat up in her chair. "Well that is where it gets interesting and confusing. I thought I just had to work out the formula a bit more too, until I found a the right pattern in the timing. When there's a difference in the settlement amounts, it's never the same machines or the same amounts, but it does always seem to be that the ATMs are close by each other. I figure the formula is still a good one, since it found this pattern, but I'll be damned if I can figure out what it means. I've been banging my head trying to figure it out." Josh laughed and she unconsciously took a defensive stance.

Josh raised his hands in defense. “Hey I’m not disagreeing, it’s just I got this image of you banging your head through a wall. I just couldn’t see you quitting until you made a hole.” She joined his laughter and shrugged her shoulders in resigned agreement. Josh shifted to a more comfortable stance. “Well I’d hate to see you bruise your skull, so I’ll be glad to take another look. Although I’m not sure I can offer much more that what you’ve done already, and the fact that even the accountants say sometimes there is just no way to balance it all and they have a tolerance built in to account for it so you might be looking for something that can never be fixed and is already written off.”

Josh glanced over the papers spread across her desk once more and sighed. “Perhaps it’s just this type of business. After all there are always transaction exceptions, exchange rates on the foreign card disputes and other quirks that take a lot of manual work to track down. There is a lot to contend with in this business, maybe we just don’t get enough data from the processor or networks to find all the differences.”

Rachel sighed. “I know that’s a possibility, but it just feels wrong.” She shook her head. “I’m just not sure that explains it all.” Josh decided not to argue with her and simply shrugged. She tried a different approach. “If it was just a matter of the business float the differences should average out over time, don’t you think?” Josh still didn’t look convinced. She persevered. “Look at this one.” She pulled the report from the bottom of the pile and showed him her notes. “It’s just a small amount but it almost looks like some of the calculations were doubled, but only for part of the day.”

Josh nodded in agreement. He stared at the report, his tone was strained. “Isn’t it possible that it was just a miscalculation or a report error, if its only one day?”

"I thought that too at first, but at some of these later reports, it happens more often and at more frequent intervals." She scanned through the documents pulling out the ones she needed. Josh scanned them over he didn't look pleased. He instinctively ran his fingers through his hair as a look of confusion washed over him. He grabbed another of her reports. Finally, to Rachel's relief he spoke.

"Okay. I see what you mean." He stood up and stretched he neck. "Could it be possible it's just the same error that's compounding with each calculation?"

"I thought of that," she jumped in excitedly; glad to finally have someone to run these ideas by, "but there would be a more definite pattern if that was the case."

"I guess you could argue that." He paced the room a little, considering his thoughts, then he turned, his face lighter. "What if it's an error that doesn't fit any pattern because it's a combination of the timing with a calculation error throwing the rest off?" He searched until he found the report he wanted. "If you look at this day, you come up short the exact amount this other day is over, isn't it possible you just transferred the data onto the wrong settlement date?"

She frowned and looked at the report that Josh was holding. She had been sure she had found a real problem, but there it was in black and white. The report he showed the data appeared to be on the wrong day. She had missed that one. Now she looked unhappy. She stared, hoping to wish away the obvious oversight. How could she have missed that? She sighed and sat back in her seat in defeat. She had been trying so hard to balance she had missed the obvious.

She blushed. "I'm sorry I wasted your time. I thought I found a problem. I don't know what I was thinking, someone was stealing the money? Heck if I'd shown this report around people probably would have started to think that I was cooking the books?" Josh let out a chuckle and she quickly joined in and shrugged her shoulders. "I did say it wasn't a perfect a system. Well back to the drawing board it seems."

Josh gave her an encouraging smile. "Hey don't get too dejected, you did some amazing stuff in such a short period, you should cut yourself a break. Why don't you do what I do when I have a problem? Leave it alone for a while, work on some other things and then go back to it after a couple of more month end reports come in. By then I bet the solution will come to you and we might have a way to better reconcile our reports. Sometimes if I over work a problem I get nowhere, but if I walk away from it for a while, the just comes to me. You should try that."

She smiled. "Yeah you're right. I've done the same thing. Guess it was just my stubborn side that was hoping to beat this problem down."

"Hey if you leave it till next month even I could probably get you some help with it. By then we should have the extra staff we need. Heck by then I might even be able to spare more time to help you with it." Josh sighed heavily. "Then again have you looked at my schedule lately? I don't even seem to have time for a proper dinner." He laughed and leaned against the wall opposite her. "Speaking of, you wouldn't want to help me out with that would you?"

"With what? Dinner?" Rachel asked confused.

"Yes Dinner." He nodded with a smile.

"You want me to cook you dinner?" Rachel exclaimed in disbelief, straining not to jump out of her chair.

"Well that wasn't exactly what I meant, but now that you bring it up."

She cut him off before he could continue. "Nice try, how about your first idea, what did you originally have in mind." If she'd had something to throw at him she would have, cooking was not one of her strength and she was not about to offer it up to her boss anyway.

Josh let out a chuckle. "Alright I know when I'm beat. I was thinking you could help make sure I eat by coming with me. See the way I figure it, if I have set dinner plans it will force me to eat." He crossed his arms. "You'd actually be doing me a favor."

Rachel was tempted to turn him down, but she couldn't think of a reason to. "Well since I'd be helping you." She started, "Ah what the heck, a girls gotta eat too right?"

Josh took a step towards her. "Hmm, not quite a glowing response but I'm not picky. Alright let's get something after work. I feel like I haven't eaten in days." She smiled and nodded. "Great. I have a few sales calls to run out to afternoon, but why don't I call you when I'm done and we can set a time and place when I have a better sense of how I'm doing for time."

"Sure I guess that works." She mumbled, wondering what she had just gotten herself into.

With that Josh walked over, planted both arms on her chair and leaned in. "You really know how to stroke a guys ego with your enthusiasm don't you."

A coy devilish grin suddenly lit up her face. "You'll never know how well." She teased playfully with a slight hint of sarcasm. They locked eyes for an instant, his breath tickling her neck.

Then he flinched in mock pain. "Oh ouch, I better get out of here while I still have the strength to leave." With that he sauntered out, throwing her a quick wink on his way out the door, then he was gone.

She went back to staring at her work, before she suddenly realized what she had done and smacked herself on the head. "Going out with the boss for dinner? What are you thinking?" She mentally slapped herself again. "How 'everything you are not supposed to do' cliché is that?" She sighed and rested her head on top of her desk in resignation realizing it would be worse to change her mind now. "How do I get myself into these messes?" She moaned into her stack of papers.

CHAPTER 6

Josh looked around the apartment. It was dark and drab. The lighting was poor and the colors, or lack of colors to be more accurate, cast a dingy air throughout the room. Dirty clothes were strewn everywhere and from the looks of it, they had probably been lying there for months. Empty beer cans, old dishes and other indistinguishable garbage had grown together such that they became part of the normal décor.

As for the floor, although Josh was pretty sure it was once the usual linoleum that lined these old apartments, he also knew it would take a shovel to prove it. He carefully picked his way through the living room and called out to the apartment owner in the other room. “God man, don’t you ever clean?” He stepped over a particularly large pile of garbage and started to push pile of dingy clothes away to expose the couch to sit on, but quickly thought better of the idea.

“Aren’t these the same dirty clothes from the last time I was here?” His face contorted suddenly in disgust and he held his nose. “Oh man! Is that the same sandwich?” He took a step back as he spoke. “It sure as hell smells like the same one.”

A deep gravelly voice sounding from just behind him momentarily startled Josh out of his disgust. “Is that why you came over here today, to bust my chops? Because if that’s the case, get a wife and leave me the hell alone.” The man’s voice was only slightly muffled as he struggled to pull on his torn shirt without tearing it the rest of the way. When he finished struggling with his shirt he simply glared at Josh and waited to hear what his uninvited 'guest' wanted from him this time.

"Relax Blaze; I didn't come here to bust your chops." Josh said with an easy smile, he was used to Blaze and was no longer put off by his gruff manner.

"Then why did you come?" Blaze grumbled with no more concern for polite chatter then he had for taming the dark brown spikes in his clean but unkempt hair. "Let's be honest, you wouldn't come here in the middle of the day unless you want something." Blaze crossed his thick muscular arms over his equally thick muscular chest. He stood over 6 feet, yet he was so broad that even men who equaled his height found his stature imposing. "Why don't you cut the crap and get to the point."

Josh held up his hands in mock surrender. "Alright, I give." He casually slid one hand into his left front jean pocket and rested the other on the only clear spot on the decaying fireplace mantle. "I was hoping you could check someone out for me. Nothing heavy, just poke around get a feel for what she's up to; make sure there's nothing going on that I should worry about."

Blaze let out an annoyed grunt. "She? You mean you want me to check out another one of your little tarts to see if she's steppin' out on you." Blaze sighed and crossed the room to the couch in two steps. He carelessly pushed aside something that oddly resembled a pizza box; then he plopped himself down, stretched back and clunked his feet onto the coffee table in front of him before continuing. "I've got better things to do than go chasing around after one of your skirts. Is that all you come to me for? Why don't you just dump her and move on to the next one if you're so worried about it?"

Blaze had a disgusted look on his weathered face. His look wasn't directed at anything in particular, it just seemed to be part of his general demeanor. He rubbed a hand across his heavily stubbled chin. As much as the thought displeased him he knew it was almost time for another shave. He had already stopped paying any attention to Josh and started shaking the various bottles strewn around for any remaining liquid. He clenched his jaw, making it appear more squared and emphasizing the small lines starting to etch across his face.

Frustrated by his lack of attention, Josh straightened and took a step towards Blaze. "Now who's busting chops?" Blaze set down the bottle he was holding and looked up at him as if Josh's mere presence imposed great hardship. Josh continued. "It's not at all like that. This time, it's company business."

Blaze grunted and raised his scarred left brow in disbelief, but before he could say anything Josh continued. "Give me a little credit would you." Blaze shot him a skeptical look and Josh sighed heavily. "I know better than to pull you into something as silly as a lovers spat again. Besides, if I needed delicacy I certainly wouldn't come to you, I learnt that lesson the first time." Blaze remained immovable, so Josh decided to change tactics.

Josh took another step forward and relaxed his stance, dropping his shoulders and his voice. "I just thought with your skills at reading people and your, shall we say connections..." Blaze snorted, but let him continue. "Fine, criminal element then, Christ Blaze you hang out with enough of them." Josh blurted, losing his patience. He took a deep breath, trying to control his frustration. "This girl is fairly new at our company. She's advanced quicker than most and today she mentioned something in passing that may be nothing, but it got me wondering. I just need to make sure she's not on the wrong side of things, working things she shouldn't be working."

Blaze swung his legs off the table and sat forward. He didn't look enthused, but he was listening. "Alright, so just what exactly leads you to believe she might be working anything?"

"It's nothing specific." Josh smiled and paced a few times his voice raised excitedly. "See, we were reviewing some of the financials and she was pointing out a few issues in some reports. Then out of the blue she jokes about her having to steal the money out of our ATMs to even out some of the numbers." He stopped and stared squarely at Blaze. "I'm sure it's nothing, just an offhanded joke. I mean she passed all background security checks and there's nothing to say she's actually stealing anything or even capable of it, but..."

Blaze cut him off before he could continue. He looked bored. "But you want her checked out anyway just to make sure she's not doing anything she shouldn't be, cooking any books or anything, maybe make sure she's not a spy for the competition or something?" After finishing Josh's thought for him, he rose to his feet and strode to the other side of the room. He was getting tired of his current company and anxious to get to his next destination.

He paced a few times near the door. He knew that if he did the job for Josh it would disturb his normal routine. He had become so embedded in his routine that it seemed to mold around him like the cushions of the old couch he had just left. Two years ago that kind of routine would have led to his death, but now his routine is the only reason he bothered to get out of bed most days.

Josh nodded. He could tell he was losing Blaze. "Yeah, something like that. Look I just want you to feel her out, see if she's capable of doing something like that. She's managed to get access to a lot of company data, but would she take advantage of it? Cause any problems?" Blaze shook his head and Josh's frustrations bubbled. "Look, I just need to be sure. The fall-out to something like that would be very bad for business, everyone's business. I need to know what she's up to that's it."

Josh aimed his words directly at Blaze, and absently rang his fingers through his well styled hair as he spoke. "At best we would lose clients if something happened and it was found out that we didn't follow-up on our own concerns. Worst case, we'd lose our bank sponsorship and if that happened, we'd be out of business and you know it." Josh turned, shrugged and nonchalantly leaned against the dusty mantel again. "Not to mention the loss of money."

Blaze glared at Josh, he looked too comfortable as he rested against his fireplace. He scanned the room, purposely avoiding looking near the unpolished frame on far end of the mantel. He took a deep breath, increasing his stature even more. Although his voice was still gravelly from lack of use, it was deep and powerful. "I get it. You want me to feel her out, make sure she's on the up and up. If she isn't, you want me to make sure she doesn't continue and the problem doesn't become public knowledge Stafford business doesn't suffer and my interests in it along with it. That about right?" His tone was blunt and direct.

Josh shifted somewhat nervously. "Well I guess I never thought of it quite like that, but now that you mention it, yeah. Nothing too heavy handed though, I don't want to scare her. She's probably innocent in all this, but I just need to be sure. Just check her out, that's all. If she is trouble, then we can figure it out."

Blaze looked less than enthused and Josh could sense he was getting ready to steer him out, so he quickly pressed on. "Come on man. This is simple for you. With your experience you could feel her out in one meeting. That's all I'm asking, one little favor. Besides, after everything you can't do me one favor, especially one that serves your interests too?"

With that Blaze cringed and clenched his jaw. Josh knew he was pushing Blaze's patience, but he also knew he was coming about as close to agreement as Blaze would ever give. Not wanting to lose it, Josh straightened and rambled the rest his responses quickly as he hurried past Blaze and out the door. “Hey, that’s great, I really appreciate this Blaze. You won’t regret it. I’ll call you later with a meeting place. If you could swing by tonight, meet us for a quick drink, check her out and let me know what you think that would be great, we can go from there. I’ll buy.” He added, closing the door behind him as he quickly hustled out.

Before Blaze could refuse, he was already gone. Leaving Blaze with a deeper scowl than the one he woke up with that afternoon, if that was at all possible. He looked around the room in frustration. “Why the hell did I ever give up smoking?” He grumbled aloud. Then suddenly his face contorted into some sort of strange look that to those who knew him usually passed off as a grin. “Thank God I never gave up drinking.”

He glanced at his watch and grunted. He was about two drinks behind schedule. He shrugged on his leather jacket, grabbed his wallet and headed out to his daily afternoon destination, the pub around the corner. If he hurried, he could still make up the drinking time he lost when Josh interrupted the normal start to his day routine. With any luck he could get back into it without any more distractions and lose the rest of his day at the bottom of Charlie’s chipped whiskey glasses.

*****

To call Charlie’s a pub was being polite. Even dive would have to be considered too high-class to describe the place, but for Blaise Ferrell, better known as Blaze to those that claimed to know him, the place felt more like home than his own apartment. His current unkempt state did nothing to prove anything to the contrary.

Charlie’s wasn’t a place where people went to meet their friends for a casual drink. People who went to this destination went with only one purpose in mind; to drink enough to completely forget where it was they were supposed to be or where they had just come from. The smoke was thick and the secrets thicker. There was a permanent stench that seemed to get worse the odd times a cleaner touched the place.

To any on-looker, Blaze wouldn't have stood out from any of the regulars in the place. A group that consisted mainly of confessed alcoholics, off-duty hookers, the odd junky that wasn't in need of a fix stronger than alcohol at that moment and of course the residents of nearby shelters and rundown low rent apartments like the one Blaise lived in that were desperate or crazy enough to come into a place like this rather than stay home. No one that frequented the place was sure which one Blaze was, and they didn't seem to care. They just knew that he never caused any trouble and sometimes he bought a round or two for the house and always kept his drinking companions well stocked. That usually made him the most popular man in the joint.

Just as Blaze finished downing his 5th Jack Daniels his current overly friendly companion started gently tugging at his arm. "Blazzze darlin'," she slurred playfully, "ain't you gunna answer that phone o' yours?" Blaze grunted in response and signaled for another drink. Since he looked like he had no intension of answering it, his companion decided foolishly to make a grab for it but was instead greeted with a hard shove from his arm as he protectively pushed her away and snatched up his phone from the table in front of him.

"This better be good." He grunted into the phone annoyed at having to talk to the unwelcome caller.

"Well I can see your mood hasn't improved much since I saw you earlier." Came Josh's light hearted response from the other end. This was in turn met with another grunt of disgust as Blaze waved off his companion's curious tug; after which he silently waved to Charlie for another drink for her as well. This seemed to be enough to satisfy and end her curious prodding. She focused instead on waiting for her drink, which he knew was the only reason for her company at the bar today.

“I take it there's a point to this call Josh.” He cringed at the sound of Josh's light laughter in his ear.

"Of course, I know you're busy so I won't hold you up. I just wanted to let you know that you should meet us tonight 10:00 pm at Renegadz. Near the bar, don't worry I'll find you."

"Well Josh about that... "

"Hey thanks again, you're a real Pal." Josh cut in before Blaze had a chance to back out. “Well I've gotta run. Remember, tonight at 10:00, I'm counting on you Blaze.” With a telltale click, Josh had hung up.

Blaze scowled at the phone for a moment until his drinks arrived, then he returned to his regular annoyed look and relaxed back into his chair. He didn't bother to acknowledge his companions glee; she had turned her focus back to her new drink and away from him and that's all that he cared about at that moment. He took a long slow sip from his, savoring the dark golden liquor as it trailed a burning warmth down his throat. That quickly erased a couple of frown lines, which was the most relaxed his face ever seemed to get. For Blaze, that was a smile.

His companion had been greedily cupping her drink as she gulped it down. Only when it was finished did she turn her attention back to Blaze. He looked down at her as she grabbed a hold of his powerful thigh with one hand and traced the chipped red nail polished fingers of her other hand along his shoulder. She mumbled something incoherent. Blaze nodded his head slightly and signaled for another drink for his companion but waved off another for himself. He took a final swig to finish off what he had and then he gently whispered into his companion's ear. "After this one Sweets, I expect you to head straight home, no stops at your pimp's place, ok?"

She obediently nodded and smiled gratefully. Then she turned her attention back to her drink as Blaze stood up to leave. She didn't see Blaze slip the bartender an extra 20 when he paid for their drinks or hear him as he leaned in and nodded towards her direction. "Make sure she gets home after this one, ok Charlie." Charlie gave him a confirming nod and with that Blaze headed out.

CHAPTER 7

With one final curse Rachel was able to stop herself from falling out as the door finally burst open. She jumped out, slammed the door shut and glared at her car. In the fading light of the new summer sun the rust almost blended into the remaining red paint. It reminded her of the powerful muscle that hid underneath its gruff and aged exterior, making it look like the glorious red sports car it was at one time. She smiled.

"My fault. I asked you to do something you don't like and you complain. What did I expect?" She said to her car chuckling aloud as she lightly patted the soft blacktop roof. "But you sure come through when I really need you, don't you ol' boy." Her car pep talk was really a stall tactic and after having to finally admit that to herself, she sighed. "One dinner and you're done, what harm could there be in that? It's not unusual to go to dinner with your NOT cute boss. Totally normal. Just colleagues getting a meal at the same time." Rachel felt reassured, so with a deep breath she turned and headed inside the restaurant to meet with Josh.

Renegadz was more of a night club than a restaurant, at least after 11 PM. Before that it was an elegant 5 star establishment and you only went to if you wanted to impress, because the prices were high and the atmosphere higher. It was known to be home to a lot of money and although not proven, it was said that very little of it came from the patrons. The source of the money was mere speculation, but since they never hired anyone outside the family, it would remain speculation.

Rachel had known what to expect from its reputation, but knowing and actually seeing it are two completely different things. She immediately found herself staring in awe as she tried to take it all in. The air was cool and light and it held a mixture of fruity and spicy smells that made you feel like you were in the Mediterranean. Much of the décor consisted of replicas of many famous Greek statues, paintings and other family heirlooms. It was rumored that some of the real pieces decorated the offices on the third floor, which was off-limits to the public.

Rachel was greeted by the host as she entered and reached the bottom of a large marble staircase. It curved upstairs where if formed an arched balcony over the main area. It also led to the restaurant's main seating area. There was seating on the main level as well, but that cleared out early to make room for the nightclub goers that would start trickling in by 10:00 PM.

"Welcome to Renegadz." The host said. He was a young man, just 21 if she had to guess. He spoke with no hint of an accent though he clearly held the classic Greek features she expected from the owners family. She smiled in return and found herself wondering how much longer the tradition would hold as the younger generations became fully integrated into American society. Rachel had to giggle silently to herself as she now found her mind wandering to thoughts of this young man sneaking off to a secret rendezvous with his non-Greek lover. "May I help you?" the young man continued.

Jolted out of her imagined thoughts, she nodded. "I'm meeting someone, Josh Tanner." The young man scanned his list and soon motioned for her to follow him. She found herself smiling as she followed him to her table. She was scrambling to take in every detail of the place as they quickly ascended the huge staircase.

When they reached the second floor, the host led her towards a small table by the center balcony; Josh was already waiting for her and smiled as she approached. She returned his smile and took the seat that the host held out for her. She nodded a thank-you to the host as he offered a nod to both and headed back downstairs.

"Glad you could make it." Josh said leaning comfortably back in his chair.

"I just about didn't make it; it's hard to crawl out of a window with a dress on, so I had to fight with the door." She replied and they both shared a knowing laugh.

“I guess I should have offered to pick you up. Well it was worth well worth the wait.” He said as he looked her over appreciatively, but to Rachel’s relief he didn’t dwell on any one part. “Are you hungry?" Josh asked as he picked up his menu.

"Are you kidding? You're buying, I'm starving." She replied as she dove into her menu. They both chuckled, but Josh had no idea she was dead serious.

They scanned their menus in silence for a few minutes before she finally stole a quick glance at her dinner companion. I don’t know what I was being so silly about. She thought to herself. He has been nothing but nice, very gentlemanly, all we are is two co-workers out for a friendly dinner. A very common occurrence these days, so sit back, relax and don’t let you mind wander all over the damn place.

She scolded herself silently and then proceeded to take her own advice, determined to enjoy the atmosphere, the food and her companion. She smiled casually. “It all looks great.” She said as she scanned the menu. She looked up and found Josh smiling at her across his menu.

“Have you ever eaten here before?” He asked, watching her intently and when she shook her head, he seemed to light up. “You’ll love the food here. I’ve been here a lot and now I get to share it with a gorgeous Renagadz virgin.”

His voice came off smooth and confident as he spoke. She got the feeling she wasn’t the first female companion he brought to this place, but she didn’t care. She was looking forward to finally tasting the famous food experience she had only heard about.

If there was one thing that Rachel rarely felt, it was jealousy, and if there was one thing she craved, it was trying something new. If Josh was in his glory showing off to a pretty woman, she was in hers by not caring. It made for perfect dinner companions.

They started by sharing a bottle of white wine. From there she definitely didn’t play the “I’ll have a salad” type of girl and she didn’t feel any guilt over either. If he wanted a cheap date, he shouldn’t have brought her here. A coy smile played over her lips as she placed her order with the waiter. She ordered something for every course.

By the time they were on to dessert Rachel was very relaxed and very full. She was having a great time; Fantastic food and to her surprise enjoyable conversation too. Josh had even let down his usual overly confident air and just had fun. However, by the third time she caught Josh looking around the bar below them she was starting to wonder if he was getting bored. She was about to ask him if something was wrong when he finally spoke.

"I notice things are starting to pick up a bit downstairs,” he said, turning back towards her. “Would you like to go down, look around a bit; maybe join me for a drink?”

She looked over the balcony and scanned the room below. The music had already switched from the preset jukebox speakers to a DJ and the bar crowd was just starting to outnumber the dinner crowd, but not by much, it was still early so there was plenty of room. She smiled but tried to control her enthusiasm. This isn't a date, she reminded herself, then she turned to back to face him. "I guess one drink won't hurt a girl on a work night."

Josh signaled for the check. After he paid, he laid his napkin on the table. "If you don't mind I have to slip down to the washroom, wait here, I'll be back before you know it."

She nodded in response; she had the last of her desert to finish anyway. She looked around admiring the view while she polished off her decadently rich Tiramisu and waited for Josh to return.

*****

Josh headed downstairs to use the washroom, but when he was done he didn't go back upstairs, instead he searched for Blaze who should be there by now. It didn't take Josh long to spot him sitting at the bar, despite the crowd starting to file in. He had a presence that stood out. It seemed to either frighten or mesmerize you, which one seemed to depend on how he felt about you.

Despite the fact that only a few hours ago he had blended in at Charlie's pub, he now seemed perfectly at home here. He hadn't yet shaved, but he had clearly cleaned up his dress. He was wearing a bomber style brown leather jacket, that although was worn enough to fit his body, it was obviously well cared for and clearly expensive. He had on clean jeans and his shirt could almost pass for bright white and free of tears or stains. For Blaze, this was dressed up.

Josh casually made his way over to join him at the bar. "Right on time." Josh said as he leaned against the bar. He was polishing off a drink when Josh found him.

"Good," he grunted without looking up, "just in time to buy me my next drink." He waved over the bartender. Josh smiled, as if it was meant as light-hearted banter, even though it wasn't. Blaze addressed the bartender in a friendlier voice than the one he had been speaking to Josh with. Josh didn't take note of this. "One more for me and he's buying so whatever he wants." He finished, pointing to, but still not looking at Josh.

"Just his, I'm not quite finished upstairs yet." Josh responded to the bartender and threw a twenty-dollar bill on the counter before turning back to Blaze.

"So how do you want to work this?" Blaze asked turning in Josh's direction. He still didn't look at him, instead glanced past him and out towards the small crowd now starting to form on the dance floor.

"I've already paid the bill and invited her down for a drink at the bar, so I thought we could meet here. I will introduce you as if we just ran into each other. You could feel her out, try determine if she's any real threat or not, then you can head out. Then I can finish checking her out myself." Josh finished with wink when Blaze finally looked at him.

Blaze didn't respond and turned back to pick up his drink that the bartender had poured. "Sounds like you've got it all planned out." He spoke into the mouth of his glass as he took a swig. He let the Jack slide down his throat before swallowing. This was much better quality liquor than he got at Charlie's and he could appreciate a good top shelf now and then.

Josh planted a firm pat on Blaze's shoulder. Blaze grunted his dislike, but again Josh took no notice. "I might as well have some fun for all the expense of this evening right?" Josh added with a smile before continuing. Blaze grunted. Josh continued, assuming agreement from Blaze, "So, I'll see you down here in a little bit." He stepped away from the bar and started to head back to get Rachel.

"I'll be waiting on bated breath." Blaze said, not caring that Josh had already turned away. He was about to take another swig, when his drink was almost knocked out of his hand as someone backed into him. "Hey." He turned to yell only to see Josh recovering from his stumble backwards.

Josh had a look of shock on his face and Blaze found himself snorting what could be passed as a chuckle. Josh stared silently at the striking blonde he had run into. She was smirking at Josh's loss of composure, which added to Blaze's amusement.

Rachel stifled a laugh and without waiting to be asked, she explained. "I got tired of waiting, so I decided to come down and find you." Blaze was tempted to turn away, but he was too curious to see what Josh's response would be. Just as quickly as he had lost it, Josh's glossy smile returned. Blaze let out a quiet grunt, turned his back to the scene and went back to enjoying his drink.

"Sorry about that, I was on my way back up to get you when a friend stopped me to chat." Josh lied, moving closer to her. Blaze tried not to choke on his drink when he overheard Josh and he tried to think if he had ever 'chatted' with anyone in his life. Much to Blaze's distain, Josh continued. "In fact he's one of our investors, owns quite a portfolio of ATMs under us. I should introduce you, that way on the rare occasion he actually drops into our office; you won't have him tossed out." Josh gently placed his hand behind her shoulder to guide her over towards Blaze.

Despite the increasing noise of the crowd and the music, Blaze had been able to hear them perfectly. Observing the unobservable came naturally to him and had been skillfully fine-tuned over the years, first as a cop, then as an ex-cop with a number on his back. Whether he liked it or not, he still had the ability. He gritted his teeth for the inevitable social niceties about to come, but he waited until Josh slid his hand from Rachel and gave him a friendly slap on the back, before he turned to play his part in Josh's game.

"Hey Josh, ol' boy, back so soon?" He even gave him a nod and a friendly voice, well a less gravely one anyway.

Josh had on his usual grin that Blaze thought made him look like a high school jock. He stumbled a bit when he spoke, thrown by Blaze's demeanor. "Yeah, I thought I should introduce you to one of our newer employees, seeing as you don't come around the office these days." Josh draped his arm around Rachel's shoulder to draw her in closer, putting her between the two of them.

Rachel stiffened in response. Things had been so casual between them at dinner that she hadn't expected to suddenly feel like a trophy on display. Despite the sudden change in attitude from Josh she managed a confident smile anyway.

"Blaze," Josh continued, "this is Rachel Ingles." He smiled over at her, his warm breath brushing against her neck. His voice was rather intimate, as if introducing a lover rather than a co-worker. "She's a real star around the office." He nodded towards Blaze. "Rachel, this is Blaise Farrell, but everyone calls him Blaze. He's one of our most favorite investors, mainly because he doesn't need anything from us and has such profitable machines."

Josh laughed somewhat nervously, he could have stopped there, but instead he rambled on. "He has a relatively small portfolio of ATMs, but somehow he manages to get the prime locations that no one else is able to. He's got the right connections I guess, but hey, as long as he's working for us, who am I to complain right?" He finally finished his awkward introduction.

There was a moment of stillness hanging in the air. Rachel broke it as she took a step toward Blaze. The movement caused Josh's arm to casually fall off her shoulder which was part of her intent. "I do believe that I'm honored." She didn't sound all that impressed, but greeted him with a smile that only hinted at her possible intent. Blaze easily read the meaning in her pale blue-green eyes. He sensed she was well aware that her greeting could be taken both as a compliment or a snide comment about his introduction or hers or both. She had intentionally left it ambiguous. Josh didn't notice but he did.

Blaze had the sudden feeling she rarely found anyone sharp enough to challenge her intentions. Blaze's face once again contorted into what barely passed as a smile, but on him he might as well have been grinning ear to ear. He even let out a definite chuckle. He nodded a hello to her then turned his attention to Josh and spoke as if she wasn't even there. "A refreshing change from your usual selection in companions Josh. I'm proud of you."

Josh let out a smirk before he could catch himself. Rachel didn't see his smirk, she was too busy glaring at Blaze. She could feel herself getting riled up, but before she could respond he turned away and signaled the bartender for another drink. The bartender quickly approached. Blaze ordered another one for himself, but simply stared at Josh in place of asking him and he didn't bother to find out what frou-frou drink Rachel would probably order so he would let Josh worry about that.

Josh nodded. “Becks for myself and...” before he could ask Rachel what she would like, she cut him off. Deciding to let go of her anger over Blaze’s insult and instead have her own fun.

“Tequila.” She said turning to the bartender, smiling sweetly, “Gold, straight up.”

Blaze had to stop himself from choking on the drink he had just taken from his glass. Rachel caught his involuntary action and her smile brightened. She pressed back her shoulders and looking even more innocent, she addressed both of them at once. “Care to join me?”

Josh smiled triumphantly, as if his night had suddenly turned around for the better and he quickly nodded. Blaze grunted his agreement and with a quick nod the bartender went off to fill their order. Feeling oddly pleased with herself, Rachel stepped away from the two men. “I’ll be back in a moment.” She stated. Without waiting for a response she turned and went in search of the bathrooms.

She had to make her way through the crowd that was starting to gather as the atmosphere was turning quickly from relaxed restaurant to hot nightspot. It was if she had been transported to a new place. There was no sign of the classy relaxed restaurant; it was now the flashy top club she had heard so much about. The idea of doing both was probably the influence of the younger generation of the family, who were no longer content with just running the family restaurant.

As soon as Rachel was out of earshot, Josh turned to Blaze and laid his hand triumphantly on his shoulder as if they were close friends sharing a victory. “Well buddy I may not need you for very long after all. A few of those it should be pretty easy for me to pump her for information myself, best truth serum for a woman." His grin seemed to morph into a leer. "I know you're anxious to get out of here, so feel free at any time after these drinks to head out." Josh turned his back against the bar and leaned back. He scanned the dance floor crowd. "Not that I won't miss your cheery conversation, but I might find other ways to pump her for information if you know what I mean." Josh added with an amused grin.

Blaze ignored the sick feeling in his stomach and gulped the last drop of his drink as the bartender returned. The bartender lined up their tequila shots in front of them, along with a shaker of salt and a bowl of lemons. Josh tossed his credit card on the bar in response. "Run a tab." He nodded towards the card as the bartender slipped it off the counter and replaced it with his Becks and Blaze's whiskey. No sooner had Blaze raised his glass to take a swig then Josh leaned in and interrupted his peace.

"Well, what do you think?" Josh asked, without waiting for an answer he continued, "I think I worried for nothing. Easily controllable, naïve, you must agree there is nothing to worry about with that one?" Josh droned on finishing more as a statement than a question.

Blaze grunted a laugh, but instead of answering right away he took a long, slow swallow, savoring every moment before finally acknowledging Josh. "I wouldn't be so quick to dismiss that one." He casually tossed without taking his eyes off of Josh's reflection in the mirror behind the bar. "I think there might be more there than the likes of you is used to handling."

Josh let out a friendly chuckle, taking Blaze's response as a joke. "Yeah, there is a bit of fire there hey?" Josh added with another dismissive wave. "Good thing we have these equalizers here." He said nodding towards the tequila.

Blaze let out a grunt, his face back to its usual scowl. Josh took it for agreement and nodded proudly. Josh suddenly straightened and involuntarily puffed up his chest after spotting Rachel heading their way. Blaze noted the change in Josh's attention and he too watched her approach from his vantage using the mirror rather than turning his head. He didn't notice his own automatic reflexive actions where he too straighten in his chair and even ran a hand over his heavy stubble before setting his down his drink.

Rachel was too focused on the actions around her to notice her admirers. The people, the music, the lights; all seemed to heighten her senses and feed her creative spirit. As she made her way through the crowd she found herself creating an entire history around the looks a couple gave each other. This hobby was great for passing time during long waits, but led to inevitable frustration from a date who felt he wasn't getting all of her attention.

As she approached the bar, she turned her attentions back to her companions. Blaze appeared to be casually sipping his drink. Josh on the other hand was practically leering at her, but with his schoolboy grin, she'd rendered him harmless besides. Besides she'd never gotten involved with anyone she worked with before and she wasn't about to do it now. Of course she rarely worked anywhere long so she didn't usually have to find out, with that thought she mentally smacked herself. She soon saw the tequila on the bar and a wave of childish competition washed over her. They don't stand a chance, she thought to herself.

Rachel approached the two men. Josh was leaning casually with his back against the bar. His half leer, half grin was still on his face; she got the impression that he thought that look was somehow irresistible to women. It wasn't. Blaze had his back to her; he signaled his order of another drink as he downed the last of his current one. Rachel had the feeling he had been drinking since he got up today and that it wasn't the first time he did that. He gave her a casual sideways glance as she had approached. She assumed that was his idea of a polite greeting.

She positioned herself between the two men as she pushed the salt and lemons aside and reached over to pass out the tequila shots. "Boys." She said, nodding casually at the two of them as she raised her shot glass and waited. Blaze didn't miss a beat as he lifted his tequila. After a slight hesitation while Josh debated grabbing for the salt and lemons, he finally picked up his glass to meet the challenge with them.

With the devilish grin, she led the trio; downing her shot in one swallow, then placing the shot glass upside down on the counter she awaited the other two who quickly followed. She couldn't help feeling a little childish victory as Josh followed his with a swig of beer to cover his grimace. Her feeling was short lived though as Blaze was already signaling for another round and had shrugged off Josh's involuntary grimace with what she assumed was his usual grunted response.

With a condescending smirk he raised his eyebrow and offered her the chance to back out. "Unless you'd like to switch to something," he paused a moment for effect before continuing, "else?" He purposely emphasized the last word to make it sound like an insult.

Rachel's face reddened slightly as she now became the one being challenged. Neither one bothered to ask Josh. "Not at all." She responded with a signal to the bartender that she'd have two more tequila. The bartender then looked at Blaze who nodded for two as well. Josh ordered only one, then as if to explain his actions, he lifted his full beer. To which Blaze grunted and Rachel smiled in understanding. She had more of an urge to show up Blaze anyway and wipe that smug attitude away.

Rachel didn't like Blaze's condescending attitude and found herself strangely driven to best him, though she had no idea why. She was used to getting the better of most guys she ran up against, because with little effort she could usually get them to underestimate her, then quickly shut them down. Not Blaze, she thought to herself begrudgingly, he seemed to not be playing into her persona. She'd get him though she decided. He had no clue how much practice she'd had holding her tequila; she was going to like this game.

The bartender didn't take long to bring over their shots. Rachel assumed that with the way he was catering to them he must have received a few good tips off Blaze earlier. Rachel picked up one and was about to smile and wait for Blaze, but he hadn't bothered to wait. Instead he had already slammed his back and was washing his shot down with a swig of his Jack. She glared at him for a moment then shot hers back too, then finished her second one before he picked up his.

Blaze gave his usual grunt then nodded at her with an obvious mix of disdain and admiration. She managed a gritted teeth smile in return. She had no idea why she was letting his crass behavior get to her so much; maybe it was the tequila, or maybe it was the shock of meeting someone who couldn't manage one nice word, either way she found herself unable to resist playing it up even more. She motioned for two more shots for the two of them, and then with a gleam in her eyes she smiled and turned to Josh. "You wanna to dance?"

Josh smiled, leaned close to Blaze and spoke in a low voice. "You don't mind if we leave you alone while we go and dance a little?" He said, more of a statement then as a question.

Without waiting for a response, Rachel grabbed Josh's hand and turned to lead him on to the dance floor, but not before giving into her childish urge. In her sweetest voice she leaned back and spoke. "Yes Blaze, you don't mind do you?" Blaze scowled at her. For some reason that fact that she managed to get a rise out of Mr. Cool made her feel giddy, that plus the tequila, but she didn't care about that. She finally got one on him.

Blaze downed the rest of his whiskey and slammed the empty on the counter with a growl. The bartender eyed him suspiciously from the other end of the bar as he finished serving another customer. Blaze gave him a nod and what passed for a smile and that seemed to satisfy him. He didn't order another drink. Instead, he settled in to go back to watching the room behind him in the mirror.

The room was full, completely transformed from the relaxed restaurant it had been only hours ago into the hot trendy nightclub it was now. The rich fragrant food smells were replaced by a mixture of sweet drinks and musky fragrances. He took it all in while he spent the next few minutes debating with himself. What the hell was he so pissed off about? What did he care if some crazy woman drank herself senseless and made a fool of herself with her slick playboy boss? He didn't. If she wanted to be that stupid then who was he to interfere? He was only here to get some information from her anyway, so if she wanted to make that easier all the better.

It didn't take him much longer before he was back to his 'chipper' self. He waved the bartender over to place another order; His drink and two more shots. He felt a strange twinge that wavered between guilt and childish joy. She wasn't going to win the challenge. There was a Challenge? He suddenly stopped himself. That realization started to make him uncomfortable. He didn't rise to challenges; he couldn't be bothered to care. How did he end up in the middle of one with a total stranger. The bartender's arrival jolted him out of his thoughts.

He gratefully accepted his drink and motioned for him to add it all to Josh's tab. He dragged me out here after all, let him pay. He was about to take a sip when he caught a movement in the mirror that drew him back to stare at the crowd. It was a flash of blonde. He caught sight of Rachel. The crowd was blocking Josh, or maybe it was their angle, he told himself, but he could definitely see her.

He watched her silently as she danced. He could feel the beat she was dancing too vibrating through the wooden bar as the base vibrated up through the floors. It was hard for him to put a finger on what bothered him about her presence. It wasn't her beauty, though she was very attractive, but he found she both disarmed and put him on edge at the same time. He didn't think she was a security risk to the company, as Josh seemed to imply, but he certainly sensed she could cause mischief, so she wasn't harmless. He was drawn out of his thoughts by his companions return. Rachel smiled when we saw the shots lined up. Josh seemed a little too excited about the tequila as well even though they hadn't ordered one for him this time.

Rachel lifted her shot glass towards Josh. "Are you sure you won't join us?" She asked politely. Josh shook his head gently in response and patted his hand on his stomach as if to indicate he was watching his weight. Rachel shrugged her shoulders and turned back, giving Blaze a sideways glance. "Well?"

Blaze stared at her a moment, sizing up the situation, then he lifted his shot glass to join her. With a curt nod they shot their first one back, then without breaking eye contact, they shot back the other. Josh finished his beer and set his empty bottle on the bar with a hard tap. That seemed to bring a sudden end to their impromptu staring contest and forced a tie. They simultaneously turned to order another round. Blaze didn't bother ordering another whiskey with his; instead he went straight for tequila. Neither checked with Josh.

Josh shifted impatiently. He stared at Blaze, a frown on his face. He was starting to regret bringing Blaze into the mix. Blaze wasn't even interrogating her like he wanted. He decided to move things forward and added a shot for himself onto their order. "Blaze," he said, struggling to keep the irritation out of his voice, "I know your portfolio has been keeping you busy, so I really appreciate you sticking around with us." His trademark grin slipped into place. "I know you had an appointment tonight and with all the contracts you bring us, I'd hate to make you late." Josh finished with what he hoped would appear to Rachel as a friendly pat, but ensured there was enough force for Blaze to get the point.

Blaze gritted his teeth but chose not to notice Josh's less than subtle hint and instead did something completely out of character. He smiled; a big full tooth friendly smile. Then he turned to face them both and spoke in light tone. "Not to worry Josh, if this girl of yours is really as good as you say, I think I owe it to the business to properly welcome her." He gave Rachel a playful wink that left her mouth agape and turned back to the bar to acknowledge the arrival of their drinks.

"Besides," he continued as he passed the drinks out, "it wasn't a timed appointment, it was just a lead and I can follow-up on that anytime. This is much more important. Rachel here takes care of paying my accounts, so it's only fitting I make sure the company is taking good care of her."

Josh was left momentarily speechless. All he could do was nod with his silly grin still plastered on his face. Rachel didn't know Blaze enough to what to think, but she knew she didn't like it. He was playing a new game and she was sure she didn't want to be on the losing end. She stole a glance at Josh and then back at Blaze. Josh might be overly flirtatious and a bit of a playboy wanna be, she thought to herself, but this man was conniving and manipulative. Rachel knew she'd have to watch her back with Blaze.

Josh went back to ordering his Becks; Blaze and Rachel continued with the tequila. Rachel led the next round, making sure to spill a little as she grabbed her glass. She let out a giggle and stumbled back a step into Josh. She righted herself and smiled shyly before licking the warm liquid off her fingers and shooting back the rest of the tequila. Blaze watched her closely as he shot his back.

She knew her change had to appear subtle and natural, so she was sure not to pour it on too thick right away. She also knew her limits well and knew that it was time to start spacing her shots out more. She figured more conversation would be the best way to accomplish both, but how to get Blaze engaged was something else. To her surprise, Blaze resolved that problem for her.

"So what is it that you do for Josh exactly?" Blaze asked as he casually spun the empty shot glass around the sticky bar with his index finger.

Despite the evident purposeful use of Josh in the question instead of the company name, Rachel bit her lip and let the comment go unanswered. "I was hired from a temp agency to replace the receptionist that left, but I've since been moved into a full-time contract as sales operations assistant."

Blaze nodded almost smugly. "So basically you're Josh's personal assistant now." Rachel could feel the blood rushing to her face and was struggling to maintain her composure, when Josh surprised them both by jumping to her defense.

"Oh she's much more than that. She's proven herself invaluable to the company. In fact I've never seen anyone learn the ropes as fast as she has." Josh slipped his arm proudly around her shoulders and continued. "Why she practically runs the sales department now, we'd be lost without her."

"Very impressive recommendation." Blaze said, sounding anything but impressed. Yet somehow Rachel still managed to bite her tongue and keep her temper in check, but the tequila was making it harder for her to do that.

"Thank you." Rachel replied smiling up at Josh as she spoke, making it obvious she was answering his praise and ignoring Blaze's comments at the same time. Then with another well placed giggle for effect she grabbed Josh's hand and took a step towards the dance floor. "I love this song." She stated in her best 'typical blonde' imitation. "Come dance with me Josh." She asked with an overly dramatic pout while she gently tugged him towards the dance floor.

Josh's smile, looking suspiciously like a leer, was all that he offered as he willingly let Rachel lead the way. Making sure to slur his name just a bit, she turned to Blaze. "You don't mind if we leave you again, Blaiss, right?" She didn't wait for his response and instead giggled a thank you and led Josh away. She needed time to regain her cool.

Blaze found himself once again sulking angrily, alone at the bar. What are you doing? He scolded himself. Enough games, you're here to do a job. Not even a paid job, a stupid favor at that, so stop messing around and just get the damn thing over with. He continued to chastise himself until the bartender brought him another Jack, which he proceeded to use to douse his mood as he glowered at his own reflection in the mirror. This girl might not be stealing from the company, but she has definite plans to play somebody he decided.

On the dance floor, Rachel soon found herself dealing with a little more of Josh's attention than she had bargained for as his dance moves brought him intimately close at every beat. Well you managed to bring this on yourself you idiot. She internally scolded herself. Just what are you doing?" She mentally smacked herself and tried to block out her own internal lecture.

Why was she letting Blaze's crass comments bother her so much? He was an independent contractor, they almost never come to the office; she didn't have to deal with him on a daily basis, so why couldn't she just play nice until he was gone and she wouldn't have to worry about him ever again.

Josh managed to jar her out of her thoughts when he stared grinding to the beat of the new song. Though she loved to dance, she realized she was pushing things a little too close to the edge. If she was going to maintain some professional decorum tonight, she'd have to watch how she played this from now on.

Just then she was jostled away from Josh by the movement of the overly crowded dance floor. She quickly decided to use that as her excuse to head back to the bar. She smiled and leaned in so Josh could hear over the noise. "Things are getting a bit crowded out here, why don't we head back to the bar?" She said as she wiped the perspiration off her forehead for added emphasis. Josh seemed hesitant, but she was already heading off the dance floor, leaving him little choice but to follow.

Rachel headed back with Josh in toe. She leaned on the bar next to Blaze who looked over at her questioningly until he saw Josh come up beside her. A small grin escaped his lips, but he didn't utter a word. "Got crowded out there." Josh offered as an answer to the unasked question. "Oh great a cold beer, you are a pal." Josh picked up the beer Blaze had ordered while they were gone and saluted him with it before taking a swig. Then he rubbed it over his brow and grinned.

Blaze didn't even bother to grunt a response; he could care less why they came back. By this time he was getting tired of the entire thing. He had a sudden desire to be in his neighborhood pub, with no one bothering him but the occasional drunk falling into a table on their way out. "So what exactly is it that you do as a sales assistant, Rachel was it? Call back sales leads, type letters and such?" His voice was its usual gruffness, a little more hurried than he would have liked, but at this point he didn't feel he needed to be overly concerned with tact. She'd had quite a few and he was over this night already.

Rachel could feel her back stiffen. "Yes, it's Rachel." She replied. Every ounce of her energy went into not reaching over and strangling him. She could feel Josh leaning in, about to come to her aid. She couldn't bear the thought of looking like she needed a rescue in front of him again, so she spoke first, cutting Josh off. "Well I do a lot of learning right now as I'm still trying to understand all the aspects of the business." She let out a gentle laugh and her voice softened. "I track the ATM technician's calls and I do follow-up on sales leads for one thing. But I also do a lot of the reconciliation between the bank processing reports and the ATM settlement reports." She shifted her stance. "Most of my work involves supporting the field sales agents and making sure we meet out goals and nothing is amiss."

Blaze raised his eyebrow in polite interest. "Oh how so?" He asked with a less rushed and more pleasant tone.

"I make sure the paperwork is complete, the deal is signed and any special notations are added to the accounts when they are setup. I also make sure the orders get setup with the for new merchants with the processors and the installations are scheduled, that type of thing." She smiled towards Josh who nodded in agreement.

He looked towards Josh and nodded in approval, his response sounding almost sincere. "Very handy Josh, that's something we could have used around that place a long time ago." Josh shrugged his shoulders and Blaze turned back to Rachel. "With that many skills, how did you end up working for this one then?" Josh straightened and pretended to be insulted but knew better of Blaze to take him seriously.

Rachel found herself rushing as if to defend Josh, which surprised her. "My agency placed me with him." Blaze stopped mid-gulp and found himself staring at her almost dumbfounded. She suddenly realized how that sounded and quickly rushed to explain. "When Stafford called my temp agent, looking for a receptionist, I had just completed my last contract and was looking for another assignment. This one seemed to fit so I came in to interview."

Blaze shot back the last of his whiskey. "Now that I could see." He mumbled into his empty glass. "They go through receptionists faster than most people go through socks." He added with a knowing grin that seemed to crack the sides of his mouth as if his muscles weren't used to smiling. With this they all broke out into laughter, they all knew he was right; they had already gone through two since she had been promoted.

Blaze lifted one of the tequila shots that sat in front of them as if in a toast and waited for the others to join him, Josh lifted his beer, and Rachel picked up her tequila. "To new receptionists and to new sales support assistants." Rachel picked up a tequila of her own and Blaze and Rachel shot theirs back. Josh took a swig of his beer. Blaze signaled for two more tequila.

Rachel found herself with a strange feeling; could Blaze really keep up this pace, could she? This was a dilemma she had never had before, and she found herself echoing Josh's earlier comments. Didn't Blaze need to get going soon? She found her apprehension alarming. Diving in head first without thinking that was her comfortable norm, hesitating on the other hand, that was unusual. One look at Blaze's condescending smirk and she was instantly poised for the next round. She knew it was a childish instinct, but her pride was at stake.

Josh leaned in resting his hands on Rachel's shoulders as he spoke. "Make sure you don't try taking advantage of our girl here." He threw Blaze a quick wink. "I'm responsible for making sure she gets home alright, let alone to work in the morning." Josh smiled his sly school boy grin, lingered a little too long with his hands on her for Rachel's comfort before finally stepping back from the two. "One side effect of beer," he continued, "means I have to visit the men's room again." He smiled and he headed off, making his way through the crowd.

Rachel grabbed one of the tequila shots for courage, glad when Blaze immediately joined her. They shot them back, the silence heavy between them. She was going to have to play this up a lot faster and that was easy now that she didn't have to worry about her behavior in front of her boss. She rested her hands against the edge of the bar and leaned her body back a little, just enough to appear light and playful, her idea of what was expected of a typical blonde again. She acted as if she lost her balance and quickly tried to straighten herself. She could feel the heat rise to her face; she was not used to embarrassing herself like this and she wasn't a fan, but desperate times and all that.

"Oops." She giggled and jumped forward onto the bar, with her chest all the way across it. "Two more!" She called out, showing the bartender two fingers for emphasis. She slipped off the bar and playfully gave Blaze a little shove with her shoulder and giggled again. "One more each, while my boss isn't around to see." She then made a shushing sound with her finger on her lips. For an instant she thought she saw a flash of concern, but it was gone so fast she knew if must have been her imagination.

“So, fair play. What brings you to work for Josh?” Rachel asked, leaning in closer. She rested one elbow on the counter and unconsciously twisted a piece of her silky hair around her finger. Blaze squirmed a bit in his seat. He signaled for another Whiskey as the bartender dropped off their latest tequila order.

“I don’t actually work for the company.” He stated. She gave him a look of confusion. Before she could ask anything he cut her off. “I work for myself. I just use Stafford’s sponsorship to allow me to register my ATMs without having to build my own financial company. It saves me the hassle of maintaining and paying for my own sponsorships. I pay a little more for processing each month by not going direct, but I save on the registration fees and other hassles. With the size of my portfolio, it works out better this way. In fact Stafford is not the only company I have ATMs registered through.”

“So is this all you do then? I mean the revenue off you ATMss are enough to ssustain you?” She said, slurring her S’s ever so slightly. She didn’t even notice, but Blaze did. The tension eased from his scowl.

“I don’t need a lot.” He stated nonchalantly. “But to answer your question, no, this is just one of many side businesses. Keeps me out of trouble.” He let out what passed as a half laugh, half grunt and stared into the golden liquid in front of him, lost in thought. After a moment he turned to face her head on. His sudden intense stare caused her to catch her breath. He held her eyes captive with his deep blue ones, not allowing her to look elsewhere, probing her as he spoke. “So what are your ambitions now that you’ve found Stafford Financial? Planning on staying around long?”

“I don’t.” She stuttered, momentarily flustered. “I haven’t made any plans yet. I'm still learning, but so far I like it." She broke his stare and tilted her head back as if to stretch her neck. She took a deep breath and smiled more relaxed and at ease. "I think I'll stay, a little while anyway." She slowly met his stare taking control of her gaze. It was at this point that she could see why they must call him Blaze. His eyes seemed to flicker with the lights around him; the blue had the same intense transparent and somewhat hypnotic effect as the blue part of a flame.

As she studied him further she began to see an intelligence and intensity lurking beneath the drunkard surface that surprised her. She could feel a constant anger seething beneath his gruff exterior and she shivered instinctively. Her skin prickled and she suddenly found herself aware that the bartender had come and gone leaving them their new drinks. She had uneasiness about her as she reached for their drinks, positioning one shot in front of Blaze and picking up the other, readying for a toast.

Blaze watched her curiously; she definitely had the dumb blonde routine down pat, but he knew there had to be more behind her giggles and grins. Could she have managed to distract him from taking her seriously, from seeing her true nature? No. He decided. He couldn't have gotten that sloppy, been that easily distracted. His training was instinct now, it might have dulled, but it didn't leave him. "So what did you do before Stafford?" He continued to sip his whiskey, ignoring the tequila that she had place in front of him.

Rachel's hand shook slightly and some of the tequila spilled out. She set the shot glass down and tilted her head to look at him. "Gee Officer; a girl doesn't even get one last drink before she's interrogated?" She giggled, but stopped short when she saw Blaze's jaw tighten and his eye darken.

"Meaning what?" He snapped.

Rachel's heart beat faster. She turned around to face him. His voice had been cold, almost menacing. His stare direct and calculating. She had touched a nerve. Her hands instantly steadied. Her postured straighten. Her eyes became intense. Her mind cleared; all effects of the alcohol temporarily gone as she honed in. "Meaning since I already have the job why is it starting to feel like I'm being interviewed?" She picked up the tequila again. "Meaning, if you aren't some cop on duty, then why are you too scared to have a little drink with me?" She cocked her eyebrow to add a challenge to the dare.

Blaze stared; he looked confused, as if searching for his next move. Though she didn't know it, it was a look he never wore; next moves were instinctual for him. He grabbed his tequila and shot it back, slamming the shot glass a on the bar hard enough to get another warning look from the bartender. He waved an apology and then turned to face her. He cocked his head to match hers and then the slightest hint of a grin crept over his mouth. "Not scared, just too impatient to wait for you to stop talking and drink it." There was a moment of silence, and then they both laughed. "No interrogation, just curious about who's watching out for my investments that's all."

Rachel set her shot glass down once again. "Well then instead of acting like a cop how about you tell me a little about your investment, maybe then I'd know what I was watching out for."

"Stop acting like a cop? Now that's funny." Josh chimed in as he slipped back in behind them. He grabbed his beer, shook it lightly to confirm it was empty, and then tried to get the bartenders attention to order another.

Rachel and Blaze, both startled, spun around to look at him. It was as if they had forgotten he had been with them tonight. Rachel suddenly broke into a grin. She turned to watch Blaze as she spoke but directed her words behind her.

“Why would that be funny?” She asked Josh

“Because once a cop, always a cop, even…” Josh stopped talking when Rachel’s surprise and Blazes’ anger registered. “Oh man, I thought you knew. Sorry, guess that’s what I get for jumping in the middle of a conversation.” Josh’s apology was short lived as he finally got the bartenders attention and waved him over.

“You’re a cheap drunk Josh.” Blaze scowled.

“What? It’s not like it’s a secret, why do you think you get drinks faster than I do around this place?” Josh chuckled as the bartender smiled in polite amusement. “See.” Josh nodded towards the bartender’s reaction as proof of his claim. Blaze simply ignored his comment. “You guys want anything else before I close out the tab?” Josh asked as he motioned for the check. Blaze cocked an eyebrow in surprise. “I’ve got an early run tomorrow, training a new technician.” Josh offered as an explanation. Blaze gave him a considered nod.

Rachel nodded to her full tequila. “I’m good thanks.”

Josh smiled and turned to the waiting bartender. “I’ll have another Becks, and make sure it’s cold this time, then close off the tab.” The bartender nodded and looked towards Blaze. Blaze gave him a half smile and waved a no, but leaned in to exchange a secret joke that left the bartender smiling as he left to close off Josh’s tab.

Blaze ignored Rachel’s stare and kept his attention directed at Josh. “Didn’t you just hire a new guy?”

Josh nodded. “Yes. Patrick, but we are still down a man.”

"Why are you training the new technician? Isn't that Miguel's job?"

"Miguel's flown the coop again." Josh started, his face animated in frustration. "I can't wait to hear his excuse this time."

"You're not thinking of taking him back again are you?" Blaze insisted, a deep scowl on his face. "He's unreliable."

"It's hard to get skilled people. Besides, he's the best technician I have."

"He's unreliable."

"If he's so unreliable why do you let him service your machines?" Rachel broke in, questioning Blaze.

"He doesn't." Josh responded with a slightly condescending tone. "He's too cheap to contract our techs, he does his own work."

"At least I know I'll show up when I need to."

Josh only shrugged and turned as the bartender returned with his beer and his tab. He raised an eyebrow as he glanced at the tab, then he feigned a hurt look and covered his chest with his hand as if he was shot. "Ouch." He said, breaking into a quiet laugh. "I see you two were busy while I was gone." Rachel giggled, trying not to sound too forced. Blaze shrugged.

"Speaking of being cheap." Blaze added, rolling his eyes at Josh.

Rachel stifled a laugh and tugged on Josh's arm before he could respond to Blaze. "How about one last dance before we go?" She smiled. Josh nodded and followed her out to the dance floor.

When they were out of ear shot of the bar she spoke, her voice sounding as casual as she could make it. "So, Blaze's ATM business doesn't interfere with his work on the police force?"

Josh laughed and as they squeezed into the dance floor, he started to respond, but Rachel couldn't hear over the music, so she pointed to her ear and Josh leaned closer and shouted. "Actually we get a lot of active and former police officers that invest in the ATM business; they are very secure in handling the cash, something about carrying a gun I guess. It doesn't interfere with their work because they do most of it in their off hours and when need be, do a quick fill on a lunch hour, but Blaze isn't a cop anymore. Left under 'suspicious circumstances' from what I here, but he still has most of his old contacts and he's very good at getting what he wants."

She rolled her eyes and nodded in silent understanding. She tried to lean in and ask another question, but she had to start and stop several times just to get a word in between the thundering beat of the new song. She pouted then slowly gave in to the music. Josh moved in close, mirroring her dance moves as if they moved as one. She smiled softly toward Josh, but her eyes were bright and inwardly focused as her mind raced. She'd have to stave her curiosity, but that didn't stop her from impulsively glanced toward the bar many times.

The moment the song ended she headed off the dance floor, after a few steps she stopped and signaled Josh as an afterthought. She giggled and clutched his arm to cover her actions. Josh's school boy grin contracted into a smirk. He pulled his arm closer, bringing her and her arm closer to him. Rachel's face flushed and her eyes darted around the room. She dragged her pace slower as they approached the bar, then she smiled and pulled them both to a stop.

"I think it's time I bow out while I have my dignity intact and face my boss tomorrow." She gave Josh a wink. Josh leaned in and was about to protest, but Rachel cut him off. "Would you mind terribly calling me a cab?" Josh looked like he was debating his options. "It would make me feel much better knowing I wasn't putting anyone out and uber is so unreliable at this hour." She said answering his unasked question. Then she smiled up at him, tilting her head vulnerably towards him. Josh dropped his shoulders and sighed.

"Of course. I'll call up front. It's a little too loud here." Rachel nodded. Josh turned and slinked off to get her a cab. When he was out of sight her smile stretched into a satisfied grin and she eagerly strolled back to the bar. Her grin deepened when she saw Blaze straighten upon her approach. He threw her a nod as she approached.

"You forget your date back there?" Rachel ignored his condescending tone and smiled. He watched her intensely, waiting for an answer. When she didn't respond, he shifted his weight and relaxed his posture. "So what did you do before you came to Stafford?"

She laughed as she remembered her last job and smiled secretively. She moved purposefully as she picked up her tequila. She moved close enough to Blaze to feel the heat radiating off of him. Staring at the golden liquid, she slowly tipped the shot glass until a drop trickled down the side. "Um, just did some accounting and helped out around a Health food store chain. I'm sure it's not as exciting as your last job was." She said, never taking her eyes off her drink. Then she smiled and licked the trail off liquid off the side of the shot glass.

Blaze tried to steady his breathing as he watched her. He ignored her comment. "Why did you leave?"

Her smile turned into a playful grin and she tilted her head to face him. "I'll tell you mine if you tell me yours." She stared at him, her eyes vibrant and challenging. As if on a bad cue, Josh returned.

"Your cab should be outside shortly." His voice was loud and mildly irritated.

Rachel tossed Blaze a deliberate smile as she set her drink down once again. Then in an instant her eyes seemed to cloud over and her stance relaxed. Her hand became unsteady and she bumped Blaze with her elbow as she turned to face Josh. She giggled and pursed her lips. "Oops, my bad." Then she rolled her eyes as if pointing behind her. She reached out and held Josh's arm, as if for support. "Thank you, my hero, but don't worry, I'll be at work bright an early tomorrow." She offered a sloppy salute for emphasis. "Would you mind walking me out?" She said as she slipped her hand softly around his arm assuming his approval.

Josh smiled and offered her a little bow. "Of course. And believe me, I'll be too tired schlepping that new technician around to be holding anything against anyone tomorrow." Josh nodded to Blaze and threw him a look indicating he'd be back. Rachel ignored him. They walked a few steps from the bar before stopping.

"Oh dear. Wait here a second. I forgot my purse." Josh nodded and Rachel sauntered back to the bar and grabbed her purse. She hesitated a moment then shot back her tequila, turned her glass upside down and leaned in close to Blaze, meeting his intense stare. "Next time you try to play someone, maybe you should make sure you're not being played yourself." With that she straightened up, threw him a wink and added. "Thanks for the info." She laughed and left Blaze staring after her.

Her laugh turned into a giggle as she got closer to Josh. "Sorry, I don't know what I'd do without this." She said raising her purse for him to see. "I'm all set." They headed out. As they approached the front Rachel stopped and removed her hand from Josh's arm. "Thanks again. It was an interesting evening." She smiled and headed out before Josh had time to answer or follow her. Leaving Josh momentarily stunned.

The night air was fresh and crisp, there was a slight mist that touched her skin and left her feeling refreshed after the heat of the club. The cab was waiting so she jumped in and hurriedly gave the driver directions for her apartment. Only after the cab pulled away did she look back to be sure she was alone.

Josh headed back to the bar; he was pouting from Rachel's quick exit, but anxious to hear what Blaze had to say. Blaze was paying off his tab when Josh reached him. "Skipping out on me man?" He joked as he gave Blaze a pat on the back. Blaze was back to his grunting responses. Josh smirked and continued. "Well what do you think? Do I have anything to worry about?"

Blaze threw the cash for his bill and a generous tip on the bar and nodded to the bartender. Then he turned and studied Josh for a moment before answering. "She's not a thief of that I'm sure." Josh smiled and leaned back against the bar. "But," Blaze continued, "I wouldn't say you have nothing to worry about. She's trouble that one."

Josh's smile faded and was replaced with a look of puzzlement. He turned to Blaze, for an explanation. Instead Blaze straightened and gave him an uncharacteristic smile. "I mean she's not your type old boy, but maybe I'll check in around the office a little more. Keep an eye on her for you just the same." Then he patted Josh on the back and made what sounded a lot like a laugh. "Have a good one." He said as he turned away from the bar. As an afterthought he added, "Make sure you teach your new tech to run a test transaction before he leaves a site. If they actually left an ATM working when they were done, maybe then

I'd use your guys." Without another word, he headed out, leaving Josh alone at the bar.

Josh nodded and turned to back to the bar. He picked up his beer and slowly swallowed the rest of it while watching two scantily clad women at the other end. They were busy using all their 'assets' to get the bartenders attentions. They had their drinks, but clearly they were bartender groupies. He noted the redhead's blouse was almost see-through and suddenly he lost interest in his beer and what he had to do in the morning.

He strutted towards the pair, only looking up at their faces when he was within breathing distance. His eyes were almost see though and his trade mark school boy grin flashed with his bright white teeth. "Mind if I buy you ladies a drink?" He tossed them one wink and they turned all their interest toward him, forgetting the existence of the bartender and he was able to get a closer look at their 'assets'. Suddenly his disappointment in losing out on a night with Rachel was forgotten, two to replace one was a fair trade in his book.

CHAPTER 8

Rachel was loading the sugar and cream in her coffee as usual. She was glad Josh was in the field this morning and she didn't have to deal with any meetings this early. With Josh out and Miguel god knows where, she ran the morning schedules. She made sure to send the techs out as early as possible and the phones were currently quiet. She had a fresh pot of coffee and a moment of peace. Life was good.

"Drinking a lot of that this morning?"

The deep booming voice behind her had started her and she jumped as the steaming coffee splashed down her shirt. "Shit." She cursed and slammed her coffee down, grabbed a damp rag off the sink and turned to scold the intruder. "I waited all mor..." She stopped dead as the hulking figure registered in her consciousness. Blaze. She stared dumbfounded.

Blaze was leaning casually against the kitchen door. He smiled and folded his bulky arms. He filled up the entire entrance way. She silently took in his looming figure, tracing his shoulders as if she hadn't noticed his size before now.

"Waited all what?" He asked, prompting her to finish her thought. A confused look crossed her face, so Blaze relaxed his arms, took a step closer before continuing. "You were saying, 'waited all' and then you stopped."

His motion snapped her out of her surprise. She turned and looked over at her cup, jutted her chin out and responded. "I was saying; I waited all morning for that coffee." She looked down at her blouse and tried futility to scrub away the staining liquid. She quickly gave up and tossed the rag back in the sink and turned to pour herself a new cup. Extra, extra cream and sugar this time.

Blaze watched in amusement as she loaded in the sugar and cream. "Please, don't let me stop you." He mused.

"If you expect me to offer you a cup, don't hold your breath." She replied without looking up from her determined search for another stir stick. Seems she used the last one with her last cup. Blaze walked over to her, reached above her bent head, opened the cupboard above her and grabbed a small box off the top shelf. He handed it to her. She stiffened reflexively to his close proximity, but she took the box of stir sticks he had handed her, shrugged her shoulders, and mumbled. "Thanks."

"Who am I to come between a woman and her morning dessert?"

Rachel finished stirring and shrugged as she took a sip of her creamy sweet coffee. Her shoulders instantly relaxed and her face seemed to soften. She smiled. "Now that's a coffee worth waiting for."

"No." Blaze said as he grabbed a mug and poured himself a coffee. Black. No sugar. He took a sip and cracked his own version of a smile. "That's a coffee."

Rachel muttered what could only have been described as a 'Humph' sound and proudly walked her prized coffee back to her desk. Blaze sauntered along behind her, uninvited. She didn't acknowledge him once. She had her morning coffee to enjoy. She settled herself at her desk and attempted to act like she was alone.

Blaze settled in the chair across from her desk, stretched his legs out in front of him and proceeded to watch her as he sipped his coffee. After a few minutes Rachel stopped checking her emails and sighed in frustration before speaking to him. "Josh is out in the field."

"I know." He replied between sips. "I was there last night when he mentioned it, remember?" He said as if there was every reason that she wouldn't remember in reference to her drinking.

She didn't take the bait. "I remember, but I was assuming from your presence that you didn't."

"I'm surprised you remember anything." He continued to goad her more directly this time.

Rachel's face reddened. Her breathing more labored. She glared at him as he continued to watch her in silence. He was just sitting there, staring at her and sipping his coffee in complete silence. She wanted him to leave. She sighed heavily. "Is there something I can help you with?" She said finally in a slow steady voice.

"Nope." More silence.

"Then what exactly..."

"I'm just checking in on my investments. Had some contracts I thought I should file."

"And you thought you'd bring them to me?"

"Well, that is your job." He said, and then with an eye brow raised he added. "Isn't that what you said?"

Rachel's pout deepened as she nodded in response. "Yes, that's my job." She eyed him suspiciously, before finally slumping her shoulders in resignation. "So, where are these contracts?" She said, holding out her hand.

"They're out in the car." He didn't move a muscle, other than to sip his coffee.

She dropped her hand and adjusted herself in her seat; Still no movement from Blaze. She sighed even deeper this time, trying to make her impatience known. Hoping it would spur him on so she could get back to her day. "Well?"

"I'll get them later. Right now, I'm drinking my coffee."

"We... I... Ugh" Rachel stuttered and turned back to her computer. "Look, Blaze. I'd be happy to process your contracts when you bring them to me, but right now I'm a little busy. We are short staffed and the service calls are backed up, so I don't have time to just sit here and sip coffee with you. I'm sure no one will mind if you use one of the empty sales desks to relax and catch up on your investments." She stopped typing her latest response email at that point and waited expectantly for him to leave.

"Well then, I'm here just in time." He said, lifting his legs to allow himself to lean forward.

She threw him a puzzled look, but before she could respond she was interrupted by the phone. She looked at her phone. It was the tech support line. She picked up the line. "Stafford Tech support, how can I help you?" Immediately Rachel jumped and pulled the phone away from her ear. The yelling man's voice could be heard from where Blaze sat. Slowly she put the receiver back to her ear and put on her best smile and nodded sympathetically as the man vented his frustrations.

Rachel let him finish before she spoke. “Yes sir that is a big problem for you. I can see that you need that resolved right away. All of the technicians are on calls right now, but let me make some calls and see what I can move around so I can get someone out there today.” The caller yelled even louder and she pulled the phone from her ear again, more quickly this time. She replaced it on her other ear before speaking. “No sir, I do understand. I will do my utmost to get someone there today.”

Blaze sat up straight in his chair. He signaled to Rachel, who was trying desperately to ignore him. She signaled for him to wait, but he insisted on waving in her face. She finally acknowledged him by holding up a finger saying one minute. “Sir. Sir, can you hold on one second, I need to check something for you quickly. No, I won’t be long, just let me check one thing for you okay?” Rachel pressed the hold button and turned to Blaze, her smile had faded. “I’m kind of in the middle of something here.”

Blaze smiled. “I can see that, but like I said before, it seems like I’m here just in time. I can help you.” Rachel was about to respond, but this time Blaze held up his finger to her to have her wait. “I’ll take the service call.” Rachel shook her head in protest. He continued. “You said it yourself, you’re short staffed, you have a new tech being trained so you can’t have Josh go over there and your others are backed up. What choice do you have?”

Rachel pondered this over. She could see the hold light blinking more rapidly. It was about to ring back to her line. A look of panic was starting to cross her face. Blaze spoke in a calm and re-assuring voice. “I used to do this for Josh all the time in the early days, before I started building my own portfolio. How do you think I learnt the business?” She still looked unsure, but now the line had rung back off hold. “I’ll take the van out back and head over; you can come with me if you like. To keep me honest.”

Rachel grabbed the line.

"Sir. Yes, sorry about that, no I didn't forget about you. I just found a technician who can head over there now. Yes, that's right. No, he's loading his van now and as soon as he's ready, I'll send him straight to your store. What was your Merchant ID again? Yes. 421? Oh 6. Got it." Rachel typed the number into the service system as the man rattled them off. When his account came up she confirmed. "Get One convenience store, on Broadside, correct? Okay, I'll send him over. Thank you for your patience sir, and again, I'm very sorry about the mix up. We'll get it all straightened out for you today." Rachel hung up the phone and looked at Blaze. She started to smile, but stopped at a kind of half grin, half wince.

"So what's the problem?"

"Seems a couple of techs went to his store three days ago to replace his ATM with a new one. Problem is they didn't finish the job. They brought the new one in, but didn't make sure it was working and they left the old one there. The one technician told him, he'd be back for it tomorrow, said he needed a stronger hand cart or the guy needed to clear his truck or something. It was hard to tell through all his yelling, but best I can tell, neither one came back for it so he has the old one pulled out of the floor, but still broken down in his store and the new one lying there too." She stared at Blaze in silence for a few seconds. "Are you sure you can do this?"

Blaze stood up and waved her off. "Please, why do you think I don't use your techs anyway? I do a better job than they do. Grab the address and whatever else you need and meet me in the back of the warehouse. I'll pack up the van and I'll take you on a road trip, teach you how this stuff is really done." Blaze's voice was strong and confident. He offered her a quick salute of his hand and he headed out towards the back. With is large frame gone, her office suddenly looked huge.

She relaxed her shoulders and her smile came back. She had never been out with the technicians before, she had always wanted to see how an ATM got set up. She gulped as much of her beloved coffee as she could manage without burning her throat, switched the tech line back over to the call center, Phil would have to handle it alone for a while, pulled the merchant's repair ticket and printed off the directions. Then she buzzed the front desk to let the new temp know she was heading out on a service call and went to meet up with Blaze. She was glad there was a new temp on the phones. Coralene was starting to go back to just ignoring her again, which made her life a lot easier than when she was actively hating on her. "Road Trip." She whispered aloud, and a giggle escaped as pushed through the back doors. Even having to go with Blaze couldn't take her sense of adventure away.

*****

"I told you to take a left." Blaze grumbled something under his breath. Rachel ignored it and continued on. "There should be another access road up ahead, at least that's what it looks like on this tiny little map which I wouldn't have had to try and read if you had just gone left in the first place."

Blaze grumbled again.

"You asked for my directions. Don't get mad at me if you don't take them and end up lost." She replied, adjusting the print out on the service ticket.

"We're not lost." Blaze slammed on the brakes. Rachel jerked forward in her seat and glared at him. "There, that road will lead behind the store." He pointed off to his left. He didn't wait for confirmation as he turned the wheel and started down the narrow road.

He pulled around to the back of the store and took the only spot they could find to park. When he finished negotiating the tight squeeze between the two buildings, he threw the van in park and turned to find her glowering at him. At that he let out a chuckle and somehow managed to squeeze between the two front seats to the back. The back set of doors were Blaze's only exit due to the position of the spot and his sheer bulk.

Rachel easily squeezed out her side door. She smiled as she rounded the van to meet up with Blaze who was still struggling around some of the equipment to get him and the hand cart out. Blaze scowled at her amused giggles. "Thanks for the help." He muttered as he turned to shut the doors. Then he swept his arm to motion for her to go first. Rachel led the way to the front of the store and he followed along with the cart.

They greeted the clerk and showed him their ID badges. Right away he started complaining. "I wan zat sing out here. It takeen up my floo space. No floo space, no good for business." His accent was this, English was clearly his second and not best language.

She smiled politely. "I am very sorry for your inconvenience. I assure you, we are here to make sure you are taken care of. I have no excuse for our technician's behavior, but we will make sure that doesn't happen again." She turned to point towards Blaze. "This is one of our best technicians and we will not leave until your new ATM is ready to go." Rachel wasn't sure if the store owner understood everything she had said, but he seemed to have calmed down and decided to leave to help a customer that had just come in. He pointed to the back right corner of the store and they headed off.

"Your best technician?" Blaze cocked his head as he spoke.

"Better than telling him you were some guy that wandered in for coffee and wouldn't leave me alone now isn't it." She smiled smugly and left him with another grunt. Then she headed off to help guide him as he steered the cart around the stacks of boxes that were crammed throughout the store's tight aisles. They rounded the corner of the last aisle and both of them stopped dead in their tracks.

"No wonder this guy was so pissed." Blaze said as he rested his hand on the cart. Rachel nodded in agreement. "Now do you see why I do my own work?" He looked over the mess they had been called in to clean up. The packing that the new ATM must have been wrapped in for transport was still lying on the floor. The shavings from the bolts that were drilled out of the floor from the old ATM were spread around both ATMs and both machines took up most of the store owners precious little floor space.

Blaze sighed. "I assume this new model is the one that stays." He said pointing towards the smaller ATM that still had plastic covering the screen and key pad.

She scanned the paperwork, but it was clear that the old bulky one with the cracked screen and various profanities scratched into its dingy finish was the one to be replaced. She nodded, but Blaze had already started to position the cart behind the large ATM. She didn't offer to help; she knew from her little experience around the warehouse that even the small one, empty, weighed around a 150lbs. The other one was nearly twice its foot print and clearly never heard of lightweight materials, she couldn't imagine its weight. She could be of little help there.

"Good thing I brought the full size cart and not the usual half carts and not the usual half carts." Blaze said as he rolled up his shirt sleeves in expectation of the work ahead. "No offense, but I kind of wish I had one of the other techs with me." He said as he looked the old machine over.

“Hey, none taken. I don’t blame you. That things a monster.” Rachel backed up a step and threw her hands up in surrender. “I’ll do what I can, but you’ll have to tell me what to do because I can’t say I have any moving experience on my résumé.”

Blaze smiled and prepped the machine for the move. He cleared all the packing and various other debris from around it. He positioned the cart in the front. It was a front loader and the cassette carriage was mounted forward, making it front heavy. Blaze decided that with no one else to help lift it he needed to take advantage of gravity. He pulled on the safe door to make sure it was secured and wouldn’t accidently open as he tilted it. He unrolled the cart straps and tossed them beside the base of the ATM. “Think you can act as a support for me?”

“Sure.” She replied, her voice unsure.

He had her push the cart under the bottom as he lifted it by shoving the full weight of his body against it. He let the ATM slam down on the cart and expelled heavily as he staggered backwards. Rachel raised her eyebrows. “That things damn heavy.” He defended. “And they probably left it fully loaded, dispensers and all. Amateurs.” He complained. “I forgot how heavy these old beasts are. Still, for it to be this heavy it must have a level I safe in it.”

“I’ll have to take your word for it. We don’t get too many orders for Level I safes, but that doesn’t mean they didn’t stick one in here just to recycle it. Not too many can afford the upgrade.” She said with a nod towards the front of the store for emphasis. “But I have seen the odd one loaded and I know they barely budge with two technicians.”

Blazed jerked up the straps to ensure they were tight as he tossed her a reply. "That's because it adds a few hundred pounds extra." Rachel's jaw dropped. Blaze grinned. "Relax, this is heavy, but I'm pretty sure it's not a level I." He tapped sides for emphasis. "Loaded with a full set of cassettes maybe and whatever other supplies the idiots left crammed in the bottom storage." He scolded as he locked down the cart's breaks. "Probably even left the cash inside." He continued ranting as he readied himself to move it. "Solid steel these old ones." He said patting the top. "Dead weight." He confirmed as he braced his body tight against the cart for support. "But I can move it." He affirmed before continuing in a more instructional tone. "Now when I pull, you push as hard as you can as high on the back of the machine as you can. As soon as it starts to move, get out of the way as fast as you can; just in case."

Rachel didn't look convinced, but she still moved to the back and braced her hands against the top ready to push. She watched as every muscle on Blaze's neck, shoulders and back strained as he began to pull the top section towards himself. She pushed up and forward as hard as she could. He was using the weight of his thick legs as leverage and steadying the cart with his hips as the ATMs started to tilt. She was pretty sure she wasn't helping, and it was all him, then suddenly she felt it move. She immediately jumped back as she had been instructed. She held her breath as it finally groaned and swung over, but when it settled on the cart and held, she sighed in relief.

He slowly repositioned his body and released the breaks one at a time. It held, and the cart did what it was supposed to in countering the weight for him, but his thick arms where clearly still straining. "Now the hard part." He said, his voice straining from the exertion.

Rachel laughed, but her smile immediately faded as she turned and looked down the long narrow cluttered aisle in front of them. "Oh." She said as her shoulders sunk down and she sighed.

"I'll clear a path."

It took a while, but when he shut the doors of the van on the old ATM, they shared a sigh of relief. The tough part was done, now was the fun part, Rachel got to help setup the new ATM. They cleaned the area around the machine up first, unwrapped the plastic protecting the screen and sealing the doors shut. Blaze skillfully drilled and bolted the base in place, then ensured it was cabled properly and had power and a network line, then they turned it on.

After its start-up routine they found it was already pre-configured. Rachel pouted. She knew it was standard practice to pre-configure the ATM before it left the warehouse, but she had still hoped to get to set one up herself.

"Let's test it, make sure the setup is good and the lines lines are live." Blaze pulled out his bank card to explain. Rachel plucked it from his hand and dipped it in the slot, then looked at him expectantly as it requested entry of his PIN. "2-3-3-1." He whispered quietly as she entered the numbers on the key pad. She requested a balance inquiry and waited. After a few seconds she received an "Invalid PIN" error proving that the ATM setup was verified by the processor and that he had given her a fake PIN number. She tossed him an amused smile and he took back his card and popped it in his wallet and gave her a shrug.

The main reason it was setup before it left the warehouse was so the technicians didn't have to rush through the programming as customers buzzed about over their shoulders. It was also the way they got around the Association rules regarding entry of the master key number used to encrypt cardholder PIN numbers with a different code that is sent to the bank instead of the actual PIN number. The rules said the master encryption keys were to be entered in two parts by two separate people, neither one knowing the other person's part, but most ATMs were installed by one installer. Setting them up in the warehouse allowed them to sign audit reports that two different key custodians managed the keys the entire time. Even though standard practice is for one setup technician to do the actual setup, the second signature comes later. She had decided for employment's sake not to ask what other signatures were 'delayed' on the logs provided to the auditors.

"Let's check the rest of the setup before we load it with cash." He said as he pressed the function keys to restart it into the supervisor mode.

"Cash!" Rachel exclaimed, her face drained of color. "This is one of our ATMs."

"Yes Rachel, you put cash in an ATM."

She turned and gave him a light smack on the arm. "I know that, I meant, I forgot this one is not filled by the merchant and we can't requisition cash at this hour."

Blaze grinned smugly. "We can't no, but you forget, I fill my own machines. I always have cash. We'll use mine. You can pay me back later." He finished with a wink, then proceeded to enter the password that Rachel had scribbled on the paperwork before they left the office.

Rachel let out a laugh. "Yeah right. Stafford Financial maybe, but you're not getting anything from me." It was her turn to add a smug smile.

Blaze scanned the print out from the ATM and frowned. "Figures." Rachel craned to look around him and see what he was looking at. He held it so she could see. "They set the cassettes up wrong. See," he said as he pointed towards the bottom of the paper, "the dispenser is setup for 10 dollar bills. If I load it with 20's it will double dispense and Stafford will be short cash." He changed the setup for 20's and rebooted it, readying it for loading cash. "And you wonder why I do my own setups." He affirmed again. "Maybe if Josh stopped hiring kids..." He didn't finish his thought, instead just shook his head and grabbed his tool kit.

Rachel's mouth dropped open when he lifted off the bottom panel and rolls of twenties were exposed. Blaze grabbed a few rolls, counted it with her as witness, then proceeded to load it into the cassette. "You just carry your around in your tool kit?" She exclaimed in disbelief.

He shrugged. "What do you suggest, a large canvas bag with dollar signs on it?"

This time she shrugged. "I guess not."

Blaze closed up the cassette and loaded it into the dispenser, then he reset it into normal operating mode. Neither had the combination to the safe so before closing and locking the safe, he took out his bank card and withdrew a 20 as a final check. He resealed his remaining cash in the tool kit and they headed out. Ensuring the store owner knew it was now working.

"You're a natural." Blaze teased as they drove back to the office. Rachel beamed with pride.

"It was kind of fun." She said, her eyes sparkling. Then she tilted her head and slowed her voice for emphasis. "Don't think I'll be switching departments anytime soon, but it was nice to get out of the office. Get a taste for how the ATMs actually work."

Blaze let out a snort. "Then you should come out with me sometime on my runs. That way you could see what a professional job looks like instead of what Stafford does."

Rachel smiled. "You've got a date." She blurted enthusiastically, then realizing what she said she quickly covered her mouth as trying to push it back in. Blaze cocked his eyebrow and cracked a grin. Rachel turned her head away as she felt herself turn red more embarrassed by her reaction than to the actual words.

CHAPTER 10

Rachel and Blaze made it back to the office around 1:30. They had stopped for a large coffee and a quick bite on the way back. She had insisted on buying to thank him for helping her out with the call, but he had only accepted after she agreed that next time she went on a call with him that he'd buy. A deal she made knowing full well she would never be going out on another trip with him.

They parked the van in the back of the warehouse but decided to leave unloading the ATM until later. They were just heading toward the bull pen when Rachel nearly ran right into Josh. Josh's smile lit up when he saw her.

"Rachel, where have you..." Josh stopped when he saw Blaze behind her. "Hey man, what are you doing here?" Josh's face froze when he saw their drinks and his smile faded. Blaze stepped forward, slightly ahead of Rachel and angled between her and Josh.

"Just doing some training of my own and saving your ass."

Rachel tried not to choke on her coffee as she held back a chuckle. Josh stiffened. The two men stared at each other in silence for a moment. They were almost even in height, but Blaze was clearly bulkier. Rachel tried to interrupt their schoolyard stare down by clearing her throat. "We had an emergency that came up and Blaze helped out, so I bought him a coffee as a thank you." Rachel studied one man, then the other. They were still staring each other down. She rolled her eyes at them and sighed and was about to walk away in frustration.

Blaze turned away first, he tossed the keys to Rachel. "Might want to grab few guys in bullpen when they are back to unload that machine and get it cleared out before it gets too late. The techs around here don't tend to stick around much once they get back from the field." He smiled then headed directly past Josh, forcing him to take a step back to let him by. Then continued speaking to her. "I'll check in later. I'm gonna clean up a bit first." He threw her a wink and gave Josh a firm pat on the shoulder as he went by on his way to the washroom. Josh's jaw muscles rippled as he clenched.

Rachel smiled and started walking towards her office. Josh turned and followed alongside. "We picked up an ATM that some techs left at a customer's site. He was really angry when we got there, but we left him with a working ATM and brought back the other one. I'll look into which tech was assigned to that call. They left the place a disaster."

"Good idea." He nodded. "Maybe I should have had you on training this morning."

Rachel smiled. "Didn't go well?"

"It's not like we need rocket scientists, but I'm still debating whether he can make the cut or not. Let's just say I'm pretty sure he won't advance through the company like you did." Josh tossed her an easy smile. He stopped at her office door. She went inside and sat down. "Let me know when you find out what happened with that service call. Not that we have any techs to spare, but I think at least one needs his hide tanned. Listen I'd love to hear about your morning in the field, but I've got some sales calls to catch up on since my morning was pretty much a wash for that."

Rachel smiled and waved him off. “Don’t worry about it; I’ve got to get caught up on some things myself. I was backed up before we took the call, so I probably wouldn’t be very talkative anyway. Oh before you go, we owe the cash refill to Blaze, he fronted it so we could leave it working for the owner, we will have to replace it.” Josh nodded and headed out.

She looked at her computer and sighed. She started to weed through some of her emails but found the stacks of paper on her desk too distracting to allow her to focus on them. So she let out another sigh, and picked up a stack of the papers closes and started organizing them into smaller piles. One was of urgent items to deal with, one to file away and the other a miscellaneous pile off to the side that didn’t need attention and she could get to them later. The piles were daunting, but she managed to get through them all so when she was down to filing the last paper in the cabinet she smiled and turned to face her newly organized desk. Immediately her smile disappeared.

“I told you I had some contracts to bring in.” Blaze chuckled as she suspiciously eyed the new even larger pile that had appeared in the center of her desk. He shrugged. “It’s been a while since I’ve been in.” He added with a wink.

She cocked her head and looked up at him. “I see that. Thanks.” She added, not thankful at all.

“Well, it’s either these or we could tackle that ATM in the back ourselves.”

Rachel grinned. “I think I’d much rather tackle that ATM than start on this mess.” Blaze looked down at the large disheveled pile, covered with unknown stains and returned her smile.

“Good choice.” He nodded.

Rachel stood up and followed him out to the back. They used the loading dock ramp to bring the ATM into the warehouse. Blaze unwrapped it and Rachel grabbed the shop keys for the ATM. They opened the top first. It was full of dirt, but it looked relatively intact, maybe salvageable for parts he thought. Blaze closed it then opened the door covering the bottom vault. He immediately frowned.

“It’s an old lock; we won’t be able to reset this to the factory settings. I don’t suppose you have the codes with you?” Rachel shook her head. “Don’t suppose that Miguel came back?” Rachel shook her head again. He sighed heavily. “Better grab Josh then.”

She shook her head again. “He left on a sales call, haven’t seen him come back yet.”

“Well then I guess it’s back to the contracts. You’ll have to empty the cassettes another time.” He stared at the ATM as he spoke. “I wouldn’t leave it for too long, no telling how much cash is in them. With the way it was left at the store I wouldn’t doubt those idiots left it full.” He ran his hand over his messy cropped hair.

Rachel nodded and started to close the bottom door when she noticed a small wire trapped in the top left corner. She furrowed her brow and looked closer. Then she backed up and scrunched up her nose.

“Stinks huh?” He let out a chuckle. “That’s nothing you should see the state of some of the ones I’ve recovered from bars. You don’t want to know what causes the smells on those ones. Let me put it this way, I don’t touch them without gloves, people will mistake anything for a bathroom when they have been drinking.”

Rachel looked at Blaze and shook her head in disgust. "Didn't need to know that." She replied. "Well this definitely stinks, but that isn't what I was wondering about. I was just trying to figure out what this wire trapped here was for, it doesn't seem to be in the right place."

Blaze furrowed his brow. "What wire, where?" He asked as he moved closer to see what she was looking at. She moved out of the way so Blaze could take a look at where she was pointing. He took one look and immediately frowned. "That's not supposed to be there." He opened up the top again and took a closer look this time. "It's coming through the back hinge and is running into the vault." Blaze grabbed a drill off the shelf, then pulled a power cable down from the hook above and plugged it in.

"Wait, what are you doing?" She said, her voice sounding panicked.

"Opening it. What does it look like?" Blaze said as he knelt in front of the vault.

"Yes, I can see that. The question is why? Once Josh gets back he can pull the vault codes from the system."

"Who knows when that will be and this could mean some serious trouble for us. Extra wires in an ATM are never a good thing. I don't want to jump to any conclusions but we better not be taking any chances and this machine will probably be scrapped anyway, no one is going to want this old monstrosity in their store, we'll never resell it." She stood with her mouth slightly open in shock, he gave her a wink. "Besides, I thought you liked doing things the hard way?"

Rachel crossed her arms and pouted. She had no come back. Blaze signaled her to step back, put on a pair of goggles he'd grabbed off the shelf nearby and proceeded to drill through the vault lock, sparks flying everywhere. Metal drilling metal was never pretty, Rachel had stood way back to be safe. When he was done he set the drill aside and wiped the sweat off his brow as he pulled off his goggles. He smiled at his handy work and moved back from the vault. He looked up at Rachel and nodded over his shoulder.

"You want the honors?" He asked his breathing slightly labored from his efforts. She shook her head. He grabbed a screw driver, popped off the lock and immediately froze. A shiver ran through her body in response to his sudden tension and she inhaled sharply.

Blaze carefully opened the vault door the rest of the way and they both froze. They didn't find expected cash cassettes, nor did they find the usual stash of spare parts and rolls of receipt paper. Instead, they were met with a stench so overwhelming that she immediately choked back the breath she had just inhaled. Rachel stood speechless at the site, her face pale. Blaze looked closely at Rachel, then back at the twisted shape in front of him. He slowly straightened up and stood beside her. "Not exactly what I meant when I said these carry a lot of dead weight." He said flatly, earning him a disgusted smack on the arm from her but she let out a nervous laugh anyway.

He tilted his head in disbelief unsure if what he was seeing was really possible. One more glance at Rachel's confused expression confirmed it for him. He had joked about it before, but he had no idea it was even imaginable until he saw it in front of him. There, defying their beliefs and contorted into almost every inch of the vault chamber; was a very dead body.

Blaze took a step forward and bent down to examine it closer. The body had been bent and twisted into an almost cartoon like shape to ensure it had fit inside the emptied chamber. Even so, the man couldn't have been much over 5 foot 6, and lucky if he weighed 165 to fit in a space like that. If stature wasn't enough, his face had been twisted sideways to fit his head inside, thus making his ID unmistakable.

Blaze shook his head and let out a heavy sigh. "I guess we know what happened to Miguel."

CHAPTER 11

The police questioned everyone in the company individually. Rachel was worn out and barely able to focus by the time the officer said he had enough and she could go. She scanned the room for Blaze. He was pacing at the back of the warehouse. She headed in his direction.

A couple of officers that she had noticed had arrived much later than the first ones were speaking with him in hushed tones. She decided that he obviously knew them when she overheard him call them by their first names. He was clearly upset with one of them and the other seemed to be acting as a buffer between them. She could barely make out what they were saying, so she inched closer.

"I'm not surprised to see you mixed up in this." The portlier of the two officers said. Even in the darkened corner of the warehouse, she could see the sweat glisten off his forehead. He had a look of disgust on his face.

Blaze's tense body was arched menacingly towards the officer who had just spoken. "Of course not Pete, you never could see anything other than what you wanted to see." Blaze answered back, his voice hard.

"That's because I saw the truth about you before it got your partner killed." Pete replied, contempt lacing his words. He was considerably shorter than Blaze, and almost a caricature opposite of him. The position of his hand resting on his holster showed where his courage came from. Blaze took a threatening step towards him, but the other officer stepped in between.

"Blaze," he cautioned, placing his hand on Blaze's chest to stop him. "You don't need that kind of trouble." His tone was friendlier than what Pete had used.

"Then maybe you should keep your pet on a better leash Joe." Blaze replied angrily to the officer in front of him, never moving his gaze off Pete.

Joe turned slightly to look at Pete. "You don't know what you're talking about." He scolded the other officer before turning back towards Blaze. "Come on, let's all calm down and get back to what happened here tonight."

Blaze shifted his focus to Joe. "Maybe if you took your head out of your partner's ass long enough, you'd see the bigger picture."

Joe stiffened. "That was uncalled for."

Blaze took a deep breath and took a step back. "You're right Joe, I'm sorry. It's been a day." The Pete grunted, but they both ignored him. Joe put his arm around Blaze and led him away.

"No problem, not everyone is against..." she had heard Joe start to say before they're voices where muffled by their new far away position.

"How are you holding up?" Josh asked, startling her. She hadn't noticed that he had come over to stand beside her. She turned and slowly focused on his face. She smiled weakly. "That good huh." He said smiling softly down at her. He looked around at the thinning scene. "I think they are pretty much done with us here for the night. Most of the employees have gone home. I could take you home if you like." Rachel shook her head faintly.

He hesitated but didn't give up. "Is there someone I can call for you?" She smiled again, more warmly this time.

"Thank you, but I'll be alright. You're very thoughtful. I appreciate it, but I think some quiet and a nice hot bath would be best right about now."

Josh nodded. "I understand. Listen," he said, facing her and placing his hands on her shoulders. "I want you to know, if you need anything, anything at all, call me. You have my cell; any time of day or night. I'll be there. I mean it." She nodded and he dropped his hands to his sides. "Take a couple days off too, whatever you need." She continued to nod and they both looked around the room silently again.

He put his arm protectively around her shoulder. She looked over at his hand, then back to his face. "This is some crazy shit." He said shaking his head. "I can't imagine what it must have been like for you to find him like that. I'm having trouble dealing with it myself and I only came after the police had sealed everything off. I just can't imagine." He squeezed her shoulder gently. "Anything you need." He echoed again.

Rachel smiled. Josh gave her another squeeze and then slid his arm off her shoulder. Rachel instinctively glanced towards the dark corner of the warehouse where the police had it blocked off. They had taken the body away a while ago, but they had to wait to take the ATM until they had a truck to move it. She could see its hulking shadow. She shivered.

She turned back to where Blaze had just been. She didn't see him. Her face grew paler. The cops he had been talking with were gone too. The few remaining staff and police were almost all cleared out too. She felt her shoulders droop further. "If you don't mind, I'd like to go home now."

“Of course. Do you want me to walk you out?” She started to shake her head, but then she stopped.

“If you wouldn’t mind.” She said barely audible.

Josh gave her another comforting smile. “Of course not. Let’s get your things.” He directed. She took another glance back at the empty warehouse and shivered again. “That ATM will be gone before you come back here.” He said assuming the source of her distress. His mention of it instinctively led her eyes towards the looming ATMs shadow in the far corner. She nodded. He placed a guiding hand on her back and led her out. Taking comfort in not having to think for herself right now, she let him.

They gathered her things from her office and he walked her to her car. Rachel thanked him and motioned that is was ok for him to go. He didn’t move. “I’m okay, really.” She assured him. “I just need some sleep.” He hesitated a moment longer, then backed away a few steps, before finally turning and heading back to the building to close up.

She watched him go inside and then tossed her stuff in the open window. She placed her hand on the car door and stopped, staring blankly. She stood like that for a minute before dejectedly letting her hand drop to her side. She didn’t seem to have the energy to fight with it. She jumped when a deep voice came from the darkness just a few feet away.

“Car trouble?”

Rachel stared up at Blaze in silence before breaking into nervous laughter. Then she started shaking. Blaze deftly closed the gap between them, slipped his jacket over her shoulders and let her fall into his arms. They stood like that until her weird mix of laughter and sobs subsided. She lifted her head and stepped back, she had a crooked smile on her face as she turned to look at her car. “My door won’t open. I didn’t feel like fighting with it.” She shrugged as if that explained everything.

Blaze grinned. “I don’t blame you. We’ve opened enough difficult doors tonight. Come on.” He said walking around her, reaching into her car and bringing out her purse. “We’ll take mine. I’ll get your's home later.” Rachel didn’t protest, nor ask about how he planned on doing any of that. She was still shaking as she followed silently beside him as he guided them to his car. “Think you can point me to your place?” She nodded obediently. He smiled. “Good, I’m betting there’s a nice hot bath there, with your name on it.” She barely nodded and stepped up into the front passenger front seat of his truck as he held the door open for her. Then proceeded to drive her home as she pointed the way.

*****

“It’s me.”

“What’s going on? You’re calling very late.”

“I know. We’ve had some trouble at the company this afternoon. A dead technician”

“And you’re just calling now?”

“It took this long to get away from the police. I had to clear everyone out and make sure that nobody knew anything else was going on.”

“The police? A dead body? Explain.”

“One of Stafford’s technicians showed up dead in an ATM. Don’t worry, it wasn’t one of yours.”

There was a moment of silence on the other end as the caller waited for more details, when he didn't get them he continued. "And the police? How did they get involved?"

"There was an office full of people here when it happened. There were witnesses when it was found; the police had to be called."

"This is very bad for our business."

"I know. I'll deal with it, I swear."

"You better. We don't need any more police or press nosing about our business. We've invested a lot of time and money in you. It would be tragic to have to close up shop. You know what that would mean."

"I know that won't have to happen. I'll deal with it. It will be business as usual in no time."

"It better faster than no time."

"We are a little light on techs right now."

"I don't care about staffing problems."

"No, it was one of 'Our' techs, we need another on our side. I'm going to have trouble finding another one right away."

"Well then, I guess you'll be spending a lot more time in the field yourself."

"It'll be noticed."

"I don't care. We don't pay you for excuses. You've gotten sloppy. I don't care how it's done, just get it done." There was silence on the other end then the voice came back more menacingly. "You only have your nice little business because of our financing, remember that. I'd hate to see that change. Am I making myself clear?"

"Yes, perfectly."

"Good."

*****

Rachel sunk into her steaming hot bath. She rested her head back against the wall and closed her eyes. Images flashed through her mind. She sunk even further into the tub, trying to drown them out. After Blaze had dropped her off she had double and triple checked her locks, not so much out of fear, but more out of something to keep her from thinking about the body they had found. Lying in the tub was supposed to relax her, but relaxing only gave her more time to think about it. The pounding in her heart as she remembered how his arm fell out at them. The sudden lurch in her stomach at the memory of the contorted look of what was once Miguel, crammed inside the empty chamber.

Rachel sunk all the way under the water; she lay there motionlessly until she had to come up for breath. Then she stepped out, wrapped a big towel around herself and stood in front of the mirror, staring. It was full of steam. She wiped it away with her hand and stared at her water contorted reflection. She jumped when she heard sudden pounding at her door. She stopped and turned her head to listen. There was more pounding. She reluctantly dropped the cozy towel to the ground and replaced it with her robe before heading down the hallway. She swung open the door to find Blaze standing there and stood back in surprise.

"You always open the door without knowing who it is?"

Rachel shrugged. "Never really thought about it."

"I had your car brought back for you. Figured you might need it."

"How?"

Blaze smiled. I have a few connections. Rachel raised an eyebrow. "Relax. I had it towed here."

"That's what I was afraid of." She teased.

"What? It's not like they could do any damage to it." They laughed and Rachel stepped aside, motioning for him to follow. "It's late. I don't want to disturb you." He replied. Rachel cocked her head and crossed her arms. Blaze chuckled and stepped inside. "Right. Too late."

Blaze scanned the apartment. He nodded his head questioningly. Rachel locked the door and walked over to him. She smiled.

"What did you expect pink and fluffy and full of puppy dogs?"

"No. I'm not sure what I expected, not pink and fluffy and not dark and metal, but."

"But what?

"But nothing. I just realized I wasn't sure what to expect." Blaze smiled and turned looked her over. Her hair was dripping wet and hung down in wet wavy strands. Her robe was sticking to her damp skin. Her lips were red and full from the heat of her bath. Her eyes were a bright vivid green or was it blue, he realized she had a strange mix of both. But despite her rosy cheeks, she still looked pale and tired. “You must be cold. Let’s grab you a blanket.”

The tone of his voice was so soothing, she found herself swaying against her tired body. He grabbed her by the shoulders as her knees began to weaken and he led her over to her couch. Once she was safely seated, he looked around for a blanket, finding none he frowned. “Where…” She cut him off by pointing her finger down the hall.

“In my bedroom.” He headed the direction she had pointed. “Last door at the end.” She called after him, but he was already moving swiftly through the apartment. Past the open kitchen entrance, down the hall, turning to look at the first door. It was the open bathroom door; steam was still coming out of it. He continued past the small narrow closet door and towards the only other room, end of the hallway. He opened it and went inside, returning with the big comforter from her bed.

He wrapped it around her and sat next to her on the couch. “You’re tired.” He stated softly and she nodded, sinking back in the couch, leaning against him. She instinctively snuggled into the warmth that radiated from him. He moved his arm and settled back in the couch so she could get comfortable against him. She rested her head against his chest and curled up as he wrapped the blanket tighter around her. She mumbled something then drifted off to sleep. Blaze looked down at her, gently moved a piece of her wet hair off her cheek and watched as she settled deeper into sleep.

When her breathing changed to a slow steady rate he lifted her head ever so slightly and slipped off the couch. Then he placed her head gently back down. He stared at her a moment longer, her face was totally relaxed, soft, vulnerable. He ran his hands through his hair, then shook his head and then he proceeded to search her apartment. Slowly, methodically and thoroughly, ensuring he put everything back as he finished looking.

He read through all her book titles, looked through her fridge, he even searched through her closet and dresser, though he resisted urge to linger at her underwear drawer; He was thorough but he wasn't a pervert. He walked back toward the living room, stopped at her computer. He jiggled the mouse, the monitor stayed black. He looked back at Rachel, the computer desk was directly opposite her; she was still asleep.

He stooped down and paused, his finger hovered near the power button as studied her computer. There were large speakers on either side of the desk and their power light was green. He looked back again; she stirred but stayed asleep. He sighed and stepped back from the computer. He checked on her one more time, resisting the urge to clear away another strand of hair, then he stood up, frowning as he headed out of her apartment. He deftly locked the door behind him to took off into the night.

CHAPTER 12

Rachel awoke to daylight filtering around her. She looked around, momentarily confused, then looked down at her blanket and smiled. She sat up and looked around. "Hello?" She listened for a response. Silence. She stood up and looked around the apartment. She was alone. She frowned and let out a sigh. Then she shrugged and trudged into the kitchen to make some coffee.

She pulled the grounds out of the freezer, grabbed herself a big mug, pulled out the sugar and then searched the refrigerator for the cream. She couldn't find any, so she immediately abandoned her efforts, grabbed her keys and purse and headed out the door. She purposely avoided the mirror as she passed by. She needed coffee and didn't want any reason to delay that.

Her cell started ringing as soon as she reached her car, so she tossed her purse through the open window and dove part way in to search through her purse to retrieve it. "Hello?" She asked, struggling to hold the phone to her ear as she teetered half way over her car door.

"Rachel? It's Josh."

"Oh hi Josh." She replied disappointment clinging to her, her voice sounded strained as she struggled out of the window. "What's up?"

"Well I feel terrible asking this. I know I said you could take as much time as you needed, but I need your help. The office is crazy and the police need help digging up records of Miguel. Not to mention keeping the business going. We, I could really use your help. I know it's asking a lot, but..."

"Josh, don't worry about it." Rachel interrupted. "It's okay; I need to keep busy anyway. I'll be in as soon as I can get ready."

"Thanks Rachel, you're the best."

Rachel looked at her car, rolled her eyes and sighed. Coffee would have to wait. She headed back to her apartment to grab a shower and get ready for work. On her way up she called Amy and asked if she'd change their lunch today to a quick morning coffee break instead so she could at least get her caffeine fix before facing the office.

*****

"Are you kidding me, a dead body? You can't go back there!" Amy's face was animated as she spoke.

"Are you actually asking me to quit? I've never quit a job in my life."

"That's because you don't have to, you're a temp! How much more urging do you need than murder?"

"Alleged murder." Rachel corrected.

"Right. He killed himself and then crammed his own body inside that ATM."

Rachel shrugged in response and they both broke out into laughter. After they quieted down she sighed and looked at Amy, who was now sporting a light brown hair color with bright red tipped ends. She smiled softly. "You really think I should quit?" She said as she traced her finger over the rough counter. " It's the longest I've stayed at a job in years. I've learned so much and there's so much to do. How can I just leave?"

Amy looked at her friend with a stunned look on her face. "Rachel, someone was just murdered, it's not safe. How can you not leave?"

"It's not dangerous." Amy rolled her eyes and Rachel continued. "Yes, someone was murdered and that's terrible, but it's not like it happens every day. Hell it's more dangerous walking out to the parking garage down the street from my apartment than that place. Besides, they need my help, it's an important job." Amy crossed her arms and gave her a skeptical look. "Okay fine, it's not the job, I just want to find out what happened."

Amy unfolded her arms and sat up in her seat. "I knew it. You just can't stay away from trouble can you? Face it, you're an addict, but this isn't one of your mystery books you know. You're not invincible, stubborn maybe, hot-headed definitely, but not invincible."

"I'm not looking for trouble." Amy raised an eyebrow. "I'm not, but come on, who kills a guy and stuffs him in an ATM? There has to be a reason for it."

"Yeah, there's some crazy guy running around, that's the reason and that's what cops are for, to find the guy, not you." Amy's arms were now as animated as her face and her voice. It was awarding her some odd looks from other patrons, but her voice was low enough not to warrant complaints.

Rachel let out a chuckle. "I'm not going to go around investigating a murder, I wouldn't even know how to. I just want to stick around a bit, see what the cops find out. I want to know it's solved, so that when I leave it's because I want to quit, not because I chickened out."

Amy groaned. "Chickened out? It's not a competition. Nobody's daring you that you can't stay. I'm just worried about you."

"Well don't, I push papers around all day, how dangerous could that be?" Rachel's voice was calm. She quietly watched Amy and sipped her coffee between responses. Her mind was set, at this point she was just letting Amy vent.

Amy bowed her head and sighed. "Okay. I get it. You're staying. At least let me know what the police find out." Rachel nodded. "And any more dead bodies in any more ATMs and you're gone!" They both laughed and finished their coffees and shared key lime pie. Sugar and Coffee, what could be better to start your day of right.

CHAPTER 13

Rachael arrived to find that Josh had severely understated the chaos. The latest receptionist had called in permanently sick, even the temp agency had not seen her. A couple of the technicians hadn't bothered to show up, including the newest one that Josh had taken out for training yesterday. The ones that were left were double booked and late getting out on the road.

Rachel found Josh rushing to help the techs load up their trucks and print off their routes. The phones were ringing off the hook and no one was moving slow enough to answer them. The bull pen was in turmoil and Rachel's auto pilot kicked in. She rushed in to take over printing off the final routes for the Technicians so that Josh could help them finish loading the trucks. Then she answered the phones and transferred any non-emergencies to the appropriate voice mail boxes.

Once the techs were on the road, she ran through with Josh what she should respond if anyone asked about the 'incident' and what information the police needed. Then Josh headed out in the field to help with the work load and Rachel went to work digging up contracts, service reports and contact data. Once she had everything, she called the detective to find out how he wanted the information delivered.

After she finished faxing the documentation and answering most of the same questions the police had asked her at the scene, she sat down to catch up on her regular paperwork. She grabbed the rather large stack of papers in her inbox and slowly worked her way through. Once her inbox was under control she moved on to the next pile. It was the stack of papers she had set aside before tagging along on with Blaze to pick up the ATM. She stared at them blankly and sighed. She took a deep breath and started leafing through them until one caught her eye. She stopped and pulled it out.

It had various notes hand scribbled in her writing. It was the report she had shown Josh a few days earlier. She started going through it again with renewed interest when the phone rang and made her jump.

"Stafford Financial, can I help you?"

"Yeah, um, Josh. Put 'im on, I need to speak to 'im."

"You would like to speak with Josh Tanner?"

"dat's whad I said righ'."

"I'm sorry he's out of the office right now. Can I help you?"

"Uh no don tink s, man."

Rachel cringed. "I'm not a man."

"Ok whadev'r. Look I need to speak to 'im righ' now. Where can I find 'im?"

"He's on a service call right now. I can take a message and get him to call you. Is this Pat..."

"No message man... Lady, whadev'r." He said cutting her off.

With that the caller hung up the phone, leaving Rachel to pull the phone away from her ear when the loud click startled her.

She furrowed her brow and stared at the warm receiver in her hand. Then she jumped again when another voice startled her from her doorway.

“It’s called a phone I believe.” Blaze teased as he entered her office and sat down. She gave him an annoyed look and hung up the phone. He placed a steaming hot mug down on her desk in front of her and then took a sip from the mug he held in his hand. “Figured you could use one of those by now.” He said, stretching out his legs and making himself comfortable.

“How did you…?” She stopped before finishing her sentence and inhaled the deep rich aroma.

“Called Josh this morning to check on things, he told me you were here.”

Rachel nodded and reached for the mug. “Thanks.” She sipped the sweet creamy treat and smiled. “Perfect.” She cocked an eyebrow and sat back studying him.

“Suspicious aren’t you?” He grinned. “I watched you make it the other day, half sugar, half cream and a drop of coffee. I did put at least put some coffee in this one though.”

“Funny.” She said with a stoic tone. She took another satisfied sip. “So what are you...”

He interrupted. “I wanted to check in on things. Make sure it hadn’t become a press circus here, bad for business. Besides, I figured you’d be a little short staffed around here right about now. Just didn’t realize how short. You are pretty much the only person left working in the office.”

“Besides Coralene you mean.”

“Right, who could forget about Coralene.” He nodded and looked towards her phone. “So what was that about?” Rachel gave him a quizzical look. “When I came in here, you were staring at the phone.”

Rachel shook her head. “Nothing really, just a very odd phone call, someone looking for Josh; he rambled a lot, and then hung up. It sounded like it could have been one of the new techs…” She started and then sighed. “Just wasn’t expecting it this morning.”

“I’m surprised you’re not used to it. It’s an ATM company, brings out all sorts of crazies.” Rachel nodded and took another sip, her attention drifting back to the paper on her desk. “Am I keeping you from something?” He asked across his coffee mug.

She looked up and smiled. “I’m sorry, I was just going through my old papers and I came across a problem that had stumped me and I guess it’s still bothering me.”

“What kind of problem?”

Rachel sat up in her chair, her eyes brightened. “Report reconciliation errors. See I thought I had it figured out with a formula I came up with, but on certain days it wasn’t working. I put it aside to work on later and I guess I forgot about it until now.”

“And now it’s bugging you again.”

“Basically, yeah.” She laughed and nodded.

Blaze raised his eyebrows, shook his head and stood. “Well that’s sounds like fun, but I came to offer my technical services so I’m going to see what Josh needs done.”

"Chicken."

"Feel free to call me when you get tired of your reports and want some help with a real problem. I'd be glad to help then."

Rachel pouted and crossed her arms. Blaze smiled and headed out to help in the field, leaving her to pore over her reports. She settled in with her steaming coffee and decided to re-create her report from scratch. It took her about an hour, but when she was almost done she suddenly brightened with a realization. She grabbed the receiver and started dialing Josh's number, but before she finished she hung it up. She had no proof.

She decided she had better find some before she went to him, especially after the mistake he found going through her findings with him last time. She knew he wouldn't be able to do anything without a proof anyway. Right now all she had was an idea. She picked the receiver up again, but this time she dialed a different number.

*****

"I thought I told you to call me when you wanted help with a real problem." Blaze grumbled.

Rachel sprang up in her chair. "This is a real problem," she defended.

Blaze crossed his arms, cocked his head and stared at her across her desk. She sighed in frustration. "It is. I just need you to show me how to prove it."

Now it was Blaze's turn to let out a deep sigh. "Why do I feel like I've just been duped?" She shrugged her shoulders and tried not to smile. "Alright, show me the problem."

She broke out into a smile and walked him through her theory, using the new report as an example. "I think Stafford is being shorted funds on certain ATMs. I don't know whether it's a bug in the software or the hardware, or something else but I know that they have too high an error rate to be coincidence. The problem is I just don't know how to eliminate the options and find the proof. That's where you come in."

"Why not ask Josh?"

"Because he already thinks I'm crazy." Blaze raised his eyebrow and Rachel threw him an annoyed look but ignored his implication. "Look. You know these systems better than I do. I'll do the leg work; I just need you to point me in the right direction."

Blaze let out a heavy sigh. He picked up Rachel's report and ran through her calculations with her. "You need to check the source." He continued after she threw him a puzzled look. "The ATMs. You need to get their journals and compare them to the bank reports.

"How do I get the journals?"

Blaze smiled. "You already have them."

"What? How? I don't... Where?"

Blaze laughed at her excited ranting. "The journals are pulled every time the ATMs are filled with cash. They are sent back here and stored. They have to be stored for at least 180 days, usually more just to be safe, in case there are any disputes by cardholder's on cash withdrawals." He stopped and stared at her, his eyes narrowed as he studied her. "How can you not know this and be sitting here with a pile of reports from every ATM processor we use?"

Rachel laughed, but stopped when he didn't join her. "You can't be serious. I don't deal with the bank reconciliations or the disputes, Coralene and her girls do that and she doesn't exactly..." She didn't have to finish the thought before Blaze nodded. "But, I do review the reports for sales."

"So how did you go from tracking sales to looking for missing funds?"

Rachel shrugged and avoided his stare. "I don't like to leave a problem alone until I solve it."

He stared at her a moment longer. Then he broke into a smile. "You don't like to or you can't leave it?" He didn't wait for an answer, but she dropped her eyes. "I bet as a child you were always the ring leader when trouble was to be found."

A slow grin crossed her face. "So if I find the journals that match these I should have my proof?" Blaze inhaled deeply and nodded. "Great, how hard can that be?" She declared proudly.

Blaze groaned and swept his hand in the direction of the door. "Have fun. I'd stay and help you with this goose chase, but Josh asked me to help out on some service calls and I need to get back to them."

Rachel rolled her eyes and headed to the file room behind accounting to search for answers. She found the shelves stacked full of box upon box of journal tape rolls, marked by date pulled. There were hundreds and they clearly hadn't been touched since they had been first filed. Still, she was determined to go through every roll if she had to until she found the answers. She might not be able to help in the field or solve a murder, but she could do this.

She grabbed the first box with a date matching one of her reports and took it back to her office. This way she could sip her coffee and methodically review each one until she found something that explained the shortages. She slipped off her shoes and got comfortable. This was going to take a while.

CHAPTER 14

Josh grabbed his cell by the third ring. "Yeah."

"'ey man, you're 'ard ta reach."

"Patrick?" He turned and lowered his voice as he adjusted the phone to his other ear.

"Ya man. Bin tryin' ta reach ya all day. Called da offis and everytin. I needs ta talk wit you."

"Talk with me. You better do more than talking. Where the hell have you been?" He moved so he was out of ear shot of anyone listening.

"Whoa man. Ya need ta be chillin' I dun you lotsa favus and be callin' needin ya 'elp."

"Favors? Are you kidding? Hiring you was the favor, you've been paid good money and what do you do, you take off when we need you most. Do you even know how short you've left us? You're putting us at risk and you want me to chill? Explain yourself 'Man' and it better be good if you 'tink' you'll be getting any more help from me."

"Don' ya be talkin at me like dat man. I know whad ya be needin' and wat ya be doin' and if ya be wantin my 'elp then you need ta be 'elpin me outta here."

"Out of where?"

"Outta da Jail man."

"Where? What the hell are you doing in jail Patrick?"

"Dey tryin' ta say I bin smokin' da weed. I don' smoke dat stuff i' verie bad fa' ya."

Josh sighed heavily. He ran his fingers through his hair and adjusted the phone to his other ear. "I told you when I hired you I didn't want any drug addicts. I told you to stay clean Patrick."

"I ain' no addic, it jus' a litta weed man."

"I don't have time for this. I've got clients backed up and I'm doing service calls that you should have been doing. What do you think I can do to help you?"

"I jus' be needin' sum money, for da bail. A leedle advans. I do ya big fava, ya do me leedle fava."

Josh took the phone from his ear and glared at it, he waved off the angry store owner who was not pleased with the speed of his service. He took another deep breath and put the warm phone back to his ear. "I don't need any of your kind of favors Patrick, but I will give you your advance. How much do you need and where do you need me to bring it?"

*****

Blaze finished off the two service calls that he'd been given quickly. He had in fact resolved the first call by simply changing the man's receipt tape. The second one required a lot more work, but he didn't have time to play around with it. Since the store owner filled his own cash he gave him one of his own ATMs that he was scheduled to install later on. To avoid having to program new keys, he switched out the memory card with the original ATM so it had all the programming set. That turned a long service into a quicker pit stop.

The third call that was on his list was at a 24 hour store. He called the owner and planned to swing by later that night after the store's late rush. Then he phoned the bar owner who was expecting the ATM he had just given away and arranged to install his tomorrow. This left him with only a cash drop at his busiest site.

He looked at his watch and exhaled sharply. He didn't like to do cash runs this late in the day, but he knew it would be running out soon and couldn't afford to lose any weekend business. He packed up his truck, double checked the count in his briefcase, pulled his revolver from under the front seat and drove off.

*****

Rachel was well through her tenth box and getting more frustrated by the minute; Scrolling through roll after roll, slower and slower, stopping several times to rub her eyes. She returned the one she just finished and hesitated before grabbing another. Instead she reached for her coffee cup but frowned when she found it empty. Sighing, she decided to go on without coffee. She was half way through it when she stopped. She blinked her eyes dry from reading and looked again to make sure she was seeing what she thought she saw. Slowly a grin crossed her face and she let out a squeal.

"Got you." She shouted beaming as she grabbed the phone and dialed. He picked up on the third ring. "Josh, it's Rachel. You'll never believe what I found."

"Rachel, I'm glad you called. I was just about to call you. How are things going?"

"Well I think the phones have finally calmed down and with fewer people in the office I've actually managed to catch up on a lot of paper work. We booked out all the service calls."

"Really? I thought we had at least two we couldn't schedule?"

"We did, but Blaze took those two, along with a third that came in after you guys were out."

"Blaze? You got Blaze to do our service calls?"

"He said you asked him to help out. You mean you didn't?" She furrowed her brow and cupped the phone tighter.

"I asked him? Oh right, yeah, I, damn. I forgot all about that." Josh laughed nervously. "Sorry, must have spaced out for a minute. It's been a long day. Well that's great work, sounds like you have things under control there. Listen, I don't have much time I'm just on my way to deal with a situation that came up, but I have a few minutes if there is something you need. You said you had found something?"

Rachel hesitated and shifted in her seat. "I, um. No, I was just going to go over some old reports with you, but it can wait." Something in Josh's harried voice and hesitation over Blaze, had hold her back from discussing what she found on the phone. She figured it might be best to wait until he was back in the office.

"Okay, great. I'll give you a call as soon as I'm done, we can go over it then."

"Sounds good." She hung up the phone and looked down at her

desk. She stretched her shoulders and yawned, then shook her head and trekked to the kitchen with her mug. She found the coffee pot was as empty as her cup and she sighed. Grabbing the pot, she rinsed it to start preparing a new pot, but after her third yawn she opted to put it down and head back to her office instead. She didn't have the energy to fuss with it

She stared at her computer and the stack of papers spread out on her desk, then looked at her phone. "Screw it." She said aloud as she forwarded her phone to voice mail, grabbed her reports and the journal tape with her coveted proof and tucked them into her purse. She yawned again. She needed sleep, but she had to go through her findings with Josh, so she'd have to settle for a coffee on her way home before she could slip into her nice warm bed. She shook off the next yawn and headed out. She hadn't slept well and now it was hitting her like a ton bricks; Funny how finding dead body can keep a person up at night.

CHAPTER 15

Rachel dragged her feet up the last few stairs to her second floor apartment. She needed coffee badly but the line was too long at her favorite coffee shop so by the tme she got home she was beyond non-functioning. She grabbed her keys and tried to unlock her door, but it was already unlocked. She swung the door open and jumped back. Blaze was standing in her living room at her computer. Her face reddened and her breathing became labored. Blaze turned and looked up at her as if he was just waiting to welcome her home. Her mouth fell open. She didn't move. There was a cut on his lower lip, blood had dried on his chin and his shirt was torn. He set her notepad down on the desk where he had found it.

"What the hell are you doing in my apartment? How did you get...? What happened...?" She took a deep breath before continuing. "Are you okay?" She finally asked as she moved into her apartment.

Blaze smiled, wincing slightly. He crossed his arms, muscles bulged through the holes in his sleeves. "Which question should I answer first?"

She looked around her apartment. Nothing was out of place, except her notepad. Blaze made no attempt to move away from her desk. Her face was still flushed, but her breathing had settled. She stared at him, her scowl deepening as his grin increased. She balled her hands into fists and chewed on her bottom lip. Blaze gave her an amused chuckle as he started to thumb through her notepad again. She rubbed her hands across her face and sighed in exasperation. She was too tired to argue with him. She dropped her shoulders and softened her eyes, then walked closer, closing the door behind her. "What happened?" She asked again, staring at his face.

He touched his lip, hiding his slight flinch. "Drug addict." Rachel's eyes widened. He turned, casually walked into her kitchen and started making coffee. She followed quietly behind him knowing she must look a state. "One of my locations is unfortunately beside a popular hangout for junkies. One of them must have gotten brave off a recent hit and decided he would make a play for the cash I was about to re-load." Rachel took the coffee grounds out of the freezer when Blaze's search through her cupboards turned up nothing. He cocked an eyebrow but continued, pointing at his lip. "Sucker punch."

"Ouch." She said with a wince.

He shrugged it off. "Shouldn't have done that cash fill so late in the day. I know better" He finished loading the coffee maker and turned it on. Rachel pulled out two mugs, then trotted off to the bathroom and grabbed a wash cloth. She returned and found him stretched out on her couch. She sat on the edge next to him and started dabbing his chin and lip clean, with much grumbling from Blaze. Something about not being a child, though his pout didn't make a good defense.

"Hold still." She scolded. "Why were you loading it so late?" He looked away from her and shrugged. Rachel stopped dabbing and studied him. "You were doing our service calls first." He nodded and she put down her cloth. Then she looked at his shirt, it was torn in several places, but he appeared to have no scratches. She stuck her finger through a tear on his shirt to check further. Finding no obvious injury, No scratches, no visible bruises, at least not yet. She frowned, but just when she was about to speak her assessment out loud, he interrupted.

"Smells like the coffee is done." He stated as he stood up and headed to the kitchen to fill their mugs.

Rachel jumped in front of him to cut off his path. The smell of her beloved coffee seemed to have been enough to kick start her brain to the situation again. "What were you doing in my apartment?" She asked, arms folded across her chest.

He shrugged and walked around her. "Searching it."
Rachel's mouth fell open again. Her face reddened, who admits to that she thought to herself. She ran into the kitchen after him. "Searching it? Why?" He poured two coffees, pulled down a bad of sugar and continued to ignore her, so she grabbed his arm and tried futilely to turn around.

"What the hell do you think you are doing?" She demanded.

He turned to face her, picked up his coffee and took a sip. "I'm drinking my coffee." He grinned and she punched his arm. She pulled her hand away and shook it, wincing. Blaze hadn't even flinched. She let out a cry of frustration. He reached out and gently touched her shoulder. His voice calm and soothing, he could see the deep fatigue set in her and decided to acquiesce. "I needed to check you out, to know who's side you're on."

"Who's side I'm... what?" She repeated not able to fully follow him with her sleep deprived brain.

"Rachel." He said, staring her directly in the eyes to be sure she was listening. "Someone was just murdered. The police are pretty sure it was the technician with him. I agree. They had to be doing something to cause one to murder the other and dispose of the body so hastily. That means there is at least one criminal and where there is one, there are usually others. I needed to make sure you're not mixed up in things that'll get you killed."

Her face scrunched as she tried to process what he was saying. "Get me killed? What I'm mixed up in? What about you? You show up out of nowhere. Never seen you around the office in the months I've been there. Then we run into you coincidentally when we are out to dinner and suddenly you're coming in the office to hand in your paper work. Helping out in the field, claiming you've been asked to by Josh and now sneaking around in my apartment. What side are YOU on Blaze?" She stared him down, studying him intensely. He sipped his coffee and met her stare.

They stayed like that, silence building as each one sized the other up. After a few moments her tired eyes dropped away, she shook her head and filled her mug with triple cream and extra sugar. She gulped her coffee like it was a lifesaving tonic. Her face was still flushed but her shoulders had relaxed and her breathing had calmed. She started pacing from the living room to the kitchen, grasping her coffee with both hands; the milk had cooled it to a comfortable temperature. She stopped beside her desk; her focus was on her notepad. She didn't stir when Blaze came up behind her and spoke.

"You're a writer." His voice was still deep and soothing. She nodded in response. "So all of that is you're brainstorming?" She turned to face him; they were only a breath apart. His eyes were soft and the corner of his mouth was curved upwards. Her face flushed again, later she'd decide to blame the coffee for that. Her breathing became shallow and she lowered her eyes. She took a step back and inhaled deeply. She nodded faintly. He took a step towards her and lifted her chin with his finger. "It's good." She smiled and her eyes sparkled. He unconsciously took a step backwards, then quickly went to sit on the couch. "Not that I read stuff like that." He added as he stretched out.

"Yes, mystery novels are a different style of writing than the blurbs under Penthouse cartoons." Her smile was playful as she responded.

Blaze let out a chuckle and winced slightly; he quickly adjusted his position in response. She watched him suspiciously as his movements seemed slow and forced. He smiled casually and gave her a small shrug. "So he might have gotten a second sucker punch in."

She raised her eyebrow and crossed her arms. "And the shirt? Do you want to explain how you got those rips, yet have no scratches showing?" She moved and perched on the edge of the couch in front of him.

"Not particularly."

Rachel nodded and reached for the top button of his shirt. Blaze looked down at her hand with surprise. She immediately withdrew it and darted her eyes away. "You should take that off and let me check you over."

He raised an eyebrow. She waved him off and tugged at his shirt lightly. He sighed, grabbed at the back of his and pulled it off over his head in one move. She inhaled sharply, her eyes seemed to widen and turn a deeper shade as the blue took over dominance from the green. His muscles were well ripped; his skin stretched tightly over them as they bulged with each of his movements. He tossed his shirt on the floor. She scolded him with her glare, but instead of comment she proceeded to examine him carefully, moving closer to get a better look.

She couldn't see any visible damage, a few reddened marks that might end up bruises later, but nothing of concern. She shrugged and started to turn away, but then stopped. She leaned in closer and ran her fingers down the side of his chest to a spot slightly darker than the rest of his tanned skin. She pressed down lightly, she felt him pull back. She pressed again, harder this time. He grasped her hand, gently pushing it away. "Okay, you found it, a little bruise. I'll survive, but not if you keep poking me like that."

Rachel laughed softly, but before she could respond her cell phone rang. She rushed to her purse to grab it, just about falling over the coffee table in the process, causing Blaze to let out a chuckle. "Hello?" She panted into it once she had managed to reach it in time.

"Rachel? Sorry, did I catch you at a bad time? Is it too late to call? It took me longer than I thought to clear things up?"

Rachel hesitated as she looked over at Blaze. "Josh, um. No it's not too late to be calling. I was just... relaxing." Blaze tilted his head and stared at her. She averted her eyes, avoiding his stare. "I found something in the ATM Journals this afternoon." Blaze stood up, picked up his shirt that lay near where she was standing and slipped it back on. She shifted her weight, transferred her phone to her other ear and turned her back to him. "I wanted to go over it with you. It explains the differences in the reports I showed you the other day, but I, uh, left it at the office." She wasn't sure the only reason she lied was because of Blaze's presence. "Why don't we go over it in the morning?"

"You want another drink sweetie?" Blaze called out louder than he needed to as he headed to the kitchen. Rachel froze her mouth agape and shot him a glare over she shoulder.

"Is tha..." Josh stopped and continued in a curt voice. "I'm sorry I have caught you at a bad time. I'll see you in the morning." He hung up without another word. Rachel stared at her phone for a moment, stunned. Her face flushed. She debated calling him back as if she had to explain. After a moment she decided against it and put her phone down.

"Was that necessary?" She said as she stormed towards him.

"What?" He shrugged and casually headed to coffee pot. "Do you not want another drink? You don't have to get so riled up on my behalf sweetie. I don't mind fetchin' you a coffee when I get one myself."

She slugged him on the shoulder, despite the solid mass she encountered, she flinched and reminded herself she'd have to stop doing that. "Who say's you're staying for another cup?"

"Well if you want me to look at that report that you brought home, I'll need another coffee." She glared at him, her mouth in a full pout. He broke into a full grin. "I recognized the scribbling on the papers you were holding when you walked in. I take it you found something?"

"I don't think that's any of your concern. Josh and I will take care of it in the morning." She finished and took the mug from his hand before he could fill it. "Since you're not staying here till morning, I don't think you'll need this. Now if you don't mind, I'd like to get some sleep." She added as she set the mug down and crossed her arms for emphasis.

"Who says I'm not staying until morning?" He replied as he took the other mug, filled it and walked out to the living room. "This couch of yours is pretty comfortable." He added as he plopped himself down on it. "So where is that report?" Rachel walked over to her front door, opened it and stood there glaring at him. He looked at his watch. It was 7:30.

"I haven't had a lot of sleep lately." She defended. He didn't move. She threw up her hands in exasperation. "Why am I explaining myself to you?" He shrugged, took a long sip and leaned back on the couch. Rachel continued to glare at him. He closed his eyes. She lowered her shoulders and sighed. "If I show you, then will you leave?" The corner of Blaze's mouth twitched upwards. She let out a loud cry of frustration, "Ugh" and shut the door once more. She couldn't slam it; it was too warped and old to have enough weight for any real satisfying sound but she made the movements as if she wanted to.

"So what's been keeping you up?" He asked as she grabbed her report and headed towards him.

"I don't see how any of that is your business." She snapped, tossing him the report.

He grinned and skimmed the report she had shown him earlier. She had scribbled new notes next to some of the numbers; Dates and times, with various sums next to each. "So what do all these mean?"

"Each of these dates and times are where there are matching journal entries," she said sitting down beside him so she could point out things at the report, "and these amounts here are the totals that the journals add up to. If you see here," she skimmed her finger down lower, "they are the exact amounts that the reports are out." Rachel turned the page. "Here is another example." Blaze nodded. He seemed like he was actually paying attention to her this time.

"I see that. So you are saying that Stafford never got paid for these transactions?" His face looked more serious than normal.

Rachel's smile broadened. She adjusted her position until she was sitting in a half cross legged style, directly facing him. "But that's just it, we got paid for each one of these totals."

Blaze looked at her sparkling eyes. "Okay, so clearly you found something to explain the fact that they got paid these totals, but are still short the same amounts."

She nodded excitedly. "You actually explained it to me, the other day when you were correcting the settings on the ATM. The settings were changed. The bill denominations were all set from 20 dollars to 10, but only for a few transactions, and then they were reset properly." Blazed grunted and continued to scan through all the pages she had marked on the reports. "Don't you see?" She rattled on more excited now that she was sharing her findings with someone who was actually taking her seriously. "The ATMs were dispensing twice what they should, we got paid exactly what the ATM thought it was dispensing, but because it was loaded with 20's and it thought it was dispensing 10's the people doing the transactions received twice, so we were shorted."

He continued to examine the reports, his expression unchanged. Rachel continued. "It was done on sporadic dates from various ATMs and the cool thing is that shortly after each one of these events, the ATMs were reported in for service calls, so the shortages were either written off as acceptable losses from a defective machine or went unnoticed all together because it was pulled from the balance sheet as out of service." She stared at Blaze impatiently waiting for him to response.

After a moment he finally looked up. "And you found proof of this in the journals?"

Rachel nodded, her grin lighting up her face. "I did, each one I've recorded so far is the same thing."

"Have you shown this to anyone else?" His voice was gruff.

Her smile faded. “No.”

“Where are the journals?” He said abruptly. Rachel hesitated and readjusted her legs. She shifted her gaze from the report, to the table where her purse sat, to the front door and back again. He continued his voice more soothing. “Do you have them with you?”

She shook her head. “They’re at the office.” She replied quietly. Blaze scowled.

“I should go.” He said, standing up hastily. “Guess you can get your sleep now.” He grumbled and left her apartment without another word.

“I guess so.” Rachel answered to the empty apartment. She locked the door behind him, hesitated a moment, then put the chain on. Something she had never done before. She looked around the living room, tucked her purse under her arm and got ready for bed; Locking all her windows along the way. She realized that she had never asked him how he got in so she wasn’t taking any chances.

She didn’t get much sleep again that night despite how tired she had been earlier; every noise disturbed her. After about an hour of tossing and turning she got out of bed and headed to her computer. She moved her note pad out of the way and jumped when the computer screen lit up. She looked down at the power button and shook her head to wake herself up. She usually turned it off when she was done so she wasn’t expecting it to come to life. She shrugged, signed in and found her story open to the end of the first chapter. She had been working on the fourth.

She snapped her head to look at the darkened doorway and then back towards the blackened kitchen. She shuddered. The room was silent, except for her labored breathing. She quickly headed back to her bedroom, turning every light on as she went, after stopping in the kitchen to grab a Butcher's knife which she proceeded to slip between the mattress and the box spring. She checked the handle twice to be sure she could grab it easily if she needed to. Then she fell back into a restless sleep. She hadn't noticed the chain was no longer on her door.

CHAPTER 16

“I’m telling you Josh, they were right here.” Rachel explained as she continued her searching.

“Maybe the cleaning staff put them away?” Josh offered.

Rachel frowned. “I suppose. Or.” She hesitated.

Josh looked at her expectantly. “Or what?” He insisted when she didn’t continue.

“What if someone took them?” She asked looking around one more time.

“What? Who would do something like that?” Rachel looked at Josh, then turned and paced behind her desk. She nervously bit her bottom lip. “Rachel?” He asked more insistently. She stopped and looked at him.

“Blaze.”

“Blaze? Why would Blaze want a bunch of journal tapes?”

Rachel let out a deep sigh. “I don’t know, but who else could have done it. He’s the only one who knew about them.”

“He knew?”

Rachel nodded. “He was here when I was first looking for them.”

Josh nodded his expression one of confusion as she spoke. "He insisted on finding out about them last night after he broke into my apartment." A look of shock crossed his face.

"He broke into your apartment? Are you sure?" Josh looked at her in disbelief.

"I caught him inside when I got home." She straightened her shoulders as if defending her position.

"And you're sure you had it locked?" She nodded, so he continued, anger laced his voice. "Why didn't you tell me?" He took an harried step towards her.

She took a reflexive step backwards in response. "I didn't have a chance. I came right over here this morning and found them gone. Nothing else is missing from what I can tell, so who else could it be?"

"But why? For what purpose? He didn't have the access to the ATMs, he couldn't have changed the amounts."

Rachel thought for a moment. "Maybe he was covering up for someone." She frowned and shook her head. She paced a bit, then her eye brightened and she turned to him. "Maybe he had a partner."

Josh still looked unconvinced. "But why? If he was in on it, why would he be so sloppy?"

Rachel sat down in her chair. "It's the only thing that makes sense. He's obviously a raging alcoholic, maybe he's a drug addict too. I mean the amounts were too small to warrant any major profits, but if you needed a little something to pay off your dealer, perhaps. Junkies are nothing but sloppy when they're in need of a fix." She almost said, believe me I know, but thought better of it. "Maybe he had other plans and losing his source made him panic."

Josh's eyes went cold. His expression hardened. He turned to leave. Rachel started to get up from her chair, he stopped her with a simple hand gesture. "No, stay here." He turned around to face her as she reseated herself. She watched him with curiosity. "Does anyone else know about this?" Rachel shook her head. Josh smiled. "Good, let's keep it that way, don't want to tip our hand before we know the full extent of the problem." She nodded, her face grim. "I'm sure it's not Blaze, but you're right we have a problem internally and I need to clean things up around here before it brings the whole business down."

Rachel frowned. Josh's school boy grin was back as he tried to reassure her. "Don't worry, I'll take it from here. We've caught it early, thanks to you, but this is my job to sort out. You've done enough. In the meantime, don't worry about Blaze; I'm sure it's nothing, but you never know, so to be safe, maybe it's best if you steer clear of him for right now." Rachel nodded silently as Josh quickly exited her office.

*****

Josh headed to the back. His face was hard and his jaw flexed from grinding his back teeth. The warehouse was empty. All the techs had been dispatched to the field. The ATM with Miguel's body had long been removed by the police, but Josh didn't even think about it as he rushed towards the back. He froze when he heard a noise. He listened, till her heard more crashing. Someone was rummaging through the tool shop. He stormed back to look.

"What the hell are you doing here?" Josh's voice was menacing as he spoke.

“'ey man. I jus' come ta go ta work man. Whad ya tink? Ain't nobody 'ere thou.” Patrick's hands shook a bit as he spoke.

“They're in the field. Which is why I say again, what the hell are you doing here?” Josh moved closer to Patrick, but still kept his distance, as if he didn't want to 'catch' anything from being too close.

“Man, I to' ya. Ima 'ere ta work.”

“Are you insane?” Josh strained to keep his voice low. He moved menacingly closer. “Do you really think I'd let you anywhere near this place again, let alone work for me? I just bailed you out of jail. You're risking everything we've got going here. You're out and if you know what's good for you, you'll never come near me or this place again.”

Patrick stared at Josh, his easy attitude was gone. “Ya owe me Man. Afa all I dun fo' ya.” Josh waved him off. Patrick rushed Josh and grabbed his arm. “Ya don' know wha' ya doin'. I know thins ya don' be wantin' certain folks knowin' wha' ya doin' 'ere.”

Josh wrenched his arm free, grabbed Patrick by the neck and slammed him against the wall. “And you seem to forget who pays your bills and who we're both working for.” Josh moved his face closer to him. “Don't you ever fucking threaten me again if you know what's good for you.” Josh slowly released Patrick and took a step back. “Now…”

“Josh Tanner, please call the front desk.” Blared the overhead speakers, interrupting him. Josh snapped his head around in reaction, he gave a quick scan of the room. They were still alone. “Josh Tanner, please call the front desk immediately.” His scowl deepened.

"Wait here. I'm not through with you." He threatened Patrick. Then he rushed to grab the extension above the work bench.

"What?" He shouted angrily into the receiver. "Yes, this is Josh, I'm kind of in the middle of something here." He paused as the receptionist answered him. "What do they want?" He paused again and then spun around, looking back to where he had just come from. Patrick was gone. He cursed under his breath. "Hang on, I'll be right there." He did a quick scan inside and just outside the back of the warehouse just to be sure. He couldn't find the technician anywhere, so he rushed to the front reception area to greet the police.

*****

Patrick raced out the back door of the warehouse, looking back frequently. He wasn't about to wait around for Josh. He snuck around the side to where he'd parked his dirty green Honda. He turned on the engine, slipped it into gear and spun out as fast as he could. It wasn't a quiet car, but it was fast. It had clearly taken a few beatings, but it was dependable enough to get him out with his hide intact. He was glad he hadn't traded it for his last fix. He never would have been steady enough to get away from Josh on foot, but this car had already gotten him blocks away in the same time it had taken him to reach it.

"Da' man gonna regret no' treetin' me righ'." He muttered to himself as he patted himself down looking for a smoke. When he didn't find one he threw open the glove box to search there. He wasn't watching the road or maybe he would have noticed the car swerving towards him in time.

He felt the jolt before he heard the deafening sound. He wasn't totally sure if it was the car that was spinning or his head until it stopped. He couldn't move. He was already well into coming off his last hit and his body couldn't move quick enough to react. The door swung open. He faintly realized he was being dragged from the car and into the other waiting one. He wanted to ask them what they wanted, but all he could make his mouth do was stutter a few W's, before he blacked out from the concussion.

CHAPTER 17

Josh met the Police at the front. There were two officers, one he recognized from the night the body was found, the other he hadn't seen before. Josh slipped into his school boy grin. "How can I help you gentlemen?"

The officer he had recognized from the night before stepped forward. "Mr. Tanner, we have a warrant for the arrest of one of your technicians in the murder of Miguel Conterna." He handed Josh the warrant. "Is Leon Patrick Palmer here?" Josh scanned the warrant and shook his head. He hadn't realized Patrick had been a middle name.

The second officer jumped forward. "We were told he still worked here."

Josh looked up and studied the two for a brief moment. "He did, the problem is he got himself arrested, then he showed up here earlier looking to work. I kicked him out. I don't need that kind of trouble working here. We can't have anyone who poses a security risk working in this type of business. We'd lose our licenses, not to mention our reputation and customers."

"He was here? Why did you let him go?" The second officer demanded.

Josh's posture stiffened, his smile hardened into a forced grin. "I didn't know he was under arrest. You had him in your custody, why didn't you keep him?"

The first officer stepped forward, putting himself between Josh and the second officer. "We understand you didn't know, unfortunately he was released before his warrant was processed through the system. We need to bring him in as soon as possible. Do you know where we might find him?"

Josh shook his head again. "You might try his home, but I have no idea where that is. I'd have to pull his personnel files."

"That's okay, we have those. Your office sent them over yesterday. We have someone looking there now."

"Then you know more than I do." Josh's trademark smile was planted on his face.

"What about anyone he might have hung out with at work, did he have any friends here?"

Josh stared into space, considering the question. Then he shook his head again. "No, sorry. I wasn't that close to the technician's personal lives, so I can't be sure. Although I know he trained with Miguel. I'm not sure that I noticed anyone else he might have hung out with. He was pretty new here, so other than passing his original back ground check, I don't know much about him."

"If you think of anything," the first officer pulled out his card and handed it to Josh, "please give me a call."

Josh read over the card. "I will, Detective Jamison. I'm sorry I haven't been much help."

"That's okay, but if he comes back, be sure to call us immediately. Don't have anyone try to speak to him or stop him yourselves. He could be very dangerous."

Josh gave him a look of concern. "I'll be sure to alert the staff of the situation. Thank you."

The two officers nodded and headed out. Josh turned to the receptionist.

"You heard what they said, please be sure to call me immediately if they or anyone comes back looking for Patrick." He turned to head back to his office, then as an after-thought stopped and added, "and of course don't do anything yourself, just call me." The receptionists face was pale, she nodded weakly. Josh grunted and headed back. He knew it was unlikely she'd show up for work tomorrow. He was starting to lose count of how many receptionists he'd hired this year.

*****

Rachel had just picked up her headset to make another call to accounting to try to track down the missing journals when Josh popped into her office. She looked up and gave him a weary smile.

"Any luck?" He asked as he scanned her now messy desk. She shook her head. "Well don't worry about it. I think in light of the events that have happened I'll be doing some house cleaning around here anyway. We'll change all the ATM access codes and passwords." Josh sighed and straightened his shoulders. "It's going to be a lot of work, but it's necessary. Any problems we had should be gone after that." He stepped closer and lowered his voice. "Of course if you do spot something else, I expect you to come directly to me, I know right away. We don't need this type of thing to go unchecked."

"Of course." Rachel nodded.

Josh smiled and gave her a wink. "That's my girl. I don't know what I'd do without you." Rachel shrugged, but she still had a concerned look on her face. "Like I said, don't worry about it. We have a lot of work to do to get things back on track and I'll need your help with that. It's really too bad those journals went missing, especially with all the work you put into your research. However, we can't look back, we have to look forward and preventing this from happening again is more important now anyway."

"Spoken like a true salesman." Rachel mused fondly.

This time Josh shrugged and gave her his white toothed grin. "Speaking of sales," he began as he headed towards her door, "I've got a few outstanding sales calls of my own that I've had to put off with all this going on." He shook his head and headed out as he added, "No rest for the wicked."

She stared at the empty door a moment after he left, then at the headset in her hand, before finally putting setting them. "Look forward." She affirmed to herself out loud as she nodded her head. She stared at her computer a moment, then smiled and pulled up the ATM database. She printed off a couple reports. One listed all the ATMs that she had come up with shortages on her reports. The other was a list of all the ATMs owned by investor Blaise Farrell. She read them over made sure the location information was ordered by route, then tucked them into her purse and headed out.

*****

Rachel left the 5th location on the list. She had ordered them by zip code in hopes to make it easier, but now she wondered if she should have reviewed a map first. Maybe crossed a few off Blaze's list. There were 30, and not all were in the best neighborhoods, she could see what he had been talking about when he mentioned it not being a good idea filling them with cash too late in the day. She slowed the car as she got closer to the address she was looking for. She cautiously eyed the rundown buildings, very few had any visible addresses, and the ones that did were so covered by graffiti that she had to squint to read.

She pulled up in front of the place called Charlie's pub. She stopped her car, looked at her watch and nodded, it should be open by now. She looked up at the entrance to Charlie's Pub. The sign actually said Charl 's ub with several of the letters burnt out, but it was still recognizable. She turned off her car, grabbed her purse and looked the place over. The windows were so grungy that any light from inside could barely be seen. The entrance door was presently propped open by the man passed out against it. She scrunched her nose and furrowed her brow. She clutched her purse tighter, took a deep breath and hopped out of the car window.

She stepped over the man passed out in the entrance and stopped to allow her eyesight to adjust to the sudden darkness inside. She scanned the dimly lit, smoke filled room. The bar was practically empty, but the smoke seemed to be part of the normal air in the place, like it refused to leave long after the smoker had. There were about 5 patrons scattered across the right side and two off on the left, but each one stopped and watched her as she crossed over to the bar. Rachel looked noticeably out of place. She was casually dressed, but she was clearly different from the regular patrons. For one thing, she was upright, for another, she had recently washed.

She had on faded low-rise jeans and a form fitting t-shirt, light green. It reflected in her eyes making them seem to sparkle and brining the green out in them, despite the dingy air. Her hair was tied back in a loose ponytail, but many pieces had managed to escape over the course of the day framing her face with golden blonde locks. The patrons continued to stare quietly as they waited for the bartender to size her up.

When Charlie finally walked over and asked what she wanted to drink, they went back to their own drinks once she had ordered hers. Who were they to care who drank in the place. All of them that is, except one unseen to her in the back corner who kept his eye on her while he gulped his whiskey. "You're not from around here." Charlie said as he set her Vodka cooler down front of her. She smiled, shook her head and took a swig. "So what brings you to our little neighborhood?"

She nodded towards the ATM in the corner. "I was just..."

"She was just checking up on my ATMs for me Charlie." The booming voice cut her off. She froze as Blaze spoke from behind her. Charlie looked from Rachel to Blaze and back again. He shrugged, disinterested and went back to running his dirty rag over the sticky counter and chatting with the drunk sitting at the far end of the bar. She turned around to face him. He leaned in close. She could smell the thick scent of whiskey on his breath.

"Or perhaps you were checking up on me?" He added in a low voice.

"And what if I was?" She replied, her chin pointed upwards in defiance.

He grunted. "Are you always this idiotic?"

"I beg your pardon?" She replied; her back arched indignantly.

"You heard me."

"Are you always this..." she scrunched her nose and pulled her face back, "pleasant?"

"Yes." He grinned.

"That wasn't a compliment."

"I know." He replied, the grin still on his face. "You didn't answer my question."

"I'm not going to dignify that question with a response." She turned to take another sip from her drink. He stared at her, brooding in silence. She ignored him and continued to sip her drink.

"You just did." He affirmed. "and clearly you're determined to continue with your idiocy; well you can do that without my help." He turned to leave.

She spun around. "I didn't ask for your help." She replied loud enough to cause Charlie to look up from where he was making a drink and Blaze to stop in his tracks. He slowly turned back to face her. He had a big grin on his face. Charlie cocked his head at the strange site. He had never once seen Blaze smile. Blaze nodded towards Charlie, who then went back to his work. Blaze leaned against the bar, giving Rachel a once over glance, his smile faded as he looked into her defiant eyes.

"No." He started his voice low and deep. "Clearly you didn't or you wouldn't be wandering around in seedy bars all by yourself with no idea what you might come up against." He studied her further. "and my guess is with no clue what you're even looking for."

Rachel huffed and crossed her arms. She glared at him, opening her mouth several times, but no response seemed to come out. Blaze grunted and walked away. She bounded behind him, following. "So what would you do then?" She called after him. He stopped and turned, the strange grin returning to his face.

"That's just the point Luv. I wouldn't do anything. It's not my business." He leaned in closer and lowered his voice. "And it's not yours either, so maybe you should just stay out of it."

She stiffened and faced him definitely. "Is that a threat?" She asked. Blaze let out an amused chuckle. She raised an eyebrow.

"I don't waste my time on threats." He said, his voice deep and reverberating and his eyes dark. "You asked me what I would do, I told you. If you don't want to take my advice, that's your problem." She reflexively pulled back from him. His eyes brightened and voice returned to its normal gruff tone. "Now since you are perfectly happy on your own, I'll be on my way." With that he motioned as if tipping a hat he didn't have to her and headed out of the bar. He motioned to Charlie before he left, pointing the money he'd left on the bar.

She raced to grab a ten from her purse, threw it beside her drink and rushed after him. She caught up with him outside and grabbed his arm to stop him. He spun around fist ready at his side, but immediately stopped himself upon seeing her and glared at her instead. She dropped his arm, but stood firm. "And what if I were to ask for your help?"

"And why would you do that?"

She shrugged and looked down before answering. "Maybe I value your opinion."

Blaze stared at her intently. She smiled up at him, her eyes bright. They looked clear and almost see through like the Caribbean Ocean in the setting sunlight. He looked down the street. The activity was increasing with the impending darkness. The few remaining hookers in the pub were leaving to claim their spots on various street corners. Even the drunk who had been passed out in Charlie's doorway, had disappeared; likely gone in search of a safe place to pass the night away. He sighed heavily.

"Whatever help you need, you can tell me about back at my place." Rachel hesitated, her look uncertain. Blaze grunted and rolled his eyes. "It's around the corner and safer than talking out here on this street at night." Rachel looked towards her car. Blaze let out another grunt that sounded a little like his laugh. "Believe me no one around here steals something worth less than their own shit." He turned and headed down the street. Rachel huffed at the insult to her car, but as she took in her surroundings she quickly caught up and kept pace with him all the way to his apartment.

Blaze turned into his building and headed up the stairs. She hesitated to follow him into the dark stairwell of the mostly dilapidated building, but with the light fading fast outside she had even less desire to stay on the street alone. She took a deep breath and hurried up the stairs behind him. He lived on the top of the second floor, directly across from the stairwell. She looked from the stairwell to his apartment with a puzzled look as he unlocked the door.

"It's easier to dispose of unwanted visitors this way." He replied to her unasked question. She nodded, a look of concern on her face, and followed him into his apartment. He flicked the switch to his only source of lighting; a bare bulb that dangled precariously from a ceiling fixture with several screws missing. He didn't bother to respond to the look of horror that sprang to her face as she looked around his living room. She opted to hang close to the front of the room. He easily walked straight through to his kitchen without disturbing a stitch of dirt.

She looked around the dingy apartment and then back to the door she just came through. She took a deep breath and just about doubled over coughing. Blaze came out holding a beer and stared at her. She straightened and looked at him, her face contorted. "I don't even want to guess what corner that smell is coming from." She choked out. "No wonder you wanted to stay at my place last night."

Blaze grunted and pointed to the kitchen. "You don't like it the cleaning supplies are in there."

She shot him a disgusted and confused look. "You have cleaning supplies?" She shook her head and looked around again. The walls were completely bare of anything but dust and faded spots of various sizes where pictures might have once adorned them. Other than the remnants of a couch and table, there was scarcely any other furniture, not even a TV. "What for, I don't see anything IN here to clean?" She added as she finished her scan of the room.

The only personal item that could be seen was a small framed photograph on the far edge of the mantel. She picked her way precariously through the garbage for a closer look. She had to squint and lower her head to make anything out through all the dust that covered it. She could see two men and a woman. She could swear one resembled Blaze, but much younger. She was about to pick it up to confirm her suspicions when Blaze grabbed it from her. She jumped back, surprised by his sudden appearance, he had crossed the room quickly and silently.

"Oh I see. It's okay for you to break in and search my entire apartment, but I can't even look at one picture?" She complained, but Blaze only grunted and reset the photograph on its perch. She snuck another peak at the photo. It was a black and white picture. In it she could make out a dark haired man cuddling with a beautiful Philippine looking woman who was sitting on his lap leaning against a motorcycle and Blaze was standing in tight beside them both, they were all smiling. She looked over at Blaze and started to ask him a question. "Who..."

She immediately stopped when Blaze turned his back to her. He crossed to the couch and shoved all the garbage onto the floor in one motion. A brief look of embarrassment crossed his features when he glanced at her, seeing the room through her eyes. He flipped the cushions over and sat down, then took a long swig from his beer. His look became vacant as he stared off into the distance. After what felt like an eternity of silence, he spoke. "That was my old partner and his girlfriend. We were undercover at the time. That picture was taken shortly before they died." He took another swig of beer and remained silent.

She looked from Blaze and back to the picture but didn't ask another word about it. Instead she crossed the room and sat quietly next to him on the couch. He offered her a swig. She accepted the bottle, took a swig and returned it to him. They remained like that for a few minutes, until Blaze spoke again. "So why were you checking out my ATMs?" Rachel shook her head and was about to speak when he cut her off. "You were at all my sites this afternoon." She sat up, her eyes wide with surprise. The corner of his mouth upturned into a grin. "The owners called me about some woman asking questions, they described you. Then you showed up at Charlie's, it was an easy puzzle to put together."

She sat back, shrugged and gave him an acknowledging smile. "I was following some leads."

"Leads? Cops follow the leads; you follow your streams of consciousness." He said flippantly as he took another swig.

"Well my 'streams' led me to shortages in the ATMs didn't they?"

She said her posture combative. Blaze shrugged. She shot him a scowl. “Do you want to hear this or not?” He rolled his hand towards her indicating for her to continue. She cocked her head and went on. “I was following the ATMs that had shortages, or at least I was going to do that after I checked up on yours.”

“Why?”

“Someone stole all the journals I found with the proof of the shortages. So, I thought if I followed them that I’d get some idea of why those ATMs were used and if I knew why, maybe I might find out who.”

Blaze nodded. He focused on her face. “So why my ATMs?”

She squirmed and shifted her position on the couch. “Well I thought maybe…”

“You thought maybe I did it.” He cut her off before she could finish. Her face flushed and she nodded without looking him in the eye. He grinned and polished off his beer. He was about to toss it on the floor, but with a quick side glance towards her, he instead pushed a clear spot on the coffee table and set it down there. “So did you find anything following my ATMs around?”

“You need to clean once in a while.” She replied staring at the bottle he had set down that seemed to have already blended into the rest of the garbage. He rolled his eyes and sat forward on the couch. “Besides the fact that you’re a slob? No.” She admitted with a shrug.

“Well then, how about we follow the other ATMs. You have that list too I presume?” He asked. She replied with a coy grin. He nodded and stood up. “That’s what I thought.” He added as he headed to the door. He stopped suddenly, causing Rachel who had followed close behind to bump into him. “How about we take my truck?" He added after she had righted herself.

She didn't bother to be insulted and tried to ignore the tiny voice reminding her that she was supposed to be avoiding him and should be calling Josh. Instead she nodded and they headed out, his place might be a mess but his truck was more reliable than hers, even she had to admit that.

CHAPTER 18

“Having fun yet?” Blaze asked with a sideways glance.

Rachel ignored his sarcasm and continued with a smile. “I can see why you would miss this so much.” She adjusted her position another time as she tried to get comfortable. She was starting to feel numb.

“Who said I miss it?” He replied as he continued to stare at the empty store. He looked too comfortable lounging in his driver’s seat. She looked away from him and turned back to stare at the store as well.

“Quite the hopping place isn’t it?” Her voice laced with sarcasm.

Blaze nodded and let out another grunt. “Maybe we caught them on a bad day.”

“Maybe we caught them all on bad days.” She added as she continued to scan the store for any signs of customer traffic. This was the third store they had staked out. She shifted anxiously in her seat, waiting wasn’t her favorite thing. Patience was not a skill she had. She turned her head and studied Blaze to pass the time. He was calm and perfectly still. His features weren’t relaxed, but they weren’t tense either. His sculpted jaw gave a slight muscle contraction as he occasionally ground his teeth. He looked like he could sit like that for hours without moving. She on the other hand was not doing as well.

She turned to look at the store again, a customer finally entered, the first one they had seen in the last hour of waiting there. She squirmed again in her seat. “I don’t understand it, how can all these locations be so dead?” They have the highest volume sales.

“Are you sure these are the ones you marked on your report?” Blaze asked as he shifted in his seat trying to get a better look at the number on the store.

She spun around to glare at him. “Of course I’m sure.”

He looked at her and grinned. “A little defensive are we? You lost the journals after all. I was just double checking.”

Her face flushed. “I didn’t lose them, they were taken. There’s a difference” Blaze raised his hands in mock surrender. She pulled the report out of her purse and retrieved the lone journal she had taken home in her purse the other night. “I still have the one I took home the other night and my original report notes. See?” She held them up for him to see. He cocked his eyebrow in surprise.

“So you did have it with you.” She turned to look at the store. He smiled again as she avoided a response. He let her off the hook, he knew the answer anyway, she hadn’t trusted him or Josh. He changed his line of questioning back to the matter at hand. “So the question still remains. If these are the busiest sites Stafford has, where are all the customers?” Her face was still flushed from being caught in her deception. She nodded in response.

They continued to watch the store for another hour until her constant squirming annoyed him to the breaking point. Within that time only one more customer had gone into the store, neither one had gone near the ATM. She sighed heavily and Blaze glared at her. He turned on his truck and put it in gear. She smiled as they drove away; this was the last site they planned to visit. She stretched out and settled back in his soft leather seats.

His truck, in stark contrast to his apartment, was pristine. Unlike her car there wasn't a stitch of rust anywhere. His truck was new, with all the conveniences her old car didn't have; like air conditioning, which Blaze now turned on full. The spring might have been colder than usual, but summer had long turned into a stifling and the night air was hot and humid. She adjusted the vent so it was blowing directly on her face. She closed her eyes and smiled, enjoying the cool breeze. Blaze glanced at her the air was blowing her long hair around her face. He shook his head, let out a sigh and frowned.

"What do you think we should do next?" She asked her eyes still closed, not seeing his frown.

He clenched his jaw tightly, his scowl deepened. He shot her another glance. Her face was relaxed as she enjoyed the air conditioning and the rocking motion of the truck. He looked back at the road and stared off into the night ahead. He lowered his head and let out another sigh, then straightened in his seat and grunted. "Nothing. It's a dead end."

Her eyes flew open and she jumped up in her seat and turned towards him as far as the seatbelt would let her. "Nothing? Are you kidding me? One technician is dead, there is a trail of stolen money from our busiest ATMs that seem to have no business. How can you say we do nothing?"

His lip quivered. He clenched his jaw harder. "There is nothing for to do. You are not a crime fighter. You're a sales assistant; just a temp at some piss ant little ATM Company. You do not go chasing murderers." He spoke harshly as he stared ahead on the road.

She ignored him, she was used to people's unhappy reactions as she charged into things. "So we go to the police then, tell them what we know, maybe we'll be able to find out more." He didn't reply and instead continued to stare straight ahead and drove on in silence. She let out an exaggerated sigh. "You were a cop once, aren't you even a little curious? Don't you have some contacts we can ask?" She pleaded.

Blaze slammed on the brakes and stopped the car at the next light. He spun around to face her. His eyes were dark. "And you're not! Just because you write about detectives doesn't mean you know anything about them. This isn't a game and I'm not a cop anymore. Just what is it that you think 'We' should be doing?" His voice cut her sharp and deep. He glared at her, before throwing the truck back into gear and driving on. He gripped the wheel so hard his knuckles were white.

Her mouth hung open in surprise. His tone had never been so cold and cruel before. She turned away from him and stared out the side window. Her face flushed and she shivered as her breathing became fast and shallow. She faced forward and shifted in her seat. She bit her bottom lip and shivered again. She tried to deepen her inhalations in an effort to control her breathing. He lowered the air conditioning in response to her shivers and they drove in silence for the remainder of the ride.

He pulled in behind her car and parked. The streets were relatively empty. The street hookers would have either picked up tricks or moved to a busier location by now. The junkies would have had their fixes and already found a place to ride out their high and the drunks would have stumbled off to their favorite place to pass out. So as far as streets go, this was one of the safest in the neighborhood. Blaze turned off the ignition but kept the lights shining on her car.

"Thanks." She said quietly as she undid her seatbelt and grabbed for the handle.

"You're not going to leave this alone are you?" He asked, his voice sounding strained.

She stopped and turned to look at him, putting on her best innocent smile she replied. "Why wouldn't I? It's a dead end, you said so yourself."

His frown deepened. "Do you ever leave anything alone once you start?"

She hopped down from the cab of his truck, grabbed her purse and smiled up at him. "I have no idea what you're talking about." She said before closing his door and walking over to her car. She hopped in the open driver's window, threw him a small wave, started her car and drove off.

He lowered his head onto his steering wheel and groaned. When he sat up he found himself staring up at Charlie's decrepit sign, flashing, welcoming him. Charlie's was always the last light off on the street. He turned off the lights and hopped out of his truck. He wasn't worried, everyone around here knew his truck and no one was stupid enough to touch it. Someone had tried once, the never tried again.

As he reached the door of the pub he stopped. He looked back at his truck, then down the street in the direction Rachel had just headed off and then back at the pub door. He lowered his head in resignation and let out a deep sigh. Then he turned and headed back to his truck, took out his cell phone and dialed. It was picked up on the third ring.

"Hello?"

"It's Blaze."

"Oh hey man, how the hell are you?"

"Fantastic." He replied sarcastically.

"Talkative as ever I see. I heard Petey say he ran into you the other night, some technician murdered over at your place or something. You alright?"

"It's not my place. I just deal with them sometimes and yeah, I ran into good ol' Pete. We had a nice friendly chat."

The man on the other end of the line let out a laugh. "Yeah, heard that too."

"I need a favor." Blaze said, running his fingers through his hair.

"Of course, you don't even have to ask man. You know I've always been behind you. They had no proof, no right to do that to you. They needed a scapegoat and they shafted you because of it."

"Thanks, I appreciate that." He shifted uncomfortably and loosened the grip he held on his phone. "Look the murdered tech, I need to know what you've got on that. I have some money invested there and I want to make sure I don't lose it. It's not like I have a lot of it to waste, you know what I mean."

The man laughed sympathetically. "Yeah, I hear you and without a pension I can imagine. I'm not working that case, but I'll see what I can dig up. Should I call you at this number?"

"Yeah, that'd be great, thanks." He shifted the phone to his other ear.

“Hey, I meant what I said, you don’t even have to ask, anything you need. I’ll get on it right away.”

“I appreciate it if you’d keep this...”

“You don’t even have to say it. I never got this call.”

Blaze smiled. “You always were the man John.”

“Yeah, Yeah, that’s what Jake used...” The caller stopped. “Sorry man.” He said, Blaze didn’t respond, so he continued. “I’ll call you as soon as I hear something.”

“Thanks.” With that Blaze hung up and started his truck. He drove off in the direction Rachel had gone, but instead of turning west at the lights like she had, he turned east, and headed up town towards Josh’s place.

*****

Rachel was fuming as she drove home. “You’re not a cop. No but you were!” She argued aloud. “How dare he? Who does he think he is? A drunken slob, that’s who!” She turned into the parking lot, her tires squealed a little as she rounded the corner. She sunk down in her seat, her face flushed. “Oops.” She apologized aloud as she looked around to see if anyone noticed. No one had. She parked, hopped out and smiled. “Sure, I can leave things alone; when they’re resolved.” She smiled smugly and headed into her apartment.

Inside she grabbed a cup of milky sweet coffee and sat in front of her computer. She pulled out her notebook and started to brainstorm. She laid out everything she knew and everything she didn’t know. She ran through a bunch of what if type scenarios and listed thoughts that ran through her mind as she wrote out her cast of characters. Writing helped her release her frustrations and flesh out some ideas.

It was early dawn by the time she finished. She had a lot of ideas scribbled throughout her notebook and had added several scenes to her novel. She was too tired to focus anymore, even too tired to bother turning off her computer. It was still dark outside, but she knew it was only a matter of hours before her alarm would go off. She turned off all the lights and headed to bed. She was asleep before her head hit the pillow.

*****

Blaze rang the bell and banged on his door until Josh answered. When He finally opened the door, Blaze pushed past him and went inside. Josh made a sweeping motion with his hand. "By all means, come on in Blaze. It's so nice to see you."

Blaze stopped about halfway into Josh's entrance hall and turned to face him. His face was deeply creased with his usual scowl, but Josh could see the intensity in his eyes and he immediately dropped his school boy grin. Josh quickly buttoned his shirt that he had tossed on to answer the door. His jeans were loosely fastened and the top of his underwear could be seen.

Blaze sized him up and nodded his head towards the back rooms. "She's going to stay back there while we talk I assume." Josh grinned, of course she will, they always listen to me. Blaze ignored the innuendo.

"Good." Blaze said as he headed off to the right of the stairwell and into the kitchen. He reached into the fridge and grabbed a beer. "This all you got?" He had disgusted look on his face as he held up the Heineken bottle.

"Maybe if you'd have been invited, I'd have stocked up on that swill you drink." Josh had followed Blaze into the kitchen and stood in the doorway; his hands tucked in his back pockets as if leaning on them. His head was only inches from the top of the door jam. Blaze took up the entire space, his muscle mass was clearly more defined than his, they were both obviously in good shape though his was more athletic and lean and Blaze's was more bulk. "Now if you're done insulting my beer, I'd like to get back to my date. So will you kindly tell me what the hell you are doing storming into my place in the middle of the night?"

Blaze put the beer down on the counter, unopened, and crossed his arms. "I want you to tell me what kind of scams you are running at Stafford."

Josh's face turned red. He took his hand out of his pocket where it had been resting and stalked towards Blaze until they were mere inches apart. "You dare storm into my house and accuse me of running scams? I'm the one who pulled your washed-up drunken ass out of the gutter and got you into the business. Not too many people would give a dirty ex-cop a job. Without me you wouldn't be able to earn a decent living."

"You don't own Stafford." Blaze said casually.

"Maybe not in name, but we both know who runs it." Josh said, his chest puffed up.

"Do we?" Blaze leaned in closer. "Why don't you tell me?" His eyes were steady and menacing.

Josh stared back, his eyes darting behind Blaze and back again, after a moment he took a step back and leaned against the kitchen wall. His school boy smile returned. "Blaze, what is all this?" He said leaning against the counter and tucking his hand back into his front jean pocket in an effort to look casual. "Come on, you got me with my pants down, quite literally. I have this hot chick waiting for me in the back and believe me, she's raring to go again. Why don't we talk in the morning after you sleep whatever this is off? We can figure out what this nonsense is about, I'm sure we just have some sort of misunderstanding going on."

Blaze stared at Josh in silence, sizing him up. He stalked out of the kitchen, not so accidentally bumping against Josh as he passed by. He stopped a few steps away; he kept his back to Josh as he spoke. "You might want to re-consider the location of some of your ATMs. Seems your busiest sites rely quite heavily on the patronage of its two customers to make all those withdrawals. Pretty risky venture if you ask me." Blaze turned his head slightly to look directly at Josh. "Personally, my busy sites are the ones with lots of foot traffic. Guess I'm doing something wrong there." As soon as he was done he walked straight out of the townhouse. He didn't bother to shut the door behind him and didn't look back.

Josh looked at the beer Blaze had left and the open front door and scowled. "Pig." He said under his breath as he put the beer back in the fridge, perfectly lined up with the others. He headed back to his bedroom, stopping only to shut and lock the front door on his way. He unbuttoned his shirt as he walked, a grin was plastered on his face to cover his deep seething anger. "You're master's back babe. I hope you were a good girl while I was gone." He entered the room then shook his head. "Oh you've been a naughty girl. I'm going to have to punish my little slut."

His date squealed with glee and she immediately sprung back into her position on the bed. "I'm sorry Master." Josh ripped off her unauthorized shirt and pulled out his paddle. She moaned with delight. As he watched her ass turn rosy pink with each smack of the paddle, all thoughts of Blaze were gone.

*****

Blaze was fuming by the time he reached his truck. He raced the engine as he started it and put it into gear. He peeled off, but was still careful not to ding Coralene's car as he backed out of the driveway. He had recognized it right away when he arrived, she had it when Josh had him check her out last year. He offered only a look of disgust as he tried to ensure no images of the two of them together crept into his mind. He headed off in the opposite direction from his apartment.

CHAPTER 19

Blaze stared up at the apartment. The lights had gone off about 10 minutes earlier. He looked at his watch. A couple more hours until the darkness started to lift. He clenched his jaw, then turned off his phone, locked his truck and headed up. He wasn't sure if she was asleep yet, but figured her bedroom was far enough away from the entrance that if she did wake up, he'd hear her before she'd find him. He cracked a half grin as he approached the second floor. Her apartment took him no time to break into; he shook his head with disgust at her cheap locks.

He listened for any sign of movement, when he didn't hear any he went straight for her computer. He noticed the power light was still on. He moved the mouse and the monitor immediately lit up. Her document was still open. It hadn't been like that the last two times, she must have been tired he noted to himself as he started scrolling through it. He stopped when a paragraph caught his eye. He started reading it to himself.

"I couldn't believe this low life junkie had just insulted me. I mean damn it! I was giving him the money, was that really necessary? There was no way I was going to let him get away with that. I may be blonde, but I am not dumb. He didn't know who he had just pissed off, but he was about to find out. Sweaty, stinky, little creep; Beside being sick of him shaking that stupid gun in my face, there was no way I was going let all those kick boxing classes go to waste. After all, I paid good money for them. As I kicked the gun out of his hand, all I could think of were Amy's last words on about this job, 'It's a no brainer'. Why do I listen to her?"

Blaze couldn't help smirking. *Diving in without thinking, even her fictional self has poor judgment.* He thought before he started searching through her desk until he found her notebooks. He pulled them out and started scanning through them. When he found the most recent one, he put the rest back and flipped through to the most recent entries. There were a lot of scribbled streams of thought; jotted words, questions and various statements in no particular order. He continued to scan the pages but stopped on the last page. His face contorted into a scowl that contained a mixture of concern and puzzlement. He focused on a list of names broken down into two columns. Under known players she had Josh, himself, the technicians and various others from the company. On the unknown side she listed Stafford owners and technician's cohorts. She also had two words circled and starred with a series of question marks; Money Laundering and Skimming."

Grumbling, he put the notebook back where he found it. He searched around a bit more but found nothing new that interested him. A sudden noise made him turn towards the back of the apartment. He froze as he listened. He soon heard another noise. She must be waking up. He swiftly and quietly rushed out the front door, locking it on his way out. He'd have to do something about her locks.

*****

Rachel bolted awake. She remained seated, listening in her bed. She wasn't sure if she heard a noise or dreamt it, so she slowly stepped out of bed and listened. She didn't hear anything so she walked to her bedroom door and turned her head towards the living room and listened again. She still didn't hear anything but she couldn't shake the bad feeling she had, so she grabbed her robe, slid on her slippers and slowly snuck down the hallway. She paused as she neared the opening to the living room; she froze and tilted her head; Silence. She peered around the corner and noticed the dim light from her computer. Immediately her brow creased and her lips formed into a frown. She tightened her robe around her waist, crouched and did a spring leap into the living room.

The room was empty. She searched around and found nobody. All was quiet and aside from her computer, nothing seemed out of place. She stared at the computer screen and shook her head. She had left it on, but as she went to shut it down she paused to scan her document. It was on page 21; she had left it on page 43. She spun her head around and looked towards the door. It was closed. She went over and checked the handle, it was locked. She started to turn away, but noticed the dead chain wasn't on. She hesitated before turning double checking the deadbolt, then slipping the chain into place. She walked over, shut her computer down and headed back to bed. She didn't sleep.

After a few hours of tossing and turning, she finally got up and made herself some coffee; very strong and very dark. She scowled at her mug, she wanted her cream and sugar, but she needed it full strength. The caffeine was the only thing keeping her eyes from drooping and the bitter taste was giving her the kick she needed to get moving. She showered at top speed and in less than 20 minutes she was out the door on her way to the office. She arrived to a parking lot that was empty except for one vehicle; Josh Tanner's. He always seemed to be the first one in.

Rachel dragged herself into her office. She looked around and smiled when she found the place empty. She noticed Josh's office light on but went straight for the kitchen to put on a pot of coffee. As it brewed, she leisurely made her way to her desk, where she checked her email in peace and quiet. The sound of her phone made her jump. It echoed through the empty office. She picked up the receiver quickly to silence it. It was a customer; she took down the information and scheduled it in the technician's database for when they arrived at their normal hour.

After hanging up, she headed off to the kitchen and just about collided head on into Josh as she rounded her office door. She let out a small scream of surprise and jumped back, holding her hand to her chest. Josh grinned his easy grin and leaned against the wall.

"Sorry, didn't mean to scare you. Just came to see who was in with me so early, should have known it was you when the phone got answered so quickly." He let out a casual laugh.

She smiled weakly, her breathing still heavy from the surprise. She let her hand fall to her side as she composed herself. "I was just heading to the kitchen for some coffee."

"Oh great, I'll join you." He motioned his hand to indicate she should go first. She smiled politely, trying to stop from clenching her teeth, and headed towards the kitchen. "You're looking a little... tired today." Josh said with as much tact as he could.

"I didn't get much sleep, something woke me up and I couldn't get back to sleep. That's what I need the coffee for." She smiled again, this time it was more genuine, the smell of her waiting coffee urging her onward.

"What woke you up?" He asked, but she didn't respond and instead entered the kitchen and headed straight for the coffee. She grabbed the cream and sugar and a mug for herself and one for Josh. She turned to offered him the mug and noticed his sulking appearance. She sighed and set his mug on the counter before responding.

"I'm not sure, I thought I heard a noise in the apartment, but it turned out to be nothing. I think I just must be a bit jumpy from all the running around earlier." She inhaled the fresh aroma deeply as she poured and dressed her coffee as usual, looking forward this one much more than the one she had choked down earlier at home.

"Running around?" He asked, taking the pot from her when she handed it to him.

She took a slow long sip from her mug. She closed her eyes and let the warm sweet liquid slide down her throat. It was better than any meditation. After a moment she looked at Josh, who was waiting expectantly for her reply. She waved it off as she spoke. "Nothing really, I just ended up visiting some of those ATMs. You know, the ones that I found showing shortages on their journal receipts. Anyway, I didn't find anything so it was pretty much a waste of time. All in all it was pretty boring and I think sitting in that truck cab all that time gave me kinks that kept me from sleeping properly." She took another glorious sip from her coffee.

"I thought all the journals were taken?" He asked nonchalantly as he poured his coffee.

"They were, but I had my report and one of the journals still in my purse. I had jotted the terminal IDs on the report, so I just pulled the addresses off the database from there." She took another long sip from her mug then turned and started to head out of the kitchen.

Josh stopped a look dawning on his face as her earlier words registered. "Truck cab? You mean you finally replaced that old heap of yours? I didn't think we were paying you that well." He laughed at his own joke before picking up his coffee and moving to join her.

"Not mine, we took Blaze's truck." She said before taking another quick sip. "He wouldn't drive in my car." She added after swallowing.

Josh raised his eyebrow. "Blaze was with you?"

"Yeah, I know you said to steer clear of him, but I sort of ran into him while I was going around to the sites and he just sort of invited himself along." The caffeine was starting to kick in, that plus her fatigue had her extra chatty and she muttered on at a break neck speed. "Which I guess was good, he might not be the greatest company, but turns out that some of the ATMs are not in the nicest of areas. So I guess any company was welcome, especially one his size." Feeling he had satisfied his ask, she took one last sip before turning and walking back toward her office.

"You might want to reconsider your choice of company." Josh insisted, keeping pace with her. Rachel nodded half-heartedly, gulping her coffee as she walked.

"I mean it." He said as he outpaced her and stopped in front, blocking her path. "I don't think he should be spending so much time around the office. I don't trust him." She gave him a puzzled look, so Josh continued. "He works with us yes, but he doesn't exactly have a spotless reputation. Not all the cops are in love with him, especially the ones that were here the other night and we don't really need any more attention right now." She cocked her head and Josh shifted his weight but didn't respond. "Besides, he's a drunk."

Rachel examined him in silence. His face was serious, not a sign of his trademark school boy grin. His features were almost forming a scowl, which didn't sit well with his normal look and his posture was stiff, not his usual easy stance. She finally responding, taking his concerns more seriously now. "Why do we let him sell ATMs under Stafford's sponsorship then? Isn't that a security risk?"

Josh let out a heavy breath and crossed his arms defensively, resting his cup on his arm. "He was an ex-cop when I first met him, a little down on his luck, but nothing major, so I gave him a break." He shifted his weight, uncrossed his arms and softened his tone. "Look, I'm not saying he's a criminal or a security risk to the company. I'm just saying I'm not sure he should be hanging around here all the time and I certainly don't think you should be alone with him. I'm just worried that maybe his drinking is getting out of control and that we need to watch him, like I said, we have enough trouble to clean up around here."

Rachel took a quick sip, considering his words a moment before waving him off with a light smile. "Well, you don't have to worry about me, besides I'm not in any hurry to hang around the oaf anyway." She confirmed confidently as she walked around him and towards her office. Josh caught up and grabbed her arm to stop her. She turned and gritted her teeth; she didn't like to be grabbed.

He let go of her arm, but moved in closer, looking around quickly before he spoke. "I probably shouldn't tell you this, but Blaze showed up at my place last night, drunk out of his mind, ranting about money and demanding access he shouldn't have. He even tried to threaten me for it." She eyed him skeptically, but she unconsciously took a step back. "I'm not trying to scare you. I'm just saying that being alone with him is a risk I don't think you should be taking. Who knows what a bitter ex-cop is capable of when they're drinking that much. Just watch yourself."

Rachel considered Josh's words carefully. She rubbed her tired dry eyes and let out a small sigh. "Thank you for your concern Josh, but I'm sure he's not a threat to me." Though as she said it, she felt a strange prickling sensation crawl up her back. She shook it off and gave him a tired smile and lifted her shoulders as she inhaled deeply. "Besides, I can take pretty good care of myself." She added confidently as she turned and sauntered into her office. Josh didn't look happy, but he didn't follow her inside either.

"At least call me when he's here, I need to watch his movements within the company. We have some very sensitive accounts that have heard what happened and we don't need to lose their business on top of everything else." She nodded and Josh headed off in a huff towards the warehouse.

Rachel sat down at her desk and scanned through some of the thirty new emails that had arrived since she went to get her much needed coffee. She took another swig from her coffee, draining it. She stared into her mug to confirm her fears. It was empty. She set it down, looked over at her flashing voice mail light and sighed. "This is going to be a very long day." She complained to the empty doorway then she let her head drop forward on to her desk and groaned softly.

"That's never a good sign."

Rachel bolted upright at the unexpected but familiar and welcome voice. "Amy! What are you doing here?"

"That's a nice greeting." Amy said taking a quick look around before shutting Rachel's door and sauntering over to the seat in front of her. "I came to see if you're still alive." She giggled. "We got another call for a new receptionist, seems they're dropping like flies around here, I thought I'd better come by in person."

Rachel joined Amy's infectious laughter as she took in her friend's newest look. Amy had added brightly colored hot pink streaks to her look and a few wild curls. "I see you couldn't take the demure look for very long." Amy replied with a simple shrug and shook her head softly, causing the curls to bounce around her face as if showing off her latest look to her best friend. "So what are you doing here anyway, not that I don't love the break, but you could have sent another replacement by phone." Rachel eyed her suspiciously. "You're checking up on me aren't you?" She tried to sound reproachful, but her laughter cracked voice gave her intent away.

Amy let her delicate laugh resonate with Rachel's for a minute before finally answering her. "I came because I'm worried about you." Rachel let out a chuckle. Amy leaned forward, her expression grim. "I'm serious Rach. The police called the agency and I have to say it kind of freaked me out. This is much more serious than you led me to believe. The guy they are after for murdering that tech is not only still on the loose, but he worked for this company. I came to get you out of here."

"And just in the nick of time too, I badly need a decent cup of coffee." Rachel laughed off Amy's concern and grabbed her purse as if getting ready to leave.

"I meant permanently." Amy said; her voice stoic.

Rachel studied Amy; she wasn't backing down and she wasn't returning Rachel's smile. She set her purse down and sat back in her chair; her expression one of surprise. "You actually want me to quit? What about the contract?"

"Forget the damn contract. Let them find their own scapegoat." Amy kept her voice low, but her hands were animated.

Rachel leaned forward, her arms resting on her desk. "Scapegoat? What's that supposed to mean? What aren't you telling me Amy?"

"What aren't I telling you?" Amy replied, emphasizing the word I, her expression one of shock. "You are the one who didn't tell me the murderer worked here. And you failed to tell me they were sticking devices into the ATMs to steal money from people's accounts." Amy crossed her arms and continued. "You also neglected to tell me they are looking into your background; they were particularly focused on whether or not you knew that junkie that tried to kill you on your last job." Amy uncrossed her arms and leaned in closer. "The company's probably trying to cover their asses so they don't get shut down because of the thefts. I'm worried about you, what else didn't you tell me?"

Rachel sat back and smiled. "You worry too much Aims. They're checking into everyone's background, it's their job. Someone was murdered; they have to be thorough. It doesn't mean I'm being used as a scapegoat or that I'm even as suspect. It just means their investigating all avenues." Amy looked doubtful, but Rachel continued. Her posture relaxed and her smile gentle. "What did you mean when you said sticking devices into the ATMs? I don't remember seeing anything else in the journals." Rachel was staring off in the distance, lost in thought.

"What journals? I have no idea what you're talking about, the police said something about a skimming device used to read account numbers being in that ATM the body was found in. I don't know, they didn't have anything specific about it, it wasn't a complete device, but clearly there is a lot more going on than you told me."

Amy realized Rachel was only half listening to her, lost in thought. She snapped her fingers in front of her. "Hello? Earth to Rach?" Rachel turned her attention back to Amy and nodded, so she continued. "I don't think it's a good idea for you to be working here. Don't think just because you're a hard worker that this company wouldn't throw anyone they had to the wolves if it saved their business. Particularly that Josh Tanner, I don't trust anyone that smiles that much."

"That's only because you haven't met Blaze yet." Rachel

mumbled sarcastically.

"Blaze?" Amy's expression instantly became less concerned and more interested.

Rachel ignored her friends probing gaze and pressed on. "Don't worry about it. The police are just asking everyone questions. Yes someone was murdered, but they know who did it and they'll arrest him and everything will be back to normal. As for someone putting devices in the ATMs that's news to me, but I'm sure the company is not a part of it. It's probably why Miguel was killed in some kind of double cross or something." Amy was about to protest, but Rachel cut her off. "What if I promise to get out the moment I feel like I'm in any real danger? Would that make you feel better?"

Amy rolled her eyes. "Like you'd stop long enough to sense any trouble before you're knee deep in it." Rachel chuckled, but didn't argue. After a bit more sulking Amy eventually gave in. "It's pointless to argue with you anyway." She threw her hands up in surrender. "Besides, if I kept it up, you'd probably take it as a dare and stay just to spite me."

Rachel laughed. "I'm not that bad." Amy cocked her head and crossed her arms. Rachel Shrugged. "Okay, maybe I can be a little stubborn."

"A little?" Amy chortled.

"Fine, a lot." Rachel gave in and they broke into easy laughter.

"If I can't convince you to go, I'd better head out of here myself." She rose from her seat. "I have another receptionist to locate." She smiled and reached for the door. She turned her head towards Rachel before she opened it. "Although I'm not sure I want to send another employee in here." Rachel shot her a scolding look. "I'm just saying." Amy added with a smile as she headed out. Rachel watched her go and automatically grabbed her mug for a sip. She frowned and dropped her head back on her desk. She forgot it was still empty. She let out a heavy sigh and groaned into her desk.

"That bad already?"

Rachel jumped again at the now familiar gruff voice. She scowled. "What are you doing here?"

"That's a nice greeting. Guess you don't want this coffee I brought then either?" He was grinning as turned to leave.

Rachel's eyes lit up and she called out stopping him in his tracks. "Blaze!" He smiled and turned back around. "Don't be so hasty, since you already have them."

He held up the two large coffee's up high so she could see them. She stared longingly at them. "Nice to see you too." He winked and walked her coffee into her waiting hands.

She didn't take her eyes off it until she'd taken a long deep sip. When the hot liquid stimulated her senses, she leaned back, closed her eyes and smiled. He let out a grunt for a laugh, took a long sip of his and nodded knowingly. "Apparently nothing a coffee can't fix."

She opened her eyes and stared at him. Her face was starting to get its color back and she was beginning to feel more alert. She relaxed into the back of her chair and gave him a smirk as she cradled her coffee. "So is this a bribe for me not to call in the dogs or just to obtain some more information?"

Blaze clutched his chest and winced. "Ouch." He said as he stumbled over to sit in the chair that Amy had sat in just moments before. She rolled her eyes at his dramatic display. He quickly subjects. "You're popular this morning; I'm beginning to suspect you'll take coffee from just about anyone." She gave him a puzzled look. Blaze wiggled in the chair for emphasis. "Still warm."

"Ah." She replied nodding her head.

Blaze waited for her to provide an explanation of her previous visitor. Instead, she studied him over her cup as she slowly sipped the sweet rich liquid. After it was clear she wouldn't elaborate further he finally spoke. "So what's this calling in the dogs business?" He asked a look of mild interest on his face.

She tried not to choke on her coffee as she held back a laugh. She watched him carefully as she debated how to respond. "I'm to call Josh if you show up here."

Blaze arched his brow and cracked a grin that was almost wide enough to be considered a smile. He set his now empty coffee cup on the corner of her desk, sat back and folded his arms loosely behind his head. He gave her a slight nod and a wink. "Better give him a call then. I wouldn't want to be the source of trouble with your boss." She glared at him; her brow furrowed and lips pursed. "What?" He added with an innocent shrug. "I'm just looking out for you."

She tried not to choke on her coffee. "Right." Blaze's grin looked more devious as he tried to act above suspicion. "Well you can wipe that smirk off your face, because I'm not calling him."

"Why Not?" He asked, unfolding his arms.

"Because you'd like it too much if I did." She replied without a second of hesitation.

Blaze chuckled, but he didn't deny it, so she nodded smugly and gulped down the last of her coffee. She tried to squeeze one more sip but when it came up empty she frowned. Then she locked eyes with him, staring in silence. When she finally spoke, her tone was direct and even. "So what kind of information are you trying to collect from me today?"

Blaze sat in stunned silence, as he searched her now very alert and observant eyes. After a moment, he gave her a lopsided grin. "Not your first cup of coffee I see." He gave her an easy shrug and continued. "What makes you think I want anything?"

She tilted her head and raised her brow. "Because you don't do anything without a reason."

"Ouch." He placed his hand over his heart again as he started to protest, but Rachel cut him off.

"Blaze." She grunted giving him a scolding look. He broke into a full grin, but didn't reply. She sighed in annoyance and shifted in her seat. He let out a chuckle, not trying to hide his amusement. She scowled and reached for the phone.

"I gather from your cheery disposition that your other visitor didn't come bearing gifts too? Guess he doesn't know you as well as I do."

"She." She corrected nonchalantly. "And nice try." She finished moving her hand away from the phone. "I'm surprised to see you so chipper this morning; I assumed you'd still be sleeping off your little binge." Blaze's familiar scowl returned. A devilish glint sparkled in her eyes. "Josh told me about your little visit to him." Blaze grunted and she grinned. "He was worried about me being alone with you."

“Worried?” e replied sarcastically. “He’s just pissed that I interrupted his little ‘play’ date.” He lowered his voice to a hard menacing tone and leaned towards her. “As for me sleeping it off, you can think what you want on that, but I thought you were smart enough to put two and two together. Apparently you don’t look at your watch when you’re dropped off or maybe you think I had a secret flask with us all night.” He stood up and turned to storm out but was stopped in his tracks as he almost mowed over Josh, who was now standing in her doorway.

“Everything alright in here?” Josh asked with a playful lilt in his voice as he looked from Blaze to Rachel and back again.

Blaze scowled. “Yes everything’s alright, why wouldn’t it be?” Blaze’s voice was thick with his barely contained anger. His stare was intense and his muscles were taut beneath his fitted shirt. Josh shot Rachel his school boy grin and a nod as he placed a friendly arm around Blaze’s shoulders and began to walk him out of the doorway.

“Why don’t we go to my office to talk.”

Blaze scowled at him and grunted. “Why would I want to do that?”

Josh dropped his arm and gave him a friendly pat on the shoulder and continued to flash his all too familiar grin. “You seem upset. I want to chat about it. I certainly don’t want one of my best investors leaving the building upset now do I?” He looked back at Rachel and gave her a wink. “I’m sure Rachel has a lot of work to do, so I thought we could talk in my office. Where we could sit down and relax a little. It’s more comfortable there anyway.”

Blaze seemed to tower over Josh, Blaze’s severely foul mood

gave him an added air of size and strength. Josh's demeanor did however suggest a confidence that made it seem he was hiding an equal intenseness he could call upon if necessary. The two men continued to stare each other down. Josh maintained his oddly casual grin and Blaze's scowl seemed etched on; neither one giving up their stance.

Rachel watched them with an odd mixture of amusement and dismay. She found herself with an odd grin on her face. It was like falling and knowing you're hurt, but you laugh anyway. Although she desperately wanted them to leave and give her some peace and quiet, but she couldn't turn away either. She immediately had images of school boys facing down on a school yard over who had the bigger 'stick'. She quickly covered her mouth as a wayward giggle escaped. Neither man looked at her, but Blaze's posture stiffened as if he had heard. He finally acquiesced and gave Josh a slight nod and marched off; Josh in tow. Leaving Rachel to only imagine what they could possibly talk to each other about but being too happy about having her peace and quiet back to care.

CHAPTER 20

“What kind of bullshit games are you playing here Josh?”

“Wait, hang on just a minute.” Josh tried to quiet Blaze down as he rushed to shut his office door. “Can you keep it down just a bit?” He added as he walked back towards him. “There’s enough trouble around here, we don’t need to add to the chaos.”

Blaze took a firm stance in the middle of Josh’s office and glared at him. “So do you want to explain yourself?” Josh stared at him innocently protesting with his expression. Blaze had no patience for this. “You asked me to help you investigate your little ‘problem’ and now you’re playing games. Suddenly you want to be called when I come in to the office? You better start explaining yourself and it better be good or you better start watching your back.”

Josh clenched his jaw; his smile stiffened. His eyes flashed with anger briefly before he gained control. He took a deep breath, walked over to his desk and sat on the edge of it. He lowered his head and relaxed his shoulders. “Look man, what can I say I overreacted a bit.” Blaze crossed his arms, unimpressed. Josh lifted his hands in a half shrug, half surrender motion. “Okay, I overreacted a lot, but you have to understand the stress I’m under. I’m trying to keep this business going, keeping our accounts happy, all while trying to counteract the damage of from this business with the ATM.”

“You mean the murder.” Blaze studied Josh as he spoke.

Josh cocked his head and shot him a confused look, then waved his hands dismissively and continued. "Yes, of course, very tragic. My point is, I'm just trying to keep things together here and I don't want to worry about my employees mucking about making things worse."

"I'm not an employee, and I'm supposed to be making things worse?"

"That's not what I meant, but you are encouraging them." Josh stood up.

"Them?" Blaze sighed impatiently, his scowl seemed to etch deeper into his jaw.

"Fine, Rachel. You are encouraging her to go running around stirring up trouble, looking into things that she knows nothing about, when she should be doing her job." Josh ran his fingers through his hair and sighed.

Blaze remained immovable. "And she's not doing that?"

Josh sighed and threw up his hands in surrender, walked around his desk and sat down. "Of course she is, it's just..."

"It's just that you'd rather she mind her own business." Blaze said, cutting him off. Josh nodded agreement. "And I mind mine." He added, Josh didn't reply.

Blaze sighed again, his face softened as much as it did most days and he let his hands drop to his sides. "I get it. You're stressed." He started as he walked toward Josh. He leaned forward, setting his hands on his desk. His eyes staring directly into Josh's. "But don't think for a moment that you can play me Josh. Remember, I don't work for you and I most certainly don't owe you anything, so you can stop pretending I do. I suggest you be a good boy, do your job and don't you ever speak to me like that again. If you do that, you won't have any trouble from me."

Josh seemed to leap out of his chair and puffing up his chest as he did. His cheeks were red and there wasn't a sign of his smooth charm. He opened his mouth to retort, but stopped as Blaze stood up and matched his posture. The two men stared each other down while they sized each other up. Josh quickly came to some realization and his easy grin returned. "Blaze let's not get worked up over a simple misunderstanding. I tell you what, next time we're out; the beer's on me."

Blaze took in Josh's smile, shook his head and gave him a grunt. "I've got some appointments to keep." He said and turned to leave, before adding one more thing on. "And watch the rumors you spread about my drinking habits, you have a few you might not want spread around either." Without another word he stalked out.

"Great, love those deals you bring in." Josh called after him, but the moment Blaze was out of sight, his smile morphed into a sneer. He grabbed his phone and quickly placed a call. As soon as the man on the other end picked up he spoke. "It's Josh. We need to talk."

*****

Rachel hadn't weeded through many emails before she was rubbing her eyes so much she finally had to stand up and stretch. She stared at the doodling she had done when Amy was in earlier. She had drawn a dollar sign and circled it over and over, beside it she had a single word "skimming" with a question mark. She frowned, grabbed her mug and headed towards the kitchen. She had to make a quick grab to recover it when she collided with the indignant Blaze who was storming his way out from Josh's office.

"First you bring me coffee, now you're trying to keep me away from more of it." She teased as she dusted herself off. Blaze didn't even offer her a grunt. She stepped back, crossed her arms and looked him over. She cocked her head but didn't say anything further.

He sighed and relaxed his shoulders a bit at her reproach. He tried to control his voice as he replied. "Sorry."

She nodded and offered a sympathetic smile, she knew where he had just been. She didn't press him on how things had gone with Josh. "What's skimming?"

Blaze shook his head in confusion. "Huh?"

"Skimming, from the ATMs, how is that done exactly?"

Blaze's tension seemed to drop away from his stature and his face cracked enough that it looked like the start of a grin. "Planning something I should be worried about?"

Rachel let out a chuckle, more of a chortle really and gave him a gentle slug on his shoulder. "No, just curious is all." Blaze raised his eyebrow and cocked his head expectantly. She shifted her weight. "Someone mentioned it." He stood firm, crossed his arms and continued to stare. She sighed and shrugged. "Okay, so I was told that the police were asking about it in their investigation."

"Told by who exactly?"

"The woman from the temp agency I work for. She was here this morning, worried about me. She told me the police were asking her questions and she said they mentioned it regarding the ATM we found... Miguel in."

He relaxed his stance and looked off into the distance. "Hmm." He uncrossed his arms and shifted his weight. "Interesting."

"Interesting? That's all I get?" She said, exasperation dripping from her voice. His expression turned into a full grin as he nodded. She let out a loud sigh and tapped her foot impatiently.

He chuckled. "I have to check something out first, but I'll get back to you with an answer to your question after that." She frowned. "I promise." He added with a two finger salute. She stalked off in a huff to get her coffee. Blaze cracked a grin and made his way out the building.

*****

Rachel started to pour herself coffee but after taking one whiff, she dumped the pot in the sink and reached for the coffee grounds. No sooner had she got them down, than reached up and she put them back. She quickly placed her cup in the dishwasher and rushed back to her office to grab her stuff. She didn't bother to shut down her computer or forward her phone. Her eyes were bright and alert and her step was hurried as she decided to sneak out of the office.

Having successfully avoided Josh seeing her, she ducked out of sight as deftly made her way out past the Coralene's crew and out through the empty receptionist area. Luckily with all their work, no one was covering the front. She chuckled and shook her head at the abandoned post. Amy hadn't been able to fill it yet. The last two replacements that had been in were very low caliber, clearly Amy had been sending in her disposables now, knowing there was no point at pulling from her top list and burning those resources.

She stopped, pushed open the front door and looked around. The lot was only half full, fewer visitors had been coming around and more staff had called in sick. She scanned it for signs of Blaze's truck. She frowned and stepped out into the lot. She quickly ducked when she saw his truck pulling out from the back parking lot. She raced to jump in her car and start it up. She covered her mouth and looked around quickly out of reflex when the tires squealed.

She kept her eyes glued to the back of his truck as she raced to follow. Her breathing increased into rapid short breaths as she tried to keep from slamming her foot on the gas to catch up to him. She tried to keep as far away from him as she could and crossed her fingers as if sheer will would keep him from noticing her unmistakable car. She followed him like that for about a half an hour before he finally slowed. The truck was pulling into the driveway of a run-down house when she neared. She pulled over, parking down the street opposite the house where she could still see the truck and the front of the house but wasn't right in front of it.

She ducked down in her car as the truck cab door opened. Her mouth hung open and her body froze. It wasn't Blaze she had followed. In fact she didn't even recognize this man. In her rush to get out she hadn't realized it was a different black truck. She quickly scanned the area and frowned. She realized she had spent more time concentrating on not losing him than paying attention to where she was going and now she had no idea where she was. She started to panic. Her focus was instantly sharper as adrenaline raced through her. She examined the truck. Now she could tell that it wasn't new at all and was nothing like his truck. In fact it was probably about 10 years older than Blaze's and had a lot more scuffs and dings. She looked back at the house and laughed nervously, then ducked further and covered her mouth when the man turned her way.

She sat still for a few seconds more, till curiosity got the better of her and she snuck a peak at the man she had accidentally followed. He hadn't seemed to have spotted her so she looked closer at him. She noted his tightly cropped hair, his tattoo laden arms and his dead stare. He walked to the back of his truck, stopped and looked around. Rachel ducked down again. She held her breath then slowly peaked up again. He was opening the back tailgate and struggling to pull something out. When she realized what it was, or rather who it was she stifled a gasp and dove as far down as she could go. It was the bound and weakly struggling body of Patrick, the technician that everyone was looking for. She had only met him once, but despite that and the obvious bruises he was still unmistakable.

Rachel continued to crouch as low as she could. She looked around and noticed her purse tossed on the far side of the passenger seat. She slowly stretched out her arm as far as it could reach, but she still couldn't reach it. She leaned back, dejected and bumped her head on the steering wheel, then immediately froze. Silence, luckily she hadn't hit the horn.

She dropped her head down and shook it on the seat as if to mimic a scream without actually screaming. Then she carefully crept and stretched forward until she was finally able to reach her purse. She put it on the floor and slowly unzipped it, as if the slightest sound would give her away despite how far away the truck and the men were. Her breathing was labored and her senses sharp. She slipped out her cell phone and dialed as quickly as she could.

"Hello?" She whispered. There was silence at the other end. "Hello?" She whispered again, her voice straining to be as loud as she could safely make it. Nothing. She pulled the phone away and looked at it. No Service. She let out a quiet "Grr". She slowly stretched the phone to different positions around the car to see if that somehow could grab a signal. No Service. She had to cover her mouth to prevent herself from screaming in frustration.

She threw the phone on the floor, ducking instinctively when it crashed onto the exposed metal at the bottom of her passenger door and made a loud clanging sound. She held her breath and froze. She didn't hear anything, so she slowly peaked out the window. No one was there. She looked around the street. Empty. She looked back at the house, it was closed up and the truck was empty.

She sat up a little further and took a longer look around the street. Not only was it deserted, but it looked like the only people still left in the neighborhood had simply squatted out the original occupants. The house the truck was parked in front of was run down. Two of the windows were boarded up and the remnants of paint on it looked more like rot then color, but it still looked fairly solid which made it the most well kept home on the block.

She looked around self-consciously. Her car would have fit in perfectly except for the fact that it was directly across from the house and it was occupied. She needed to get out of there fast. She took a deep breath, and sat all the way up. She threw her car in gear and slowly drove off, keeping a close eye on the house. When she got around corner she turned right and stopped, out of view of the house. She rifled through her purse and found a pen and quickly wrote down the name of the street and what she remembered of the truck's license plate on the back of a gum wrapper.

Then she drove on, taking turn here and there when she found a road that looked like a major through way she took it. She drove like that for about 20 minutes until she managed to stumble into an area she recognized. She immediately pulled the car over and dug her cell phone out from the bottom of the passenger side floor. She tried turning it on. It was dead. She shook it and tried again, nothing. "Damn it." She flipped it over, the batter case was cracked and the battery had fallen out. She shook her head, dropped the phone on the seat and headed home. She'd have to call from there, she wasn't about to search around for one of the last remaining pay phones and get lost again.

CHAPTER 21

Rachel inhaled sharply when she saw the white pick-up as she rounded the corner to her apartment. Every muscle in her body jumped and she slammed on her breaks. She sat frozen, staring in disbelief, her heart pounding wildly. She reached for the gearshift and threw it in to reverse but before she could pull away the truck door opened and the driver stepped out. She threw the car in park, expelled the breath she had been holding and fell back limp against her seat.

Blaze stepped out of his truck and stared at her. She didn't move so he strolled over to her window. She was holding a hand to her heart. Her breathing was labored. He placed his hand on her open window and leaned in. "Remind me never to drive with you." He complained.

Rachel stared at him, stunned, catching her breath. She looked at his truck. It was newly polished. Not one ding; not a patch of rust, couldn't be more than a year old. She started to smile, but in the adrenaline release it quickly turned into a laugh. She looked over at Blaze, he was starting to scowl. She rested her head against the back of her seat and let the laughter flow until she held her sides in pain. Her laughter choked off and she tried to catch her breath. Blaze stood up, crossed his arms and clenched his jaw.

"I'm sorry." She started to explain as she turned and pointed towards his truck. "It's just when I saw your truck just now I thought he had somehow found..." She let her voice trail off.

She looked at him and smiled. Blaze cocked his eyebrow and waited. "I'm very relieved it's you."

"Who did you think I was?"

She took a deep breath before answering him. "I thought you were the guy who took Patrick." Blaze cocked his head and furrowed his brow. "That new technician at Stafford." She rattled off as an explanation.

"The one they want for murder?" He asked, studying her carefully. She nodded. He turned to look at his truck, then back at Rachel. "and you thought that because of my truck?" She nodded and looked around, avoiding his stare. "Rachel." He said in a low voice. He continued slowly and purposefully. "Why would you think someone took Patrick? And more importantly, why would you think that guy would be waiting for you here?"

"I… I'm not sure I could explain." She stammered.

Blaze uncrossed his arms and placed both hands on her door frame and leaned ominously close. "Try."

She took a deep breath then blurted it out almost incoherently. "I accidentally saw some guy dragging him out of a white truck, kind of like yours so when I saw your truck I was worried that he saw me and figured out where I lived and came to find me." She suddenly sat up straight and was about to take her car out of park. "If you don't mind that's a prime spot I see and I've got to make a phone call, so you might as well just be on your way now." She tried to push his hands off the car but he didn't budge. Her eyes narrowed and she glared at his hands gripping her doorway. "If you want to keep those attached, I suggest you move them."

Blaze moved his hands and took a step back. "Be my guest." He motioned her forward with a sweeping gesture of his arm.

"Thanks." She whispered between clenched teeth. Then she threw her car in drive and lurched forward into her target spot. The fact that she had come home early enough to get a spot out front and not have to park in the paid lot down the street was less than satisfying at the moment. She decided to fume about that as well when she got out and found Blaze had already parked and was standing outside her car expecting to come up with her. She glared at him and he smiled. Her eyes narrowed and she stalked off towards her apartment.

"You might as well tell me everything now. I'll just find out later anyway." He said calmly as he easily kept stride with her.

She stopped, causing him to stop to avoid colliding with her. She clenched her jaw, increasing the pout in her lips. She glared at him in silence for a moment. "And just how will you do that?" She asked glancing at him. He shrugged and she threw up her hands in surrender. She let out a loud sigh. "Forget it." She said as she started walking again. "I don't even want to know."

"If you must know I was following you." She blurted out when she reached her apartment door. She unlocked it, but as she reached for the handle Blaze stopped her. He opened the door and inserted himself between the open door and her apartment. She looked up at him, her brow furrowed. "Oh don't look so surprised, like you wouldn't do the same." She affirmed as she opened the door further and pushed past him, leaving him to close the door behind them.

"Clearly you weren't following me if you thought I was someone else." His tone was slightly mocking, slightly annoyed.

She sighed heavily, dropped her stuff and plopped down on the couch. She leaned her head back and closed her eyes. "No, clearly it wasn't you, but I thought it was at the time. After I saw you at work, I decided I was tired of being kept from the truth, so I followed you from the parking lot. Well at least what I thought was your white truck. When I got there, instead of you, I found some guy I'd never seen before pull a beaten up Patrick from the back."

"From where?" He asked as he stood over her.

She rubbed her temples and took several deep breaths. "Some rundown house on some more rundown block somewhere downtown." She let her hands fall to her sides and remained quiet, looking as if she would fast fall asleep.

Blaze shifted his weight and crossed his arms impatiently. "And you're sure it was Patrick?" His voice was gruffer than he meant it.

"Quite." She whispered and nodded faintly.

"Rachel." Blaze insisted as he gently shook her. She jumped, she had nodded off. "Did you call the police?"

She shook her head, she was disoriented. "No, broke my cell phone." She straightened herself up and rubbed her face.

"When was this?" He prodded as her senses returned.

"Maybe about 45 minutes ago." She mumbled. Blaze scowled and grunted. "What?" She defended. "I was a little lost, it took me a while to find my way home."

"Great. I suppose you can't find your way back either."

"Probably not." Blaze grunted again, stood up and started pacing. "But I kind of figured I wouldn't have to if I gave the address to the police."

Blaze stopped and swung around to look at her. "You have the address?" He said dumbfounded.

"Uh, Yeah!" She replied matter-of-factly.

"Give it to me." He demanded. She snapped her head up, her eyes wide and she inhaled sharply. He took a deep breath and clenched down, trying to control his reactions. "Please." He asked in a calmer voice.

She studied him closely, inwardly debating the pros and cons of handing it over. After a moment she sighed and rummaged through her purse to recover the scribbled note to herself. She slowly handed it over to him.

He squinted as he read over the note. He looked up at her, then back at the note. "Hand writing isn't your strong suite." He complained. She pursed her lips into a scowl. He shrugged. "Sorry, you're right, at least you got it. Thanks." He nodded, turned on his heels and headed towards the door.

In a sudden burst of energy, she jumped up and lunged at the door to block it. "Wait just one minute. Where do you think you are going?" She demanded.

"Get out of the way." He warned.

"I will not!" She said as she puffed up her chest and set her shoulders back. "Not until you tell me what you are planning on doing."

He sighed and dropped his shoulders. "I don't have time for this."

"For what? We need to tell the police about this."

"I'll take care of that." He said trying his best to stave off his irritation.

"And what I am I supposed to do?" She demanded, her voice cracking slightly.

"Wait here."

"W... Wait here?" She stuttered, stunned.

"Yes." He easily directed her aside and stalked out.

She stared after him, her mouth agape, her face flushed. Her frustration at his total dismissal left her momentarily lost for what to do next. Her mind raced over the events. She quickly grabbed up her keys and was about to race after him when her home phone rang. She was tempted to leave it; she looked back and forth from the door to the phone, it rang again. She let out a frustrated sigh, shut the door and ran for the phone.

"Hello." She answered out of breath.

"Rachel?"

She hesitated, after a second a smile of recognition crossed her face. "Josh. I'm sorry about that you caught me on my way out."

"On your way out where?"

"Uh." She stopped and searched for what to say.

"Is something wrong?"

The tension released from her body and she placed her keys on the counter beside her. She grabbed a pen and began to scribble as she spoke. "No, Josh. Everything's fine. I just needed to write something down before I forgot it."

"I see. You get that done?"

She smiled as she re-read the duplicate of the note she had given to Blaze just a few minutes before. "Yes, thank you, I've got it." She set the pen down and rested against the counter. "So what can I do for you Josh?"

"I was just calling to check up on you. You left work so early and I've been calling you on your cell for a while with no answer. I had HR pull your records to look up your home phone."

"Oh yeah, sorry about that, my cell battery died. I came home to try to finish up some reports." She lied. "I wasn't getting anything done at the office with all the interruptions today."

"Oh, I understand. It's just when no one knew where you had gone I got a little worried."

"No one told you. Hmm, that's strange, I could have sworn I mentioned it." She bit her lip as she lied again.

"No, no one said anything. Well, I was just checking in with you. I don't want you to worry, you don't have to bring the report in today, you can bring it in with you tomorrow."

"Huh?" She replied with a puzzled look on her face.

"You mentioned you were on your way out, I just assumed you were coming back here to drop your report off."

"Uh, right, that." She bit her lip again and straightened to shift her weight. "No, actually I was just going after Blaze."

"Blaze was there again? Are you alright, what did he want?"

She squinted as if in pain and slumped back against the counter. "Oh yes, everything is fine. I don't want you to worry about that. It wasn't work related.

"Oh. I see." Josh replied coldly.

She pulled the phone from her ear and hit herself lightly on the head with it. Shaking her head in disbelief with how badly she was doing. She tried to clear the fog from her mind, her lack of sleep was catching up with her. "No, well you see I had a bit of car trouble. At the office," she added quickly. "And he helped me get home. It took a while to get it going and he just left. I was rushing out to try to catch him, I forgot to thank him." She pulled the phone away again and rolled her eyes as the pathetic excuse. She put the receiver to her ear in the middle of his sentence.

"...could have asked me. I really wouldn't have minded."

"I appreciate that, I didn't want to bother you and he volunteered when he ran into me in the parking lot. I figured, what harm could it do?"

"You'd be surprised." His reply was barely audible.

She picked up the scrap of paper she had just written on. She tried to hide her anxiousness to get off the phone. "Well he's gone now. Thank you for checking in on me, I really appreciate that. I'll make sure next time I need to leave early that I tell you myself, that way I know you'll get the message. I'm very sorry I worried you."

"Like I said, no problem, but I hate to leave you stuck for tomorrow. Why don't I swing by there and take a look at your car. I wouldn't want you getting stranded again on your way to work tomorrow."

"Oh Josh, that's very sweet of you, but I'm sure its fine." She shifted her weight and squeezed the receiver.

"Nonsense." He said, cutting her off. "You've been through a lot, it's the least I can do for such a valuable employee. I'll be over there in a flash. In fact I'm not far from there now."

Rachel caught her breath. "Oh."

"Yes, well like I said, I was starting to worry. I thought it best to swing by myself, just to be sure. I'm calling you from my car now."

Rachel spun around to look at the door as if she expected to see Josh standing there. "How thoughtful." She replied weakly. She bit her lip and held a her breath. "So how far away are you?" She tried to make her voice sound as calm as possible.

"Well I'm not completely sure. I've never been to your place." He said almost darkly. "But from the directions I printed off, I'd say I'm literally just a couple blocks away."

"Great." She said, her voice barely audible. "I'll see you soon." She slowly hung up the phone, barely noticing as he said goodbye.

After the call registered she raced out her front door and down hall. She leaned over the balcony and looked down at the parking lot. There was no sign of Blaze's truck. She searched down the street as far as she could see from her vantage point in both directions. No truck. She let out a heavy sigh of relief, walked back into her apartment and put on a pot of coffee. She needed to wake up and clear her head.

CHAPTER 22

As she waited for the pot to brew, she pulled the pieces of her cell phone from her purse and tried to put it back together. The battery wouldn't stay in. So she sighed and put it aside. Then she went back to the kitchen to prep her mug; Heavy cream, extra sugar. She smiled as the welcome aroma filled the room. She could feel her senses begin to awaken in anticipation.

Before the pot had finished brewing, there was a loud knock at her door. She jumped, then laughed nervously at herself as she went to answer the door. She took a calming breath before opening the door to the waiting Josh. She smiled politely and hesitantly stepped aside to let him in. He passed by her and entered her living room. She shivered unconsciously.

"Coffee." He said as he inhaled the aroma.

"I just brewed a pot." She said, then after a slight pause she added, "Would you like a cup?"

"Sure." He answered as he followed her into the kitchen.

She pulled out a mug for him and filled them both. "Anything in it?"

"Just sugar thanks." Josh smiled.

She plopped a teaspoon in his and over at him quizzically. He waved his hand so she put the sugar down, stirred his cup and handed it to him. Then she stirred hers and took a sip. She smiled politely at him over her mug. After a few more awkward sips she broke the silence. "I really appreciate you coming by to check on things, but as I said, the car seems to be working now that Blaze boosted it."

Josh placed his mug down and leaned back against the counter. His school boy grin plastered on his face. "I told you, it's no problem. I wouldn't want you getting stuck again, besides I was in the area. Shall we take a quick look at that car?"

"Ah yeah." She straightened up, smiling. She placed her treasured mug down, anxious to get underway. "Right this way." She said a little too eagerly.

Josh puffed up his chest. "Appreciation like that and you might be able to get me to do almost anything for you." He winked. She swallowed to choke back a groan, then plastered a sweet smile on and led him down to her car.

Josh had her pop the hood. He poked around under there for about five minutes before closing it down. He smiled at her through the windshield and nodded for her to come out. "Mind if I wash up?" She nodded, deftly slipped out the open window and walked with him back up to her apartment.

She pointed him to the sink in the kitchen. "I'll grab you a towel." She said, leaving him to wash up as she slipped away. She returned with a small hand towel just as he was trying to air dry his hands. He took her offer and switched to the towel to finish the job. When he was done he set it on the counter, turned to face her and leaned against the sink smiling.

"So what do you think is wrong with it?" She asked feigning interest. She tried not to stare at the water that had splashed onto her scribbled note that she had left earlier when she had made the coffee.

"Well it looks like your problem is simply engine dirt, happens with a car that old." He winked. "I'd say all you need is an engine flush."

She nodded and found herself glancing again towards the note. She quickly looked up at him and smiled. "I guess I'll be booking it into the shop again soon. Well I really appreciate your help." She stood tall and shifted her weight to her other foot. "Wow." She said looking at her watch. "I didn't realize it was so late." She smiled, her glance drifting towards the note again.

"Oh it's no problem, but I don't want to keep you if you have somewhere you need to be."

She looked at him and smiled. "No, I was just going to head to bed early, make sure I'm bright and chipper for the morning." Josh studied her in silence for a moment, his grin almost turning into a leer as he gave her a once over.

"Well since it doesn't look like I'll be getting an invite this evening, I guess I'll be going."

Rachel's smile froze on her face. Her back stiffened. She remained silent. Her gaze shifted uncomfortably from Josh, to the doorway, back to Josh and then to the wet note.

Josh cleared his throat as he straightened up. He followed her gaze to the counter. "Oh dear, I've splashed water everywhere." He said as he turned and picked up the towel. "Well that's what you get when you invite a bachelor into your home." He let out a chuckle and started to mop it up.

Rachel rushed towards him. "Oh don't worry about it." She said, adding a nervous laugh in an attempt to sound casual. "Let me."

She reached for the towel, but Josh pulled it away.

"I wouldn't dream of it." He added as he reached over and blotted the paper dry. Then he picked it up and looked at it. He glanced at it and looked up at her. "Good as new." He said, handing it to her with a smile. He tossed the towel on the counter and casually tucked a hand in his front pocket. She let out the breath she had been holding and returned his smile.

"Thank you." She said looking around the room tentatively. Josh emptied his mug and rinsed it in the sink.

"Well, I guess I'll be heading out now." He said, his head cocked to the side.

Rachel smiled a little too eagerly. "Let me walk you out." She said straightening her posture. Josh took a step towards her, casually draped his arm around her shoulders and gave it a squeeze. She inhaled sharply. Josh's smile deepened.

"What a sweetheart." He whispered softly in her ear. She stiffly walked with him like that towards the front door. Then she dipped and pulled forward to free herself from his arm as she opened the door. Making it appear as if it was an accidental result of her having to struggle to open the door. She turned to face him, putting her back towards the door.

"Thank you again so much." She said, quickly extending her hand. Josh looked at it and smiled. He slipped both hands around hers and lifted it to his lips. He leaned down and gave it kiss. Then he slowly let her hand slide through his as he let it go.

"Enchanté!" He said as he straightened and gave her a wink. She stared, dumbfounded, she tried to offer a polite smile in return, but it was weak at best. He let out a soft laugh as he turned and headed out the door. She shivered involuntarily as she shut and bolted the door. She stood frozen for a minute, as if in shock. Then as if she was suddenly jarred awake, she spun on her heals and raced to the kitchen to recover the address.

She went to grab her keys, but stopped mid way. She looked at her watch. Over an hour had passed since Blaze had left. She sat on the couch and frowned. She stared at her phone. Her face suddenly lit up. "A little duct tape fixes everything." She muttered as she searched her kitchen drawers.

*****

Blaze studied the house from his truck. When he first arrived, he had parked around the corner and took a quick surveillance on foot. There was no movement that he could see, but the old white truck that Rachel had described was still parked at the house. He had found he was more exposed on foot. His large frame made his presence on the deserted streets too obvious, so he pulled his truck into the lot across the street. Then, using the overgrown shrubs for partial cover, he sat and watched through his factory tinted back windows.

He re-adjusted his positioning a few times to try to get a better view. "Damn it." He cursed as he searched through the entire glove compartment of his truck. His scowl turned to a grin as pulled an old pair of binoculars from the center console. "Much better." He muttered to himself as he focused in on the house. Nothing. No movement inside and no movement outside. A scowl etched across his face and he grunted. He turned and tried to get comfortable as he stretched out sideways in his truck cab. Then he sat back, waited and watched.

*****

"Pick up Damn it!" He cursed as he tried the number for the third time. After the voice mail answered again he hung up and tossed the phone on the seat beside him. He pressed down harder on the accelerator, juggling his phone as it rang. He frowned when he saw the number. He hit ignore and tossed it back on the seat, then ran a hand through his hair. "You better be home." He complained aloud as he threw a quick glance in his rearview mirror before changing lanes.

He slowed as he rounded the last corner. He clenched his jaw and shifted uneasily in his seat. He hated coming down here and usually avoided it at all costs. He wasn't happy he was forced to do it now. He kept his speed steady, but slow as he drove past the house, looking around as he past. He noticed the white truck in the driveway and gritted his teeth.

He drove to the end of the street and made a slow U-turn, stopped and looked around the street. He called the number one more time. Still no answer. He swore under his breath, drove closer to the house and stopped, not far from where Rachel had parked earlier that day. He slowly stepped out and after clicking on his car alarm, he headed up to the house. His pace was quick and determined.

*****

Blaze shot up, dropping his binoculars behind the seat as he did. "Shit." He said as he fumbled around to recover them. He hadn't expected someone to show up so soon. He figured he'd watch the place a while, check things out when it got a little darker and maybe call his old pals on the police force should it turn out Rachel wasn't making stuff up. What he hadn't planned on was someone showing up before he had a chance to even look around; especially when that someone was Josh Tanner. Blaze scowled, he didn't like being forced to move before he wanted to. He grabbed his cell phone and punched the numbers with disgust as he watched Josh disappear into the house.

"Its Blaze."

"Blaze? Good to hear from you man..."

Blaze sighed heavily and interrupted him. "521 Lincoln Avenue, in the heights. Get here, now." The other end of the phone line was silent. All Blaze could hear was some faint scribbling sounds. "I won't be sticking around." With that he hung up the phone. He knew he had maybe 20 min. Now he had to get into a position where he wouldn't be seen. He slipped quietly out of his truck and looked around the abandoned lot he had parked in. There was a lot of room behind the rotting burnt out house, but it heavy with over growth. He looked at his watch, won't be dark for another hour. He knew his movements could be easily seen if anyone was watching, but he had no choice.

He walked slowly, but purposefully directly to the house, on alert the entire way. He took the best side approach he could. As he passed behind the white truck he took a quick glance around, you couldn't see in the back cab, but he was sure no one was inside. He used the truck as cover as long as he could. Finally he was in the open he tucked himself close against the house. He wasn't worried about on lookers. The overgrowth had enough cover to hide him in case anyone still lived nearby and the squatters in this type of neighborhood weren't about stick around to be witnesses to anything.

He slowly checked out each window of the house, looking for any sightlines inside. There was no one he could see, the basement windows had been boarded up and the upstairs ones showed empty rooms. "Where were they?" He didn't like not knowing, this wasn't what he had in mind and now he didn't have much time. He suddenly froze. He heard faint shouting inside. He ducked down to try to gauge the location of the voices. They had to be coming from the back of the house. He looked at his watch, he didn't have time.

He scowled and ducked down to listen near one of the boarded up windows. It had a few rotted out spots and some light could be seen coming from inside. There wasn't enough for him to see inside, but he could hear the voices slightly more clearly. They must be in the back of the basement, he thought. The voices were still too muffled to make much out, aside from the odd word or phrase that was shouted louder than the rest. "Damn it." He cursed under his breath.

"...You can't tell them that!" Came one voice, could have been Josh, but it could have been anyone, he couldn't be sure.

"...ripping them off... get you killed... they'll know... my job..." Way to choppy, Blaze's scowl deepened, this was getting him nowhere, he couldn't tell who was saying what and certainly wasn't hearing enough to make sense of anything being said. "... dead man..." Blaze froze. The blast was unmistakable he had heard enough gun shots to know their sound. There was total silence now. He heard nothing, he had nothing and time was up.

"Shit." He cursed again in a barely audible voice. He quickly headed back to his truck, took a quick glance around and started it up. He put it in reverse and let the car roll down on its own momentum. His truck had a quiet idle that was barely audible, but he knew as soon as he stepped on the accelerator the low rumble would be enough to draw the curiosity of someone close. The house was only 20 feet from where he had to drive out. Once he had it in drive, he knew fast was his only option, but one wheel squealing would give him away.

He held his breath and relied on the trucks powerful acceleration to do its job. He didn't look back till he had rounded the corner. He stopped, rolled down his window and listened. He heard nothing. He immediately drove down the road and parked at an old gas station. It was closed, and too far to give him any kind of sight lines, but he could at least catch site of any strays coming in or leaving the area. This was the only way out if you didn't want to end up further in the neighborhood. He ducked down, listened and waited.

Within minutes he caught the unmistakable sight of several unmarked cars heading closer. He immediately caught sight of Josh's car heading out, couldn't have been more than seconds before they would have gotten to the house. He gritted his teeth and slammed his hand on his steering wheel. Blaze didn't believe in luck and Josh's escape was too convenient. He fell back against his seat, placed his cell phone in easy reach and waited.

*****

"We've got a problem." The caller said immediately upon getting an answer. Then quickly added, "but don't worry I'll take care of it."

"A problem? You call me at home, disturb my evening and tell me we've got a problem and you expect me not to worry? How about you tell me what the problem is and I'll decide if I should worry or not?"

"We had an issue with a couple of technicians we used to handle the money."

"I know. You've already told us this. That was nearly a major mess, one junkie killing another. You got sloppy with your choices, but we've already taken care of that. We sent someone in to deal with it. He's 'interviewing' one now. We should know if there's anything else to worry about soon enough."

"You don't understand. The cops got a hold of him."

"We know that, but we've taken care of that too."

"No, I mean right now. Him and the guy you sent to take care of it. They cops got them."

"How do you know this?"

"Someone found out, they called the cops. I got away, but they didn't and there's something else; there was a shootout, I'm not sure your guy made it."

"What?"

"Look, I told you, don't worry. I can take care of this. Let me handle it."

"So far I haven't been impressed with how you handle things. We have entrusted a lot of our money to you and now your screw-ups have put our entire operation at risk. We think it's time we find a new laundry service. It's time to close up shop. Our clean up team is already in place, we'll deal with it now."

"No, wait! I can fix this. It's already underway, I promise, you won't be exposed."

There was a long pause, then finally a response. "We had better see some results."

"You will, I swear. I have it all under control."

"You better. You know our response to failure. We haven't gotten this far by taking unnecessary risks."

"I understand. I'll take care of it. I won't fail you."

"I hope not, because we don't give warnings."

*****

"Blaze!" She shouted excitedly in his ear, forcing him to momentarily pull the phone away.

"Rachel." He grumbled back.

"Gee, hold back the enthusiasm." She complained, but continued before he could respond. "What happened?"

"I'm surprised you don't know yourself. I half expected you to show up here." He moved his cell to the other ear it was already moist with sweat.

"I would have, but Josh is almost impossible to get rid of." She carefully held her phone as she rested against the counter.

"Josh was there?"

"He came over to check up on me. I kind of told him I had car troubles, so he came over to help me fix it." Blaze let out a reflexive laugh. "What?" She said, somewhat annoyed.

"Josh doesn't know anything about cars. I'm sure your car wasn't what he came over for."

She rolled her eyes. "You sound just like him. Do you all have some kind of competition going on?"

"What are you talking about?" He adjusted his seatbelt as he moved to get more comfortable.

"Nothing, look I didn't call to talk about Josh, I want to know what you found out." She tried changing the subject back.

"Actually you did call to talk about him." Blaze's tone was blunt.

"Oh stop stalling, just tell me…"

"That's what I found, Josh, here at the house." Blaze interrupted. There was total silence on the other end of the line. He smiled and nodded to himself. "That's what I thought."

"How did he?" She stopped herself and looked back towards the kitchen. "Shit."

"What?" He said shifting upright in his seat, carefully holding his cell close to his ear so he didn't miss a word.

She bit her lip and shifted her weight. "I think, well he saw the address while he was here. He was upset about you being here, I think that's why he really came. Maybe he thought you'd be there."

"He knows you had the address?" Blaze demanded.

"Yeah well, just because you have a hero complex and need to do it all alone. Let me tell you, you wouldn't have even known about all this if I hadn't told you." She shifted again, wishing she could shift her phone to the other ear, but she wasn't sure how strong the duct tape was.

"I know." He grumbled. "I'd be having a nice quiet drink right now down at Charlie's. Thanks."

"Oh gee, such a loss."

"I'm here aren't I?"

"Yes, and about that. What happened? What did you find out? What did Josh say?" She fired her questions off quickly.

"I had to call the cops in." He mumbled.

"That's it? That's all you got? You didn't even look around a little bit? Come on, I could have called the cops if that's all you were going to do, in fact I told you we should call them. Do you have such a need to do it all yourself you won't even let someone else be the one to call it in?" She rambled on almost incoherently.

"I thought we established where I'd be if it was my choice. I'd be will into my fifth drink by now too."

"So why go there then if all you were going to do was call the cops?" She furrowed her brow.

"That wasn't exactly my plan, but I had no choice." He sat back into his soft leather seat.

"So what do we do now? I mean the cops aren't going to tell us what they know, so where do we get answers?"

"WE don't do anything."

"Oh please, you need me." No sooner was it out of her mouth then he let out another chuckle. She pouted. "You're not going to leave me out after all I've done."

"Oh yes, you've done quite enough and I wasn't planning on leaving you out of anything..."

"Good." She said, cutting him off. Her face brightened.

"because there's nothing to leave you out of. It's a police problem now." He continued talking over top of her voice. Rachel was silent again. "The police will take care of it from here. You can go back to your life and I can go back to mine." She remained silent. He let out a heavy sigh. "Rachel." He said with a scolding tone. She remained silent. "Rachel it's out of our hands." He almost sounded like he was pleading with her. More silence. "I can hear those brain cells ticking. You need to let it go, there's nothing you can do now."

She finally broke the silence with a sigh. "I guess you're right." She drooped her shoulders.

"Yes, I am." He said softening his tone. He rested his phone against his forehead for a moment, then rolled his eyes and put it back to his ear. "You did a good job."

She beamed reflexively. "Thank you."

He grunted and shifted in his seat. "Yeah well, I'm sure most of it was dumb luck, but you did find things that nobody was looking for. Not sure what the police will end up making with what you found out, but well you did ok just the same."

"Gee, you really go all out with your compliments don't you."

He smiled despite himself. Then there was a click. "I've got to grab my other line."

"Oh yeah, sure..." She managed to say before he cut her off. She pouted as she pulled the phone away from her ear. She set it down gingerly. She switched uncomfortably between pacing the room and fretting on the couch as she thought about the phone call. This was not what she had expected to find when she started the day.

She got up one final time from the couch and headed over to sit at her desk. She pulled out her note pad and reviewed her pages of various scribbles, doodles and notes. None of this made any sense and now it was in the hands of the police. She furrowed her brow, unconsciously tapping her pen as she tried to re-order some of her pages, hoping for a flash of insight.

She was so deep in thought when her buzzer rang that she nearly knocked her chair over jumping out of it. Her heart was pounding and her face was flushed when she pulled the door open. "What did you fi…" Her voice trailed off when she saw Josh's school boy grin. "Josh." She said with surprise. She stuttered as she collected her thoughts. "Wh… Why are y… What are you doing here?" She finally blurted out. She offered him a polite smile as her breathing returned to normal.

"Expecting someone else?" He asked casually as he slipped past her and into her apartment and made himself comfortable on her couch. She watched him, her mouth agape. She automatically shut the door behind him and shook her head. "Good. Come and join me then." He said patting the couch beside him. After a moment she seemed to snap out of her confusion.

"Was there something you needed to talk about? Did something happen?" She took a step forward.

"No." He replied, his school boy grin spreading across his face as he stretched out on her couch. He patted for her to join him again.

"Josh, it's late." She said shifting her weight and loosely crossing her arms. "What are you doing here?" Her voice was calm and gentle, but her expression remained impassive. She sighed impatiently.

Josh's smile faded as he looked her over. "What's the matter, waiting for news?"

Her look turned to confusion. She tried to control her tone. "I'm not following what you're trying to say." She rubbed her temples and continued. "I guess I'm just a little too tired for a decent conversation right now. Why don't we talk tomorrow? We can meet at the office first thing; I'll even bring the coffee." She offered a weak smile as emphasis.

Josh slid his legs off her coffee table and sat up straight. "Provided there is an office left to go to that is. I suppose that depends on what they know." He stood up and slowly stalked over to her. Her arms dropped to her sides. "Perhaps you can help me with that." His voice was laced with menacing undertones. She instinctively backed up. She opened her mouth to speak but nothing came out. His grin had twisted into a sinister smirk. "Maybe you can tell me why you had that address in the Heights scribbled on that piece of paper? Or what you've told the police?"

"The Police? I haven't..." Her mind raced to sort out what he was saying. He closed in quickly when she backed herself up against the door. He leered at her, menacingly close. She jumped as her cell phone cut through the ominous silence. She glanced towards the coffee table where it lay. Josh snapped his head around to scope out her target. He saw the bandaged phone ringing helplessly and he snorted. She used his distraction to slip around him and walk swiftly towards the phone, conscious to never have her back fully towards him. "I should get that." She whispered as she slipped by. She grabbed the phone and answered as quickly as she could.

"Hello?" She panted. Josh spun around and raced towards her. He managed to grab her other arm, stopping her in her tracks. "What the hell are you doing?" She demanded as his grip tightened. She tried to pull free and was instantly jarred backwards with such force she was forced to watch helplessly as her phone fell to the floor and shattered instantly.

Her face flushed and her heart pounded in her ears. Her eyes darkened and her breathing increased. She pulled hard against him then spun around to face him, loosening his grip. She swung her hand and slapped him, forcing him back in surprise. His eyes narrowed as a trickle of blood formed at the corner of his mouth. Her pinky ring had caught his lip. She covered her mouth in shock.

"Bitch." He spat. She turned to run into the kitchen, but he leapt towards her and managed to pull her back. This time instead of giving her a chance to struggle, he landed a backhanded punch on her cheek so hard it threw her back and made her eyes water. She stumbled to the side and slipped on some of the pieces of her phone, knocking her off her feet. She hit the back of her head on the table leg as she hit the floor. All of the air expelled from her body and she lay there dazed and fighting off shock.

Josh quickly scanned the room. He grabbed the duct tape she had used in her futile attempt to patch her phone earlier. He grabbed her arms and spun her over, binding them tightly together behind her. Before she could recover he ripped off a smaller piece and taped it over her mouth. He sat back on his heels and smirked. He tossed the tape on the couch and stood up. He dragged her up from the floor and swung her over his shoulders.

He could feel her gasping for air as her dazed body fought to regain focus. His face contorted into an ominous grin. He grabbed a blanket and threw it over top of her before rushing her down to his car under the cover of darkness. He threw her into his trunk. His smile deepened with excitement when she let out a weak yelp as her body impacted with something on the floor. He instinctively rubbed a hand over his crotch as he slammed the lid down. Then he jumped in his car, jammed his keys in the ignition and brought his car to life.

From the trunk, Rachel struggled to keep awake, but with her mind unable to fight off her confusion and her lungs prevented from gulping the air her body demanded, she soon slipped into darkness. The sound of the squealing tires when he jammed on the accelerator and sped off was the last sound that registered as she drifted into unconsciousness. She didn't hear him laughing darkly as he drove off.

*****

Blaze grabbed the phone and dialed for a third time, straight to voice mail again. "Shit." He cursed tossing his phone aside and slamming his fist against the steering wheel. His scowl was etched in his features as he turned on the ignition. He revved the powerful engine and threw it into gear. He tucked his phone into his pocket, hit the accelerator and headed east; straight for Rachel's.

CHAPTER 23

Blaze stared up at her apartment. The lights were on in her apartment, but there was no movement inside. He tried her cell again; his call went straight to her voice mail. He returned his phone to his pocket and reached under his front seat. He clenched his jaw and pulled out his semi automatic. He checked the clip and the chamber. He stared up at her back windows, his glare boring holes through them. He inhaled sharply, tucked his piece in his belt and stepped out of his truck.

He swiftly made his way up to her apartment, slowing his pace as he approached her entrance. The door was closed. He tried it anyway. It was unlocked. He stepped back behind the door frame and drew his gun. He pushed the door open, ducked back and listened. He heard nothing. He slowly made his way inside. He methodically searched her apartment. It was empty. He re-seated his gun back in his belt and went back to her living room.

He looked closer at the mess he had stepped over on his way through. After a few seconds he realized it was her cell phone. He searched the area further and found blood on the coffee table leg. He clenched his jaw and quickly stood up. He ran his fingers through his hair and looked around helplessly. His mind raced as he paced the room. He suddenly grabbed her purse, dumped it out on the couch and started searching the contents. He scanned all the scraps of paper that were strewn about, stopping only to answer his phone as it vibrated.

"Speak." He demanded to the caller.

"It's me." The caller replied quietly.

"What'd ya got for me?"

"Nice to hear from you too. Jesus man, I shouldn't be doing this. You know what kind of trouble I could get into a little appre..."

Blaze exhaled sharply. "Look, I'm sorry, but I don't have time right now. I'm in a bit of a fix."

The man on the other end of the phone sighed. "Do I want to know?"

Blaze shook his head. "Not yet, but you will soon enough I expect."

"This is going to be a long night, I don't like long nights." His caller complained

Blaze clenched his jaw. "Joe!" Blaze reprimanded.

"Right, sorry." He apologized and cleared his throat before continuing. "There were two men in that house tonight. They were both dead when we arrived. One was the guy we had been looking for, Leon Patrick Palmer; the other we haven't identified yet."

"Shit."

"But here's the thing," he continued, ignoring Blaze's outburst. "The one looked like he died not long after being brought there if your time table was right. His cause of death, besides a pretty severe beating, was a lovely little cocktail of drugs that were designed for only one thing, immediate termination. By the looks of things we suspect that interrogating then disposing of him, was the reason he was in that house to begin with."

"And the one you haven't ID'd yet?" Blaze prompted as his impatience grew. He continued to juggle the phone as he searched through the rest of the stuff. He stopped, nearly dropping the phone as he read the paper in his hand. It was another copy of the address he had spent most of the night on. He grabbed the phone again, only catching the last part of what the speaker was saying.

"...had to be right before we got there. Definitely not clean or planned like the other one. It was messy and hurried, probably heard our sirens and panicked."

"Who panicked?"

"The killer who killed the other guy, the one we figure did the interrogating on Leon. Weren't you listening?"

"Sorry, dropped the phone."

The caller expelled loudly. "Look, I'm taking a big risk here, they're looking internally now. Whoever killed the hitter did it right before we arrived and got away clean. They're saying someone must have tipped him off. You know what would happen if they found out you were the one who called it in don't you?" The caller's voice was hushed, but the concern was clearly evident.

"Yes, I know exactly what they'd do; accuse me, then accuse anyone that still associates with me." He stated bitterly.

"You know we never believed that shit they claimed..."

Blaze cut him off. "Look I've got more trouble here. My prints will be all over this place, but I have no choice; You've got to get someone out to 41B Lindenhurst Boulevard at Summerset place. Oh and Joe," he added quickly, "I won't..."

"Yeah I know. You won't be there. Shit. I knew it was going to be a long night. Anything I should know?"

"Same thing I know, only that the occupant isn't here and you'll need a blood kit. Oh and she works for Stafford and she might have stumbled across the person who killed your hitter." With that Blaze hung up and stared again at the address. He looked around her apartment, then back at the paper and thought back to her earlier conversations. He suddenly leapt off the couch. He left her purse and the apartment as it was, except for slipping the paper into his back jeans pocket and rushed out.

He ran for his truck and as he pulled out of the parking lot he stopped. He looked one way down the street then the other. He wasn't sure which way to go. He looked at his watch and frowned, worry etched across his face. It had already been too long since the last time he had reached her. Time was critical and choosing the wrong destination first could be a fatal mistake. He looked right then spun out of the lot in that direction.

*****

Josh pulled as close to the back doors as he could; he quickly unset the alarm before retrieving his prize from the trunk. He didn't have to worry about onlookers; the warehouse district was deserted at this time of night. Rachel was still unconscious when he dragged her from the trunk and took her through warehouse entrance. He cleared off one of the work benches and laid her limp body on top. He retrieved some rope used to secure the ATMs during transport and tied her towards the back of the bench.

When he was done he stepped back and smiled proudly admiring his work. She was spotlighted by one of the bench lights on the back wall behind her. He had freed her hands from the tape, but had tied them with the rope and strung them above her head using one of the extension cords draped from the rafters that the technicians used for power. He had tied her legs, one to each corner of the bench legs. He looked around the dark warehouse and nodded knowingly, his smile twisting into the same sinister leer from before. He instinctively rubbed his crotch as he felt his cock swell.

Rachel was starting to stir as her lungs began to absorb the additional quantities of oxygen. he watched her for a moment longer, shifting his weight and staring at his watch. He had begun to pace. She still had not regained full consciousness. He wanted her awake. He expelled loudly and rushed over to her, giving her a shake and a light slap on the cheeks. Her eyes began to flutter open. He moved his face close to hers and sneered, then he ripped the tape off of her mouth.

Her eyes flew open and she greedily gasped to fill her lungs. She inhaled quickly, her breath stopping in her throat as the shock of Josh's twisted features began to register. She tried to move. Josh stepped back, his distorted smile grew deeper as she struggled against her bonds. She searched her surroundings wildly, her eyes beginning to focus as her mind fought to regain full awareness. Her head throbbed, but the pain meant all of her senses had returned and now she was angry.

"What the fuck are you doing!" She demanded, pulling as hard as she could with her arms. Her breathing was quick and deep, each breath more painful than the last. She remembered wincing when he had thrown her in the trunk, she tried to look towards the source of the pain, but she didn't have enough movement in her bonds. She spun her head around to face him when he began to laugh.

"Ready to start with the truth now?" He demanded, condescension filling his every word.

"You won't get away with this Josh. Someone's going to find us here." She tried her best to sound strong.

"Someone? You mean those bumbling cops? That haven't gotten anywhere without the all information you dug up for them? Ha! I'm pretty sure you didn't point them my way yet, not with your surprised reaction at your apartment." He paused and took a step towards her, his voice deepening. "No. Wait, did you mean Blaze?" He voice was dripping with contempt. He took several more steps until he was only a breath away from her.

He leaned in close, pinning her further with his body, his breath tickling her neck as he whispered in her ear. "Did you tell your little boyfriend where you'd be tonight? Was that who called you earlier?" He lifted his head so he could stare at her face. "No? Oh that's right; you didn't have had time to let him know of your change of plans before your phone accidently broke." His deep laugh rumbled in his throat, taunting her.

"Don't worry princess, I'm sure if he manages to figure anything out he'll be hero enough to charge over to my house to rescue you. Even dirty cops like to play good guy with a prize like you waiting." Rachel struggled to pull away from him. "Oops. We didn't go there now did we?" He shook his head. "Well don't worry if he does figure it out, we'll be long done here." He traced his hand around her neck. Then leaned in and traced his tongue along the same path as she squirmed even harder. "I'll leave him what's left." He finished with another laugh and jumped back just out of her reach as she tried to bite down on his throat.

"Such a shame really?" He said shaking his head and licking

his lips. "You're just feisty enough to be some real fun. The rest of the girls around here are just no challenge anymore." He deliberately ran his hand down his pants to show her his engorged cock. He smiled as her eyes widened. "Oh yes, you'd love my little collar. I could just feel you tremble with excitement as you begged your master to let you please him."

She spat at him and cried out in frustration as she strained to get free and strangle him. "You're sick. What happened to you?"

"Happened to me?" He threw his head back and laughed. Then he grabbed a box cutter off the other work bench behind him and lunged at her. Pressing it into her neck just hard enough for her to feel it. "Darling you happened to me! Everything was fine, before you had to stick your damn nose into everything." He stepped back and raised his hands, making a sweeping motion as she spoke. "I had the perfect setup here until you saunter in and wag your little tail and get everyone sticking their necks out for you."

He let out a snort as he moved closer to her, this time, trailing the box cutter down the neckline of her shirt. "I knew you were trouble, but I figured with someone as washed up as Blaze, he'd be immune to you." He flicked the first button off her shirt, it popped off easily. "Mmm, sharp." He smiled amused with himself. "I guess he wasn't as wasted as I thought." He slid her shirt open further with the blade. "Or maybe you revived him in ways only you and those pouty lips of your can revive a man."

She futilely pulled at her bound hands. The electrical cords had enough give to frustrate her, but not enough to give her any real movement. She winced as her struggles brought the blade into her flesh. She froze instantly and held her breath. Josh smiled darkly, his school boy grin now twisted into something that made her shiver.

"There, there." He said shaking his head. "Now do you see what you've done? Mmmm, yes you would be exciting. I'll bet you'd scream for me baby, wouldn't you?" He chuckled as he watched her rage build. He stepped back again to admire her.

Her face was flushed. She could no longer feel the pounding in her head. Her vision was clear and focused. Her senses heightened. She could hear every little building creek, every disgusting breath that he took. She could smell the thick stale air, musty, mixed with oil and other chemicals used to clean the ATMs. Her mind raced, her bonds were tight. She couldn't be sure of the time, but she knew it could be hours before anyone came back to work. She had to keep him talking. Her breathing was shallow, her adrenaline was pumping. She struggled once more, but this time to pull herself closer to the front edge of the bench. She arched her back slightly and let her head fall back a bit. "I would scream for you… Master." She began tentatively.

Josh eyed her suspiciously. He trailed his eyes down her arched body. The sweat that had formed on her skin seemed to glisten under the spot light. Her full red lips were moist. The ropes pinched her delicate white skin so that there was a pink ring around her wrists. His eyes grew dark and he let out a moan. His excitement was clear even from the shadows where he stood. He took a step closer to her and she licked her lips and smiled. He stared at her breasts as they peaked through, newly exposed by the missing button and emphasized by her arched movements. He moved even closer.

"I've been waiting for a man like you, to show me how to please him. Can't we go now? Get that collar you wanted?"

Another moan escaped from him, he took another step and she pulled slightly on her ties, lifting herself back ever so slightly. He stopped and she froze. All that could be heard was their labored breathing. "No." He shouted. "There isn't time for that now. I'll reward you later with that as long as you're truthful with me and help me fix this."

She nodded her head innocently. "Anything. Whatever I did, let me help you fix it. Just tell me what to do."

Josh's expression hardened and he pressed against her again. "Yes, that's my good girl. You fix your mistakes now and I'll not punish you as long before I reward you." Josh slid the knife behind another button and popped it off too. She shivered as he exposed her further. She tried to keep smiling. "That's better. Not for play, but proper dress for you to know your place."

She gave him a small nod as she inhaled deeply, she felt the cool air in her lungs and she was finally able to start to control her breathing. Josh kept the blade away from her skin, but he dangled it close as he spoke. "Now tell me. What did you tell the police about my little friend in the heights?"

Rachel hesitated and her breathing became labored again. "I, I didn't tell them anything."

Josh stopped and moved the blade closer, he popped another button. His expression was impassive. "Keep lying and I'll have no choice but to punish you harder. I thought you wanted my reward?" He said as he ground his crotch against her leg.

"I do." She said quickly. "It's the truth, I didn't tell the police anything."

"Liar!" He shouted, then reached out and grabbed her by the hair, pulling her closer to him. A small scream escaped from her. "Uh, uh. No screaming yet, it's not time." He smiled and rested the knife blade on her breast. "You must have told them, how else would they have found us?"

"Because she told me!" The reply came from the darkened shadows behind them.

Josh spun around to face the deep familiar voice. Rachel yelped again as he twisted her along with him. "Blaze." He said with disgust.

Blaze stepped partially out of the shadows. His gun was raised and pointed directly at Josh. His hand was steady and his gaze was fierce. He slowly tried to close the wide gap between them.

"Stop right there!" Josh demanded as he twisted both himself and Rachel so Blaze could watch as he trailed the blade close to her neck.

"Josh. Let it go. It's all over. The police are on their way." He lied. "Drop it now and they'll be able to make a deal with you. You could give them the money laundering."

Josh looked momentarily surprised, but it quickly turned to a look of disgust. "A deal? What, like the deal they made with you? Look how that turned out. What do you care anyway, you're not a cop?"

"You're right I don't care. Just as long you don't screw up my business you can steal all you want, but I can't have you going around kidnapping friends of mine now can I?" Blaze adjusted the grip on his weapon.

"Friends? Is that what you're calling it now?" Josh's voice was laced with sarcasm. He trailed his gaze back down to Rachel and pushed the blade in closer till he drew another trickle of blood. Rachel froze and Blaze held his breath. He then tilted the blade and trailed her blood down through her open shirt. He stopped at her bra, slipping the blade underneath, then back out before he once again spoke. He again looked at Blaze. "You'll have to do better than that. You'll never catch them for money laundering; they've probably already started relocation. You think this is the first ATM Company they've used to money their funds?"

"So they've left you to take the blame and you don't want to deal. You're making it harder on yourself. Let her go now and a good lawyer could probably get you off with a misdemeanor. You could start by claiming you had no knowledge of the scam, as for the account skimming, you could blame that on the dead technicians."

Josh scowled. "It was them! Stupid junkies. We had a perfect setup and they had to go and steal from me. Bringing all sorts of attention to themselves and for what? A nickel bag?" Josh momentarily swung the blade away from Rachel and pointed at Blaze. Blaze jerked his gun in reaction, but Josh had immediately replaced it to her neck. Josh smiled. "You were right all along Blaze, I never should have hired those idiots."

Blaze took a deep breath. "But why'd you kill them? I mean, you knew that had to draw even more attention." Blaze steadied his stance as Josh got more agitated.

"I didn't kill them. They killed themselves. I wouldn't have even known they were stealing from me if it wasn't for you two finding that body." He looked down at Rachel for a moment. "And those damn journal tapes. I should thank you for that." He whispered in her ear before turning his focus back on Blaze.

Rachel tried to steady her breathing. She focused on the knife blade and tried to slow her pulse rate, as if that would somehow make her small enough to slip through Josh's hands. She closed her eyes and tried to rest herself against his body to ease the pain building in her head. Not only was the throbbing back as her body temperature cooled and the flow of adrenaline slowed, but she could feel her head wound from earlier starting to seep as he pulled harder on her hair.

“How did they kill themselves Josh?” Blaze asked a step closer than before. He had taken advantage of Josh’s distraction to inch forward. Josh didn’t seem to notice.

“You mean you haven’t figured that out yet? I guess you weren’t very good at being a cop when you were one.” He said, almost taunting him. “Seems Miguel felt Patrick was too sloppy, hitting ATMs on each fill instead sporadically as Miguel used to do it. Guess Miguel got scared and was going to tell me about it. Patrick panicked and killed him, stuffed his body in that ATM. Apparently he was going to go back for it later and instead the idiot got himself arrested leaving his dealers place.”

“and How do you know all that?” Blaze asked trying to keep his attention off the knife blade at Rachel’s throat.

Josh let out a deep laugh, his hand shaking dangerously close to Rachel’s throat. “Like you don’t know. It was you who called the cops to the house wasn’t it. I’m sure that must have pissed you off to have to call in your old buddies. Couldn’t handle it alone?” Josh was relishing in his taunts.

Blaze clenched his jaw harder. He didn’t move his focus off Josh once. He remained silent, letting Josh continue. “Money laundering is a dangerous game. It’s not run by a single person. They have connections; Henchmen to do whatever is needed and cleaners to fix it should something major go wrong. Patrick screwed up, brought too much heat; they had to deal with him.”

This time Blaze threw the taunts. “So why did you kill the henchman? That can’t have been a good career move and so sloppy too. I would have thought you’d be smart enough to get someone else to do your dirty work.” It worked, Josh became more agitated and he was able to reposition his stance.

"I had no choice." Josh defended. "One little interrogation and Patrick spilled all of it. About our side deals, Miguel must have told him what the extra funds were for that he was taking. They ruined our operations with their petty greed. I had no choice. Patrick had told him everything and he was going to turn me in to them, but I had a plan to fix it. I was going to make it look like Patrick had escaped, like they killed each other, but then you go and fuck it up by calling the cops."

Blaze studied Josh carefully. Josh waved the blade around slightly with every angry word. He looked Rachel, her eyes were closed. She was conscious, but her breathing was shallow and uneven. "All what operations? Were you skimming a little off the boss's money for yourself Josh? Tisk, tisk." Blaze taunted as he took another tiny step forward. "I can't imagine that would make your backers very happy. No wait." He added as he took another step, sideways this time. "The bank account skimming, that was your doing wasn't it?"

"Of course it was. Do you think those idiots could have figured out how to do it themselves?" Josh's chest puffed out with pride as he spoke, angling the knife slightly. "They would have been as sloppy about that as they were about everything else. You don't steal money from them, that would be suicide and you don't steal enough from anyone to get you noticed. It's all about timing and patience. I tried to tell them. Too much and it'll get traced back to the company, too little and it's not worth the effort. You have to be smart about it."

"And you were smart weren't you." Blaze praised, inching sideways a tiny bit more.

"Actually it wasn't that hard. It was just a matter of watching the news and taking advantage of their fascination in reporting flashy crimes. As soon as someone hits a few bank ATMs or they announce another round of identity thefts; we do a quick sweep on our own. That way, it all looks like ours hits were just part the rest. Even if they manage to catch the guys, it' not like they remember half the ATMS they hit. Neat and tidy; One crime hidden by someone else's and no one's the wiser."

"Nice." Blaze offered admiringly, nodding his head to allow him to sneak another inch forward and angle his body slightly towards Josh.

"It was nice. Perfect actually." Josh responded with such venom his voice cracked. "Until you two screwed it up!" He screamed, emphasizing his words by pointing the knife tip towards Blaze. In a split second he realized his mistake and quickly turned the blade back and was about to jam towards Rachel when the shot rang out.

Everybody froze. The air was still except for the strong stench of gun powder. The first sound to be heard was the sound of Rachel's gasp as Josh gripped her hair tighter. Blaze held his breath. Then they heard the knife clamor as it hit the floor. Josh's grip fell limp and Blaze dove forward, knocking him the rest of the way down to the ground. Blaze stared down at him. Josh shuddered and then he was still; He didn't move again.

Rachel let out a whimper. Blaze spun around to face her. She had opened her eyes and was staring at Josh's motionless body. Blood trickled down her face from her open head wound. She was alive, but she was starting to go into shock. He picked up the box cutter and rushed over to her. He cut her down, then he grabbed her as she collapsed in his arms. She was shivering and her skin was clammy and pale. He gently lifted her off the bench and carried her out to his truck. He wrapped her in his jacket and pulled her close. He tried to comfort her as he grabbed his phone and dialed.

No sooner had the phone been picked up than Blaze started in. “You need come to Stafford Financial now! Bring the an ambulance.” Then as an afterthought he added. “and the coroner and hurry, she’s already going into shock.”

“Shit…” He replied. Blaze could hear his muffled voice barking orders. After a few moments, he continued into the phone. “It’s done.”

“Good…”

“and Blaze,” he man continued, cutting him off. “This time you need to be there when they arrive.”

“I know.” Blaze replied, holding Rachel closer.

CHAPTER 24

"Oh wow that's wonderful!" Amy squealed. Rachel tried to look disconcerted when her friend grabbed her and gave her a hug, but she hadn't been able to wipe the grin off her face since her agent called her.

"I don't know why you're so happy my temping days might soon be over."

"Halleluiah! I might actually get a job that finishes when contract states." Amy raised her hands for added emphasis and quickly ducked when Rachel's good hearted slug headed her way.

"Oh come on I wouldn't give that up. How could I; what would I do for inspiration? Besides, I wouldn't want to forget the little people when I'm famous." She tried to sound serious, but they quickly broke into laughter.

Within minutes Amy's got quiet and her expression serious. "So have you heard seen him at all?" Rachel blushed. Amy's face lit up. "You have, I knew it!"

"No, I haven't." She turned her face away and took a calming breath. "Well that is to say not exactly. I mean the nurses told me he came by the hospital that night to visit me after the police had all left, but I was asleep."

"That's it?" Amy blurted in disbelief.

"I think I've seen his truck a couple of times outside my apartment, but I can't be sure." She bit her lip, her cheeks were still flushed.

"Well that's just crazy. Sounds like he's as stubborn as you are."

Rachel placed her hands on her hips. "What's that supposed to mean?" Rachel demanded.

Amy waved her off. "Like I have to explain that one, the guy wasn't exactly unattractive and neither are you!"

"I'll send him a thank you note. He can take it from there." She replied, refusing to look Amy in the eyes.

Amy signed in frustration. "Why not just send him your book, that's all warm and inviting?"

"Maybe I will." Rachel crossed her arms and pouted.

Amy rolled her eyes. "Like I said, stubborn."

Rachel's eyes twinkled. "Well maybe I'll run into him on my next job.".

"I thought you said you were done temping?" Amy eyed her suspiciously.

"The book's not even on store shelves yet, let alone making me enough to live off of. Besides, you'd be bored without me." Rachel threw Amy a wink.

Amy groaned and dropped her head. "I'll look for something this afternoon." Rachel beamed.

EPILOGUE

He turned the book over in his hands as he sipped his drink. It was a pre-release edition, not due out on shelved till Christmas. He traced a finger over Rachel's picture as he read the inside jacket. He smiled and signaled for another one. Charlie sauntered over and refilled his cup.

"Jesus Blaze, I think you drink more coffee then you ever drank of whiskey." Blaze gave him a grunt and a smile, then he opened the book and began to read...

"Who the hell did this junkie think he was. That's what I wanted to know! I mean damn it, I was giving him the money from the register and now he had the audacity to insult me? I'll show him dumb blonde. Okay, Gym class, don't fail me now!"

Blaze chuckled aloud. "Good book?" Charlie asked from across the bar.

Blaze shook his head. "Troubling book." Charlie stopped moving the dingy rag across the glass and tilted his head. "Trouble in the guise of a blonde that is."

Charlie nodded his head in agreement, "Aren't they all." He replied, then returned to polishing the glass with his dingy rag. "Something a little stronger than coffee next time?" He said without looking up from his glass.

"Maybe, Charlie," Blaze mused as he nodded his head, "Maybe."

He skimmed ahead to the last page, his face contorted into a painful stare as he read...

"Okay, so the ATM business turned out to be a little less boring than I thought, but every girl's gotta have a little excitement right? Well you won't be able to say that about my next job, that one really is dullsville. What could possibly happen with interior decorating?"

Blaze let out a groan and Charlie looked up with an indifference that was akin to mild curiosity. As any long time customer knew, not much moved Charlie. "Better keep that bottle handy Charlie." Charlie shrugged and continued cleaning. Blaze cracked a smile that immediately turned to an annoyed scowl as his cell phone vibrated in his pocket. After a heavy sigh he reached in pulled it out.

"Yeah." He turned slightly in his seat as he adjusted the cell against his ear.

"I thought you were going to take care of things."

Blaze scowl deepened. "I am, but it was a big mess."

"And you're being compensated well for cleaning it up, but we thought you'd be faster."

"The police had to be involved, cleaning a mess like that takes time. You'll be back in business again soon." Blaze clenched his jaw and inhaled deeply.

"I hope so. We have a lot of investments to wash."

"Yes well, if you'd have come to me first instead of Josh, you wouldn't be in this mess." Blaze shifted on the stool and switched his cell to his other ear.

"He said he had it under control. We had a lot invested in him, we had to give him a chance fix it."

"He was unstable." Blaze said coldly.

"We know that now." The caller said, cutting him off. "Look, we won't make that mistake again. We don't want any more attention on things, which is why we're wondering why the police had to be involved."

"I had no choice; not involving them would have meant they would be running through everything you own. This way I could keep the focus of the investigation down to a Josh and his boys and away from you." Blaze's features hardened and he inhaled again, keeping his voice low and controlled. Are you really questioning MY methods?"

There was a silent pause as the caller inhaled deeply. "No. We know you're good, one of the best really, we're just anxious to get back on track that's all."

"Well you can relax; I'll have it ready in a matter of days now." He quickly became bored and started flipped through the last couple of pages of Rachel's book while he spoke.

"That's great news."

Blaze grunted. "Don't call me again. This number needs to stay clean. I'll call YOU when the cleanup is done."

"I look forward to it…" Was all the caller could say before Blaze hung up.

He ear was red, but it was more than just the heat from the cell's battery that caused his irritation. "Charlie." He called out loudly, his voice raspy. Charlie spun round at Blaze's sudden change in tone. "I'll be back in an hour and I'll expect you to have a full bottle ready."

Charlie raised an eyebrow, gave Blaze a quick once over, then nodded as he leaned back against the bar. Blaze jammed his cell back in his pocket and stood up. He rubbed his rough moist hand through his hair. It came to rest on the open book sitting on the bar. Charlie watched him as he stood like that motionless, hand on top of Rachel's book. After a few moments of this, Charlie shifted his stance and spoke. "You taking that with you?"

Blaze re-read the last sentence saw a few times. *"I know there were missing pieces, I just couldn't put my finger on them and someday I'll have to find out what really happened at Stafford Financial."* He stared a moment longer and shook his head, he wore a smile that was a mixture of caring and concern. Then he simply shrugged and walked out; leaving the book on the counter and Charlie to simply shake his head, confused.

-- The End --

www.ingramcontent.com/pod-product-compliance
Lightning Source LLC
LaVergne TN
LVHW091039080826
845145LV00002B/557

* 9 7 8 0 5 7 8 7 5 3 5 5 3 *